BAD ART MOTHER

Edwina Preston is a Melbourne-based writer and musician. Preston is the author of a biography of Australian artist Howard Arkley, *Not Just a Suburban Boy* (Duffy & Snellgrove, 2002), and the novel *The Inheritance of Ivorie Hammer* (University of Queensland Press, 2012). Her writing and reviews have appeared in *The Age*, *The Australian*, *The Sydney Morning Herald*, *Heat*, *Island* and *Griffith Review*.

† † †

'I adore Edwina Preston's *Bad Art Mother*. This is a magnificent panorama of a novel, written with an assured verve, that encompasses art and feminism, love and marriage, and makes us believe we are right there, at the very heart of a transformative moment in culture when everything is about to change. There is anger here, as there must be when telling the story of how women have been silenced in the world – but there is also a scrupulous empathy for every character: this is a humane and tender work. The conception is daring, yet Preston has the confidence and talent and assuredness as a writer to never stumble in the storytelling. I was never less than enthralled.'

– CHRISTOS TSIOLKAS

'With commanding prose, imaginative energy and fierce wit, Preston tells the lives of women artists. The focus is Veda Gray whose confronting presence, desperate stratagems and passionate engagement with her creativity offers an intense and memorable portrait.'

– JANINE BURKE

BAD ART MOTHER

Edwina Preston is a Melbourne-based writer and musician. Preston is the author of a biography of Australian artist Howard Arkley, *Not Just a Suburban Boy* (Duffy & Snellgrove, 2002), and the novel *The Inheritance of Ivorie Hammer* (University of Queensland Press, 2012). Her writing and reviews have appeared in *The Age*, *The Australian*, *The Sydney Morning Herald*, *Heat*, *Island* and *Griffith Review*.

† † †

'I adore Edwina Preston's *Bad Art Mother*. This is a magnificent panorama of a novel, written with an assured verve, that encompasses art and feminism, love and marriage, and makes us believe we are right there, at the very heart of a transformative moment in culture when everything is about to change. There is anger here, as there must be when telling the story of how women have been silenced in the world – but there is also a scrupulous empathy for every character: this is a humane and tender work. The conception is daring, yet Preston has the confidence and talent and assuredness as a writer to never stumble in the storytelling. I was never less than enthralled.'

– CHRISTOS TSIOLKAS

'With commanding prose, imaginative energy and fierce wit, Preston tells the lives of women artists. The focus is Veda Gray whose confronting presence, desperate stratagems and passionate engagement with her creativity offers an intense and memorable portrait.'

– JANINE BURKE

Bad Art Mother

Edwina Preston

Wakefield Press

Wakefield Press
16 Rose Street
Mile End
South Australia 5031
www.wakefieldpress.com.au

First published 2022

Edited by Jo Case, Wakefield Press
Book design by Duncan Blachford, Typography Studio
Printed in Australia by Pegasus Media & Logistics

ISBN 978 1 74305 901 2

A catalogue record for this book is available from the National Library of Australia

Publication of this book was assisted by the Commonwealth Government through the Australia Council, its arts funding and advisory body.

Wakefield Press thanks Coriole Vineyards for continued support

Contents

PART 1

FOOD IS A SOLID FACT 1

PART 2

CREATIVE BONES 51

PART 3

SNOW WHITE IN THE FOREST WITH THE APPLE 127

PART 4

MONASTERY MAIDEN 203

PART 5

SABOTAGE 275

PART 6

THE POEMS OF VEDA GRAY 305

Dedicated to the feminists of my mother's generation, the mothers of my friends, for paving the way, getting the laws changed, and making possible the conversations we are having today.

Helen Myles, for her work in women-centric healthcare and childbirth education in Melbourne in the 1980s, and for first alerting me to the word 'feminism';

Carolyn Lloyd, one of the original pram-pushing front-bar-stormers of the Graham Hotel public bar in Melbourne CBD and the Manhattan Hotel in Ringwood, 1972;

Liz Preston, upon whose bookshelf I first discovered *A Room of One's Own*.

BOOK LAUNCH

I don't remember much of Mother's book launch, just the flash of the newspaperman's camera. Flash! it went, fixing us in time. Flash! Flash!

I've still got the photograph the *Age* used. I keep it in my Cartridges box. Mother's got a big glass of wine in her hand and she's blinking and talking at the same time. Her eyes are closed and her mouth is open and the combination isn't flattering. The *Australian* found a worse picture, in which she looks like a crazy Picasso woman, with bits of her face in the wrong places. No one, looking at her in those photos, would like her or feel sympathy for her.

I don't remember Mr Parish's speech. My subconscious must've deliberately erased the words he used to put Mother's book to death. There was the picked-over head of a pig in front of him, I remember that. A lump of dead pork on the cover of someone's *Veda Gray*.

He cleared his throat and drank a gulp of wine and then he read Mother's sonnet, spelling out the first letter of the first word of every line, making sure no one could fail to understand.

It was 1970.

Germaine Greer had yet to publish *The Female Eunuch*.

Mother wasn't a respectable woman.

PART I

FOOD IS A SOLID FACT

MILK

In the beginning, I thought my mother was a book. A paperback, with a cream and orange jacket, and a picture of a small milk-bottle-shaped bird. The book just happened to have a mass of golden, wavy hair. It ate packets and packets of chocolate digestive biscuits. It regularly heaved and shifted and made low rumbling sounds, and sometimes sharp high barks.

But I was happy: I was getting all the milk I needed, I wasn't cold, I wasn't hungry.

Sunlight came through my eyelids. The book had a comforting heartbeat. Its pages turned with a papery *whoosh, whoosh.*

And then Mother yawned and the book fell from her face.

I broke off from the breast and wailed. Mother was not a book at all and she was enormous. Her colours weren't orange and cream and black; they were pink and gold and grey. She had a big mouth and small, sharp teeth. Her face contained nothing that was familiar, nothing I could get a purchase on. She was utterly, utterly strange.

And I never got used to her strangeness. Mother never settled into a reliable shape. She's always been unfathomable: woods I can't see on account of all the trees.

You won't believe any of this, Ornella. You don't think it's possible to recall things from such an early age. But it pays for the brain to be forgetful, or maybe we wouldn't recover from the trauma of being born.

And I remember that too: being born is unbearable. It's terrifying, the worst thing that ever happens to us. The weight, the terrible squeezing weight, and then, just when you think you can't take it anymore, the sudden paralysing weightlessness. The massiveness of space and air. And the *cold*, it's so *cold*!

Better to be a marsupial, born into a pouch, always able to climb back into a warm pocket of fur. Humans just get spat out into cold white nothingness and can't ever go back.

But you've never imagined being a marsupial, Ornella. You've never imagined inhabiting anything except your own brain and body, plain and simple. Your first memory, you say, is of your mother yanking a pair of tights over your nappy, propelling you across the floor on your backside. From then, there is nothing in your memory banks until a Grade Three skipping contest. Before you knew it, you were an adult. In between, I imagine lots of grey bitumen, greaseproof paper and orange peel.

When it comes to my earliest memories, the only one I concede to you is the one about Mother being enormous.

'Owen,' you say, shaking your head. 'Your mother was not a large woman. She was pe*teet*. Pe-*teet*.' When you say this, you bring your thumb and forefinger together, like you're pinching out a lateral from a tomato plant.

Yes, you're right about her size, I give you that. In the one photo I've got of her from this time, she's small and compact and wearing a chequered dress with buttons down the middle. I'm in a carry-cot but Mother isn't holding the carry-cot, she's holding a tiny leather suitcase. She isn't going anywhere – not yet – and the suitcase is not full of clothes, it's full of her poems. Unfinished mostly, but lots of them, on scraps of paper and half-filled notebooks. Her legs look long for a pe-teet person. But her hands are little paws; the fingers don't properly wrap around the suitcase handle. They're an embarrassment, those hands, those fingers. It makes me sad to see them now, even in a photo. She was supposed to have a piano-player's fingers. 'It doesn't matter,' said Papa, 'it's what they write that needs to be elegant.'

Soon after this photo was taken, Mother says I became her enemy. I didn't mean to be her enemy. It was not something I planned on or decided. But I had discovered my arms and legs and I climbed onto couches and ripped pages out of books that were lying there. I did the same to those on the bottom shelves of the bookcase, chewing their corners til they were moist and soft. When Mother settled down to a quiet afternoon read, the only thing I wanted to do was *eat her book.*

Which leads me to Papa.

My early interest in eating, and the iron constitution that allowed me to digest, unharmed, seventeen pages of Balzac's *Cousin Bette* (a book that goes on too long anyway, Mother always said), was a source of great pride to my Papa. He boasted of how he'd opened my mouth one day and pulled out a lump of orange rind, a three-inch-long piece of hessian, and a £2 note. After that, he removed the washing powder from the laundry floor, and put all his penny pieces up high on a shelf.

Papa kept my very first baby romper suit too. I don't know why. It's very dirty and not really worth preserving. It's in a trunk with his father's war medals and a miniature silver-plated soup-ladle he was given for charitable services 'undertaken under the auspices of the Salvation Army, Bourke Street, Melbourne, December 1966,' says the soup-ladle.

I've got a million memories of the kitchen where he cooked this charity meal. These are bigger and more colourful memories than the ones about Mother. They feature what seem to be *vats* of olives and anchovies (though surely they're only large tins); slabs of bacon and orange freckled ham hocks that look like orthopaedic shoes.

There I sit, pinning olive eyes to a potato with toothpicks.

I loved the smells in that kitchen, the height of the ceiling, the way the steam covered people up when the lids came off pots. No one took any notice of me when I was in there. I got to do just what I liked, just be a person among other people, everyone doing jobs of their own. The kitchen was my invisibility cloak.

There were actual spaces you could disappear into in the kitchen. There was a gap between an oven and a fridge that I discovered when a marble rolled in there and I crawled in after it. In that gap, puddles formed and dried and formed again, and a curious cottony mould grew on the lino. Once in there, I didn't want to come out again. There was cold steel on one side of me, humming gently, and warm steel on the other, still. And I remember how secret and safe I felt, pressed in between those two contraptions. I unrolled the curious cottony mould from the lino and made it into a ball and wedged it between the bottom of the fridge and the floor. I peeled off another and did the same. But then, prodding and wedging and blowing my breath against the metal, I suddenly felt the fridge begin to move. I caught a glimpse of white shoes and felt the wheels grating on the floor. There was a slow clamping pressure against my stomach and my ribs, a great squeezing that grew more and more intense. I had to suck in my breath and jam up my shoulders, and I suppose I must've made a squealing sound, for suddenly the fridge lurched violently away, and the white shoes were upon me. I had *light* again, and I had *space*, and I was lifted into arms that smelled of oranges. And the person who belonged to those arms rocked me and pressed me into her neck and said, 'My *God*, Oh my *God*!' and that was you, Ornella. My first memory of you.

MILK PIE

Garlic was just an exotic word before 1956, says Papa. Sausages were fat and bread and offal scraps, wound through Grandma Blanche's mincer and stuffed into intestines. Milk pie is the way Papa describes the culinary world he grew up in: spongy, creamy, white.

Starting out in life, Papa knew the following dishes off by heart:

Boiled Rabbit, which required 1 rabbit, 2 onions, 1 carrot and half a turnip, and could be served with a parsley or white sauce;

Brown Stew, which had a similar list of ingredients, but also stewing steak, and dripping;

Marmalade Pudding, which he still cooks in wintertime;

and *Roly Poly*, which involves something called *Suet*.

These four dishes came from a book of Grandma Blanche's called *Teach Yourself to Cook*, published by The English Universities Press. Also in the series were *Teach Yourself Household Electricity*, *Teach Yourself Astro-Navigation*, *Teach Yourself German* and *Teach Yourself More German*, and last, but not least, *Teach Yourself To Fly*.

Papa possessed none of the more applied and manly volumes, but with *Teach Yourself to Cook* in his swag, he lurched around the countryside after Grandma Blanche's death, laying bricks, killing rabbits and stealing vegetables from gardens. He got too much creek-water in his system and was so skinny you could hook your hands up under his ribs.

When he came to Melbourne, the city was getting ready for the Olympic Games. There were going to be fencing competitions in St Kilda Town Hall and weightlifting at the Royal Exhibition Building. On Swanston Street all the street-stalls had been vacated, or relocated, or put out of business via fines. It was a time of flags and gloves. Queen Elizabeth was everywhere: in profile on penny pieces, in touched-up photos in *Women's Weekly*. No one could say she wasn't lovely: the hint of blue in her eyes; her pale, smooth English skin.

On St Kilda Road, the plane trees spewed out their spores and made the commuters sneeze. Papa went for a walk and saw little inscrutable changes afoot in Melbourne. Places that looked suspiciously like art galleries (Papa was not sure) were popping up in buildings that had been haberdashers or dental surgeries. A woman in a black skivvy and green-and-red peasant skirt swished past on ballet slippers. A door banged open in the side of a wall and three men came laughing down some stairs, carrying musical instruments.

One day in late October, at the ripe old age of nineteen, Papa approached a restaurant called *la Coccinella*, having haltingly translated the half-English, half-Italian advertisement for a kitchenhand taped to the glass. He had applied a large quantity of hair oil. He had borrowed a suit from the Salvation Army. He knocked. A tram clattered past like a centipede in lead boots. The door opened. 'Then my real life began,' says Papa.

You were fifteen, Ornella, and you didn't like the new kitchenhand; you hated it when Nonno promoted him to first courses and desserts; you hated it even more when your parents decided to 'adopt' him. Papa says this like a fact, but surely a nineteen-year-old boy's too old to be adopted! In 1956, a nineteen-year-old boy was a man. They must've felt sorry for him. He was small, and a little bit dirty, and he looked like he needed caring for.

The whole situation made you miserable, Ornella. Papa even got his name changed by deed poll and he called your parents *Nonno* and *Nonna*, which were *your* words for them – because they were so old, so grey, their English was so bad, (so embarrassing).

But what kind of Italian family has no son? Papa was a prime specimen of native Australian-ness rolled up in unfulfilled filial longings.

Papa didn't forget his other life though. He didn't forget camping under Princes Bridge: the sound of water lapping at the pylons, the smells of brick-dust and clay and possum droppings, the violent rattle of traffic overhead. There was a scar on his wrist from a piece of glass or a razor blade. He was always, at heart, a small man, hoping for the best, never quite despairing.

WEST BRUNSWICK PROGRESS ASSOCIATION HALL

It was you, Ornella, who begged Papa to attend that fateful dance of 1958. Nonno wouldn't let you go on your own. A girl had to be chaperoned. Once through the door of the West Brunswick Progress Association Hall, you abandoned Papa. Naturally. (Who could blame you? He was not your keeper. And Carlito was waiting for you, with his full repertoire of masculine wiles.)

Papa made his way to the refreshments table. He took a fruit punch and rolled a cigarette one-handed, which he proceeded to suck on, propped up by a wall. I imagine him like Humphrey Bogart, with his top button done up and the waist too high on his trousers.

Mother, sitting a few feet away, also smoked. But while she smoked, she scribbled in a small book in her lap. In between attacks of writing, she sat almost entirely still, inhaling and exhaling cigarette smoke.

Papa had never seen a woman writing so publicly, in a notebook. It shocked him.

Mother didn't notice him until her cigarette went out. Then she looked up, waved her dead cigarette at him and he obliged. The flame went *poof!* between them like a French movie, and his metal lighter made a click as the apparatus fell back into place. In that moment of illumination, Papa saw Mother's eyes, a bit yellow in the reflection of the flame – 'tiger's eyes,' he says – which always embarrassed me, for in reality Mother's eyes were a very boring grey.

'What are you writing?' Papa asked.

Mother glared at him and stashed her notebook back into her purse.

'Do you like to dance?' he persisted.

'No,' said Mother. 'I'm here with my friend.' She brushed away some ash that had fallen into her skirt and pointed to a plump woman in a green dress, whirling on the dance floor. 'That is Esmeralda,' my mother said. 'She's a pharmacist's assistant.'

'And what are you?' Papa didn't mean it rudely. He didn't really know how to talk to girls, let alone women. And Mother was definitely a woman.

Mother puffed her smoke in a different direction to let him know she wasn't impressed. 'I'm a girl at a dance. Talking to a very short man who is dripping his fruit cup all over his shirt.'

And then she got up and left, and Papa discovered she was right and went immediately to the Gents to clean himself up.

That might've been the end of it, but later in the evening, outside, Papa saw her again and this time she and her friend were having an argument.

Esmeralda was yelling something at Mother about a 'blue fox'. She was shaking a decrepit-looking wet fur article in one hand, and angrily smoking a cigarette with the other. What Mother had done to her blue fox stole – for that's what it was – Papa was never sure, but he had to intervene, he says.

He had been taken in by those yellow 'tiger's eyes'. He needed to be gallant and valiant or, at least, memorable. He stepped in front of Mother just at the moment when Esmeralda threw her cigarette at her. It missed Mother but it got Papa in the chest, then fell to the ground. Papa put it out with his foot, glared at Esmeralda, and took Mother's arm.

The two of them proceeded haughtily up Sydney Road, not looking back, Esmeralda shouting out behind them.

'I didn't put her stole down the toilet,' Mother finally said. 'I dropped it in. Accidentally. I was trying to wash it.'

Papa said nothing, so Mother took a silver decanter out of her purse and offered him some whisky. 'My name's Veda. What's yours?'

They walked together for hours that night, Veda and Jo. It was not a cold night, so there was no good reason to huddle together, but at last Papa got his arm around Mother's waist. 'What were you writing, back there at the dance?' he asked.

She took out her last cigarette and lit it. 'A poem,' she said.

Papa had never read a poem in his life. Even at school (he left at the age of twelve) he had apparently missed the classes where poetry got read.

When Mother said she was writing a poem, Papa's mouth made the shape of an 'O'. He didn't quite take his arm from around her waist, but he was suddenly too nervous to kiss her.

Some days later, Papa attended Mother's first poetry reading.

The venue was a private apartment at the Aquarius Hotel. It wasn't a grand hotel, but it had been once: little flakes of gilt came off the plaster and there was a marble entrance hall. Now the third-floor rooms were rented out for dubious purposes, and the second-floor rooms for such curious events as poetry readings.

Mother had to learn her poems off by heart because her hands shook too much to hold the paper. When she finally stood up to read, she reeled slightly. But then she cleared her voice and looked straight out at the audience. 'This first poem,' she said, 'is called "Just My Type".'

Do you remember her voice, Ornella? It wasn't like anyone else's – not like you imagine a poet's, that's for sure. It wasn't like *cream*, or *honey*, or *liquid gold*. It was like a high-quality rasp – it filed away your defences. And her poem, when she began reciting, was all on the ascent – a crescendo of feeling, and rhythm, and momentum, and then a sudden capsizing that dropped the audience and left them momentarily hanging, all those fluttering, hapless poets Papa immediately resented for their educations and vocabularies. When she finished, Mother made a mock-bow, and the audience clapped, and, after several more drinks and congratulations and offers of other reading opportunities, Papa steered her to a taxicab.

He took her home that night to her flat in East Melbourne and put her under the covers of her unmade bed. She reached out to undo his trousers, but he avoided her and went instead to inspect her kitchen. There was half a pint of off milk in her refrigerator and a can of baked beans in the cupboard. Mousetraps littered the floor. Papa poured the milk down the sink and washed out the bottle. Then he walked the five miles back to Coburg.

REAL ESTATE

Papa had been part of your family for two years and you'd got used to him. He had become the quintessential Italian son, and he'd started bringing Veda to family lunches. Veda had a skinny chest like a griddle pan. She lived on custard and butter-beans and cigarettes, Papa says; she ate her peas one by one. Nonna must've desperately wanted to feed her.

Nonno wiped his big grey moustache with his napkin and nodded. You could see his singlet through his shirt. Mother smoked and wasn't paying attention. Nonna pursed her lips and ladled seconds onto plates.

They were very boring. They were talking *real estate.*

'Where exactly is it, this place, Joseph?' said Nonno.

'Acland Street. St Kilda. Right near the seaside. Luna Park.'

Nonna poured an inch of grappa into her husband's black coffee. 'You cook Italian food, Joseph?' she said.

Papa nodded again and shrugged his shoulders as if to say, what else? Nonna beamed. Ornella scowled. Mother looked wistfully into the deepening dark of the garden.

123 ACLAND STREET

123 Acland Street was a steaming fishbowl in summer and a brick of ice in winter. Papa opened lunchtimes Monday to Friday and for lunch and dinner on Saturday. People came. A trickle, never a rush. Papa alternated between 123 and La Coccinella. This went on for a year. It was tiring, but he loved it. His days were full. His life was busy. He had a *girlfriend who was not only beautiful, but smart too!*

Mother still lived in her flat in East Melbourne. She had a secretarial job at Goodwin & Franck Solicitors on King Street. The transformation this job had wrought in her, said Papa, was amazing. She was now a wearer of straight grey skirts and pale pink seersucker blouses. There still wasn't much food in her one-person-sized Frigidaire Mini, but there was fresh milk, and usually a couple of eggs and a plastic dish of butter. She loved typing, she told Papa. She loved punching the keys into their necessarily lexical (and yet strangely numerical) patterns. Mother could plant seventy-five words a minute, without error, from the keys of her Optimat Portable onto the archival-quality paper of Goodwin & Franck. *Ding!* For lunch, she fished into her beige Glomesh cigarette container – filled half with Menthol and half with Peter Stuyvesant – and drank a cup of coffee. Sometimes, she bought a tuna salad sandwich from Corn's Deli. The afternoons rolled on tediously, and sometimes – when her in-tray was empty – Mother rolled a piece of 100 gsm cream stock with embossed gold and red letterhead into her Optima and wrote some lines of poetry, just because she could; because no one was watching, because occasionally she became terrifyingly aware that being a secretary was being *paid to waste her life*. Sometimes, said Papa, Mother made poems purely out of chopped-up legal terms and phrases. 'My gobbledegook poems,' she called them.

Equitable estoppel,

Libel libel libel

Limitation of liability

Nonfeasance, reasonableness, nonfeasance

Mother earned £9 a week; she paid a considerable sum to have new curtains hung in her flat and bought herself a chest of drawers made of cedar, which she lined in paper sprayed with Arpege perfume. She and Papa had become engaged, and with that notion of herself as a *fiancée*, she had trimmed her wild edges. She still had a temper (she had thrown several desserts at Papa in their time together) but she was doted on now by Nonno and Nonna – even though you, Ornella, always suspected her of fraud. She was *as fit for marriage as a porcupine for a carriage*, you said.

Papa continued to live out the back of Nonno and Nonna's in Coburg. A man and woman, unmarried, might not live together in 1959. Besides, if Mother married Papa, she would have to leave her job. She didn't want to leave her job. She enjoyed her financial independence and the way Mr Goodwin deferred to her on issues of spelling, punctuation and syntax. Once a week, on Sunday mornings, Papa and Mother had sexual relations in the too-soft double bed in Mother's East Melbourne flat; she assured him she had everything in place to prevent conception. Papa asked no further. He says Mother seemed to like the arrangement, though he could never be sure as, at the end, as a general rule, she sat up, opened the curtains and brushed her hair vigorously for about half an hour, saying nothing but looking very cross.

Demure in her work guise as Miss Gray, at home Mother said exactly what she thought: she nicknamed Mr Goodwin 'Cane Toad' on account of his acne scars and Franck 'Cherry Ripe' on account of his repulsive red mouth.

Ultimately, when the time came, she was happy to get married and leave Goodwin & Franck, because of Mr Franck. Franck criticised her handwriting. He commented on the cuts and colours of her outfits. He liked to dally in the office out of hours and find ways to prevent Mother from leaving. Once, he patted her on her bottom when she stood next to him taking dictation. Papa always said the name 'Franck' like he was eating something disgusting and needed to spit it out.

ROSA

123 Acland Street was slow in finding its clientele. People wove from the beach to the streets and sometimes made it to the restaurant, where the fan whirred overhead in summer, turning the hot air round and round, and the icy wind from the sea filtered through the many draughts in winter. But often it was empty.

Papa employed one waitress.

Much to your disappointment, this waitress was not you, Ornella. You would've liked the freedom. Instead, you were holed up at home being Nonna's *slave labour* in the kitchen and learning the arts of marriageability. A marriageable woman needed to know how to cut and pin and tack and reinforce seams. Nonna had an overlocker. She could alter a pattern to 'fit like a glove'. She knew high-quality store-quality. She had worked for Manton's, even if it was as an underpaid piece-worker. So Papa left you in Coburg to sew and hem and instead employed Rosa Ferros, squat as a toad, plain as a chicken-house (until she smiled, and then you were dazzled by her beauty).

Rosa was an Italian Ashkenazi Jew who spoke an obscure Italian–Judeo dialect as well as English and Italian and Yiddish. She bustled into the restaurant as though evaluating it for higher purposes of her own. She proved an ultra-efficient waitress, passionate about food and generous with her smile. She smiled and nodded approvingly at her diners, and called out their orders to Papa through the hatch-window as though each were a declaration of good taste. She never picked them up on their bad pronunciation and forgave them when they used the wrong cutlery, added too much salt, cut up their spaghetti with a knife and fork. She smiled and they fell in love with her and ate whatever she recommended. Though 123 had no coffee machine, she brewed strong, dark coffee in the French way on the kitchen stove for them.

Rosa Ferros was also an artist.

A peasant artist, she called herself; she was self-taught and a bit folksy. But her images were moving. They caught your attention. She mainly drew scenes from Southern Tyrol where her whole family had been exterminated in the Bolzano Transit Camp in 1944. She had escaped long before the atrocities. In 1938 she had been freighted off to Melbourne as a proxy bride. It was soon after Mussolini had published his Charter of Race and her father had lost his job as a government official. Now she couldn't look at a picture of the Dolomites without breaking into tears. She loved her proxy husband,

Michele Ferros, as soon as she saw him from the porthole on the *Jervis Bay*. They had no children and he died of stroke only three years into their marriage. She would never love a man again, she said.

That was the story of Rosa's survival and freedom. She never saw the landscape of her childhood again, she never remarried, and she never located a single relative. So she painted out her personal losses in oils and watercolours and harsh charcoal line-drawings.

It was Rosa Ferros who got Papa onto the subject of Art. It was Rosa Ferros who took Papa to the *Antipodeans* exhibition and introduced him to James Parish.

THE ANTIPODEANS

The Antipodeans Exhibition was held by the Victorian Artists' Society in East Melbourne. Papa didn't know anything about art, knew only from Rosa that *abstract art threatens the future of art and civilisation*. The only artwork Grandma Blanche had had in her house was a reproduction image of a boy and girl, in eighteenth-century dress, holding a dead chicken in their cupped hands.

Rosa yanked him by the arm. 'Come and meet my friend, Mr Parish,' she said.

With his widow's peak, beaked nose and crest of greying hair, James Parish resembled an owl, thought Papa. A wise owl. An educated owl. An owl from the very top of the tree. He enthusiastically shook Papa's hand as though Papa were the very person he had hoped to meet that day. 'Lovely,' he said over and over. 'Lovely! How lovely!' He hooked Rosa and

Papa into an arm each and off they went, through the exhibition, James Parish giving them his commentary.

'Are you an artist too, Mr Parish?' Papa asked finally, when they seemed to have come to the end of the show.

Mr Parish disengaged himself. 'Oh lord, do I look like an artist?'

Papa stumbled. 'I don't really know what an artist looks like.'

'An artist can look like anyone,' confided Mr Parish. 'A door-to-door salesman. A vacuum-cleaner repairman. A taxi-driver. But no, *I'm* not an artist.'

'He *is* an artist,' said Rosa. 'Mr James Parish is a poet, like … what do you say? Like Alfred Lord Tennyson.'

'I'm no such thing,' said Mr Parish.

But Papa could tell Mr Parish was very important. Only the very important could pretend so well that they were no such thing.

'Ah! *There's no money in poetry*,' said Mr Parish, '*but there's no poetry in money, either.* Robert Graves. I'm happy with my slender little volumes and my handful of reviews, thank you.'

'You're a poet?' said Papa. He started to say something along the lines of, *my wife is a poet*, but didn't. They weren't married yet and, *my fiancée is a poet,* didn't have quite the same ring. (And then, after all, *was* Mother a poet? Or was she a legal secretary? He wasn't sure.)

'Indeed, I am a poet,' said Mr Parish. 'In spite of myself. I *wanted* to be an artist, did I not, Rosa? I tried valiantly. I studied. I primed my canvases. But no, unfortunately I had no talent. I am not a brother of the brush. I have to be content to be an avid collector of paintings. In the meantime, I write my little poems and publish them and hope I can capture in words some of what these gentlemen capture in paint.'

He turned back to the walls where Arthur Boyd's *Phantom Bride* hung.

'See!' he said. 'Look what Boyd can do! This is the difference between the art-forms. A painting can be apprehended at once, in its entirety. A poem cannot. Boyd's painting is both beautiful and painful to look at. Don't you find that?'

Papa strained his eyes at the painting: an ugly little flower-girl was offering flowers to a floating bride whom an unpleasant-looking gnome tried to hold down. What was the meaning of this painting? *Men are so ugly,* was Papa's instant feeling. *And they are forever trying to hold down their women.* He thought of Mother, only five hundred yards or so away, in her East Melbourne flat. What was she doing now? Filing her nails? Warming milk in the saucepan? Penning a line or two that expressed, obliquely, her own hopes – as a woman, as a bride? What did this painting mean? What was he, as a man, in the face of this painting?

He wanted to ask but Mr Parish steered them on.

'There's good art and there's bad art,' Mr Parish continued. 'That's the end of it. Figurative art is art of the human condition, that's why it speaks to me. But there's no reason I won't, one day, be moved by a Pollock or de Kooning. Then again, my wife achieves the same thing with her bloody *icky-bana.* Anyone who can do a bit of flower arrangement is uttering a prayer of sorts. Don't you think, Rosa?

'Mrs Parish makes a beautiful flower arrangement,' said Rosa soberly. (She felt an urge to defend her sex. There were no women artists in the Antipodeans exhibition, and Mrs Parish's flower arrangements *were* beautiful.)

'My problem ...' continued Mr Parish, 'is that non-figurative artwork makes the ordinary viewer feel stupid.' He considered a moment, 'It's undemocratic, in fact. That is my objection. It is *undemocratic*.'

Papa had never had a conversation like this before. Now he felt his inadequacies, the terrible gaps in his education, his country stupidness.

'Abstraction,' nodded Rosa, 'is just decoration. It is an American fashion and will pass.'

This then was their uniting theme, Rosa and Mr Parish. Papa couldn't otherwise make sense of their connection. Although he wasn't quite clear what *abstraction* amounted to, he understood that on this point they were allies.

In the end, Rosa had the better reason to resent the abstractionists. She was an immigrant female artist in post-war Australia. She would not be exhibited alongside the men. Not the big men nor the small. She would have to make an entirely new category for herself. But Papa would let her paint a mural of the Dolomites on the southernmost wall of 123. Soon. They would talk of it in weeks to come, in fact. And it would prove a drawcard for the restaurant.

In the meantime, when she went home that evening, Rosa selected six art history books from her shelves and brought them in a string-bound package to 123 the next morning. Papa eagerly untied the string.

THE DOLOMITES

So Papa became an art student of Rosa Ferros and James Reginald Parish. James Parish even gave Papa a John Perceval work on paper. The work was sketchy, unfinished-looking – he didn't really understand it – but it was the first artwork Papa had ever owned, apart from a poster of Popeye.

Papa put it on the wall at 123 and stepped back to check if it was straight. He wasn't entirely happy. 'Makes the wall look bigger and barer. Being on its own like that.'

'Well,' said Rosa, watching him, 'work hard, become rich, buy more.'

Papa squinted. It wasn't a big drawing.

'Or buy my unsold works on paper: then you have wall-paper, floor to ceiling!'

'Would be good to have more colour,' Papa said.

'Shame Parish didn't give you a Perceval in oil, huh? One of them big waterside colourful ones.'

'Colour,' said Papa. He thought of Van Gogh. Everyone knew Van Gogh: his madness, his tragedy, *his colour*.

Rosa stuck a fork into a jar of olives. 'Thing is: what you need here is not sad-eyed paintings while you eat dinner. Not crazy-face people whirling round your head. You want fields of wheat. You want waterfall and pebbles and sun. You want Nature. This is where food comes from. Nature. You got to think like a *restaurateur*, not like a art critic, Jo.'

Papa thought about this. He talked to Mother about it.

After work now, Mother came straight to 123. She sat at the window-seat, with a book in her hand – 'posing', Papa joked.

At close of business, she and Papa would catch the tram home to East Melbourne. They would get off the tram at Clarendon Street, curl up in Mother's bed, and in the morning, Mother would slip off to work and leave Papa snoring his rasping child's snore till he woke, all of a start, sweating, wondering where she was.

It was practice for marriage, Mother said, though of course, she would have no job to go to once she got married, no reason to get out of bed.

Mother loved that Papa was learning about art. She had started scouring second-hand bookshops for art books, bringing home treasures: Vasari's Life of the Artists; a beautiful unbound collection of Eugene van Guerard plates that set her back several weeks' wages.

'Get Rosa to paint a mural,' said Mother. They were in her East Melbourne living room on the new yellow-buttoned sofa. It was hot. She got up and her nightdress stuck to her bottom. She trotted into the bedroom for the latest collection of art magazines she had got cut-rate at Blundell's Books. She flicked through them, tossed one after another aside. 'Here,' she said, thrusting a dog-eared magazine in Papa's lap. 'Diego Rivera. Look. Communist mural art!'

'I don't like this much,' said Papa. 'It's very crowded.' He turned the magazine around and cocked his head.

'Something crowded might make the restaurant look full,' said Mother.

Papa turned the page. And Mother saw he was struck by something. She leaned over his shoulder to see.

It was an image by a Brazilian painter called Candido

Portinari. *The Hill*, 1933. 'Something like that,' Papa said, holding it out to her, 'that would work.'

The hill in Portinari's painting was rich brown in colour and very steep; people walked up it with goods balancing on their heads, ice blocks or cans or milk-jugs. In the left distance, the sea beckoned. In the foreground, a sullen woman looked out a window. The painting felt *easy* to look at to Papa: the curves, the angles, the literalness. People would understand it. They would be calmed by it and reassured by it and they would be happy to eat pasta alongside it. 'Something like that,' he said again to Mother.

'Sure I do a mural,' said Rosa the next day. 'You want St Kilda Beach? You want Esplanade, seagulls?'

'No,' said Papa. 'This is an Italian restaurant. I want Italy.'

And so Rosa painted the Dolomites.

Rosa's mural proceeded in fits and starts. She made sketches and tore up sketches. She started outlining the mountains, then painted over the outlines. She decided on a grid, and then decided that she couldn't possibly work within the confines of a grid. In the meantime, the restaurant was closed because there were dropsheets over everything and the place stank of paint.

Mr Parish arrived at unpredictable times and smoked a pipe and bossed Rosa around.

'Rosa, that mountain looks like a bloody camel's hump!' 'Too much foreshortening in the foreground, Rosa! That hut's about to roll into the valley!' 'What are you doing, Rosa! It isn't Stonehenge!'

He was enjoying himself. Rosa took no notice.

She threw herself into action, hauling in ladders, kicking away dropsheets and slowly but surely bringing to life her craggy, much-loved Dolomites, until finally there they hung, in their entirety, tremulous, snow-capped, against a crisp winter sky that was just turning dark.

Rosa's mural was a hit. Two days after its completion a reporter from the *Melbourne Herald* came with a photographer and a flashbulb on a stick and before they knew it, Rosa and Restaurant 123 were in the papers, Rosa looking a little squatter than she would've liked but beaming her famous smile, and the peaks of the Dolomites rising behind her in soft drifts of pinkish cloud. The restaurant was never empty again.

THE WEDDING MENU

You know the story from here. 123 was a success. Papa started making money. Rosa got a few clients: one wanted the Cappadocian Caves in her dining room; another wanted the south of France, *trompe l'eoil* style.

Mother and Papa were married at St Peter and Paul's Church in South Melbourne in 1959. There was confetti, or rice, because you can see it in a black-and-white photograph, raining down on them. Mother's ducking her head and Papa's laughing up at it. There are other photographs, but I don't know whether to believe them. A portrait shot of the happy couple, for instance: Mother's mouth slightly parted to reveal a millimetre of white teeth; Papa gazing proprietorially down at the top of Mother's head. Is there any truth in that photo?

Papa looks like a conman and Mother looks positively sedated. And what's going on with their heights? Papa, looking *down* on Mother? What, did the photographer stand him on a milk-crate?

Then there's a photo of the family gathered around the wedding cake: not the croquembouche pyramid that Nonno had planned, but a three-tiered Anglo monstrosity – inch-thick icing with a slab of fruit-cake inside, the kind of cake that will survive decades wrapped up in a piece of tinfoil. I bet there were fifty-three dessert plates untouched at the end of the night.

The cake was provided by the Grays, Mother's family, who weren't convinced by Papa and his adopted Italians, and were clearly dubious about Veda, their black sheep. There are no photographs to document that, though. It was you who told me how, when Nonno tried to kiss *both sides* of Grandmother Gray's face, she pulled herself back in shock and knocked a floral arrangement off a table.

What other photographs were *not taken* that night? Well, after dinner and toasts, Mother proceeded to get completely drunk. She didn't end up in the tree ferns out back of La Coccinella, on her haunches, vomiting (as I would see others do over the years) but she did explode briefly over something she thought she heard somebody say that she didn't like and didn't agree with, and didn't think ought to have been said at a wedding. It might've come from Gray quarters; it might have been something about Eyeties or Roman Catholics. And she didn't leave elegantly for the Menzies Hotel, smiling from the windows of the cab, like the photographer would have us believe.

She trotted to the taxi with her wedding shoes swinging in her hand, and when she threw her bouquet, it ended up stuck in the canvas awning of a neighbouring shop. The expense of the Menzies Hotel ended up being a waste. Mother spent most of the night with her head over the toilet bowl. Father told me this fondly but sadly.

What should I believe then? I choose to believe the wedding menu. You kept this, folded, for years. I found it when cleaning out your house in Richmond. And menus can be trusted. Food is a solid fact.

The wedding menu:

Gli antipasti: offered on trays with the obligatory champagne. (Actually, Italian sparkling wine. Nonno now had a 10 pm liquor licence, though with the odd condition that he only serve Australian wine, a condition he did not observe.)

Capelle di funghi ai gamberetti
Carciofi con maionese all'Arancia
Crostine al dragoncello

You slaved for hours for all those tiny little shrimp-stuffed mushrooms, didn't you, Ornella? Carlito laughed at you as he smoked in the kitchen doorway and you pinched and tucked this fiddly finger food and he called you *la domestica*. And did Mother and Papa ever thank you? No, not properly, never. *Never!* Mother picked up a piece of crostini, took a bite, and put it back on the tray.

I primi:

Polenta pasticciata con il gorgonzola

o

Passato di spinaci alle nocciole

You toasted the hazelnuts. You wound the spinach through the foodmill. Your mouth was taut and grim. Nonno was laughing and happy in the background. The kitchen was a place to sing, he said, and he sang, badly. You were grimacing, but you kept working.

I secondi:

Pollo al vin santo

o

Spezzatino ai piseli

This was Nonno's area. You untied your apron. You smoked a cigarette in the courtyard with Carlito. Nonna found a splash of oil on your pink silk dress and yelled that you were stupid for wearing it in the kitchen. You'd wanted to wear dark blue silk, but Nonna said that was married women's silk and not suitable.

I dolci:

Budino di albicocche al caramello

o

Crema al mascarpone

You made these the day before. Nonno sent you up to King and Godfree to get Vin Santo. The man at the till asked after

Carlito and nodded and laughed when you said Carlito was 'good as gold'. He made a doubtful shape with his mouth.

It was on the way home from the wedding that Nonno began feeling a strange burning sensation in his jaw and throat. Nonna said it was all that laughing and singing. But then it spread, there was a heaviness in his left arm, and he said he thought he'd drunk too much – his head was odd, he was dizzy. Nonna said he needed to watch it: he ate like he didn't care about his waistline, and he drank like a fish. She'd been telling him for years to do more exercise, drink less alcohol. He didn't reply. She put her hand on his forehead and it was cold and wet and his breath was coming in short little bursts. By the time they reached Thornbury, he was dead.

30 OCTOBER 1985

Dear Mr Ferrugia,

Let me first thank you for meeting with me last Thursday to discuss your mother's work. Further to our conversation, we have set a tentative date for publication of *The Poems of Veda Gray* of 8 May next year. I attach the intended contents list for your perusal. Where untitled, poems are identified by their first lines. We are planning to include 316 of the 410 you originally sent us. This will include all from her original book in their intended form.

I reiterate that we feel very grateful to you for allowing us to publish your mother's work – it is daring and experimental and casts new light on mid-century modernism. I understand too that this project brings up difficult memories for you and appreciate your preparedness to assist.

In response to your question re readership: there is currently a genuine excitement occurring in feminist scholarship and art curation, and a renewed interest in overlooked works of female authorship. Certainly, we will use this broadening interest to our advantage in marketing.

Further to the poetry, your mother's letters to her sister, as we discussed, are a piece of literature in their own right. We have communicated our thanks to the estate of Matilda Bryant for bequesting these, but await your opinion before proceeding with publishing plans on that account.

As requested, I now forward this correspondence from your mother to her sister in as close to its original chronology as possible. I hope you find her letters as vivid and interesting as we have.

Yours truly,

JULIA GRAHAM-HAMMOND
Bacchae Publishing
Carlton
Melbourne

EXTRACTED LETTERS FROM THE CORRESPONDENCE OF VEDA GRAY (FERRUGIA) AND MATILDA BRYANT, 1961–62

10 NOVEMBER 1961

Dear Tilde,

Have just come inside from bright sunshine in the backyard, tomato plants covered in green baubles, beginnings of a 'kitchen garden' evident in fronds of dill and mint (such a hardy wanderer once it gets going!) – all of which sounds idyllic had I not, wheeling up to come in, nearly garrotted myself on the washing line. (One hardly conceives how the accumulation of wet white flannels turns the whole apparatus into a death trap.)

At least now we are in spring, things will dry (clothes, mud &c). Owen is always dirty, but having quickly learned the futility of washing dirty articles only to have them soiled again within minutes, I am no longer applying myself fastidiously to that particular treadmill. A little freedom is good for children (apparently) but they have too much of it here, where a park, if it springs up by order of a civic authority, is immediately transformed into a battleground with stones, sticks, slate or firecrackers.

It is of constant surprise to me, Tilde, that I now find myself in this stolid little house in Fitzroy, feeding pennies into a slot to run the gas. You have always said I was contrary by nature. If I had started out poor, no doubt I would now be married to a rich man – although perhaps, lacking the charms to <u>net</u> a rich man, I am overly optimistic.

Instead our mother got a drop-out daughter and a son-in-law who wears an apron for a living. Didn't I just thwart her brilliantly? Send her my slummy old love, will you? Jo will sell the St Kilda restaurant soon and I'll send her a present with the proceeds. (Diamond necklace?)

Love Veda x

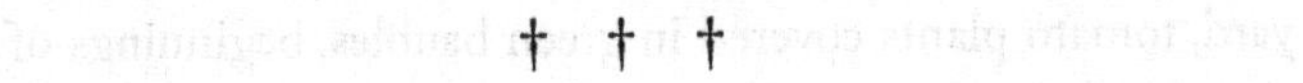

30 NOVEMBER 1961

Dear Tilde,
Have just got in from the Parishes'. I believe I've mentioned them – he, the famous poet and she, the wife. Spent the weekend at their Estate (there is no other word for it: it is vast though there ain't a paddock in sight). On said Estate we get 'in touch' with Nature. Jo looks at paintings he doesn't have the words for with Mr Parish, and foodstuffs (which he does) with Mrs. P. We went for the whole weekend, which means we must suit ourselves, and wander, and fill in time as best we can. I, for my part, am at a loss to do much there but walk and smoke, fearing the 'pose' of settling at the window with my notebook and pen. For, as I am never asked of my own literary prowess (except by Mrs, occasionally, in whispered undertones) I cannot bring myself to foist the 'fact' of it (dare I call it 'fact'?) into the Parish consciousness.

They are friends of a different cut – (may one describe a friend like a trouser?) Much better to chat about food, or to prove myself a discerning reader of other people's work. I acquit myself intelligently enough in literary discussions. I have given opinions on the latest offerings in Southerly and been agreed with, though with reservations. Mr Parish has a new collection he hopes will come out late next year. He expounded on that, as much as poetry of one's own might be expounded upon. I did not mention my second-rate readings in second-rate rooms with second-rate poets, where I briefly thought myself a rising star before it became apparent that it was the same eleven men poets, every reading, and I was in fact getting nowhere very fast in their company.

Mr Parish is an entirely different species. They pay him to speak on the radio and sit on boards of charities and philanthropic organisations. His poetry gets reviewed in America and Canada and Britain. It's an honour really just to be taken seriously by him in conversation. We have had several lively debates, such as Ern Malley, that old chestnut, where I find him a harsh critic of MacAuley and Stuart. He says C-C (of Meanjin) is absolutely a snob, and every rakish detail I extract from him I put under my bonnet to savour later. (I have been rejected by C-C so many times that I can no longer pencil the address on an envelope.) I am happy not to speak of my own 'work' really (I can barely even call it such, not even to you, for fear that it might shrivel in the face of being taken seriously).

You would be bored to tears by the literary bent of our conversations, but to me, they are such a breath of fresh air, so full of first-hand anecdote and educated opinion. It makes me feel part of the literary world, even if as an interloper. Still, I am red-faced with shame when I recall the secret 'package' I lay on Mr Parish's desk that time, creeping away afterwards and hoping for a word of encouragement. Which was, as I believe I told you, unforthcoming. Perhaps the package 'blew away' or 'disappeared up the chimney' – it was fairly lightweight, after all. I nurture a mild vanity that the sheer brilliance of my poems was overwhelming. Still, I blush now. (I will come back, must attend to a roasting chicken that needs carving, gravy-ing … and the child is at large with crayons …)

Back. Owen asleep like a wind-tossed angel – all devils look like angels when asleep – so let me tell you more of our new friends the Parishes. Mrs Parish I like very much: she is hen-pecked (might a woman be 'hen-pecked'? I turn it over in my head and think it perhaps unacceptable to say …) She is brown and dour, tall and square, with shoulders like a man's, and beautifully set hair. Pale brown twin-set that forces her shoulders into a stoop as though the tension in the knit is too tight. I have put her in poems once or twice, as you can see above. I like her but I don't know what to make of her: she is a figure of both ridicule and respect.

The 'wild' of Park Orchards is beneficial for Owen, who totters in from the outdoors, tumbleweeded and sunburnt, to eat large portions of bread, dripping, apples from their own trees &c. And that is before lunch! I am not quite so blasé, however, as to forget ponds, dams, disused mineshafts … In fact, I cannot even read contentedly, for I must look up and spot Owen continually, and then put things down (pages flutter, place is lost) to run over and check he is indeed behind that tree and hasn't crossed some boundary line, past which reside snakes, bunyips, men with shotguns …

It is living in Fitzroy that has made me alert to every sound and possibility; before, they were mere stories from unimaginable places. Just last week, a little girl some houses down was attacked by her mother's lodger, a tall thin apparently average man I had been in the habit of saying hello to!

The lease we will soon take on in Hawthorn is just across the Yarra River from Richmond, near the Skipping Girl lights you commented on when last here: a big old house split in two, of which we will take the front portion. There is a bay window and big shadowy trees in the garden. Paperbarks in the street. The tram runs nearby, straight into the city.

If you ask me how my 'work' proceeds in the midst of everything, I can only tell you: short, unsatisfactory stints mainly. There is so much to do around the house. And yet, when I find myself with an uninterrupted few hours, I'm panicked, can't get a thing down. I open my notebook, and a great wave of exhaustion overcomes me. Is it that the thought of work tires me, or that my own work bores me so much it puts me to sleep? I suspect some subconscious avoidance is at work. When I have time, at a desk, in silence, the whole enterprise of Poetry (capital P) becomes preposterous. Like pretending to work at the Parishes': a pose. And now I am writing in alliteration.

I only tell you this because I know you will encourage me and pepper me in praise that, deserved or not, will spur me on to more scribbling!

Meanwhile, on the home front: I went out and bought two slabs of steak yesterday, and came home and fried the whole thing up with potatoes and mushrooms. My husband was delighted to be served a meal he was not involved in the making of, and O choked on a piece larger than it should've been – Jo leaned across the table in a flash, had O by the chops and his hand down his throat and up came the offending article, hardly chewed as that boy does not chew but <u>inhales</u> food. God help me, what a palpitation of the heart: I felt weak eating the rest of dinner.

Things like that make me feel I am an imposter as a mother. Surely other mothers pay better attention. Is it like that for you, Tilde? I hope Owen can't tell!

I have hardly enquired about Frank's work, or Marigold's nuptials. You must send back big, thumping letter full of detail and laughs,

Veda x

21 DECEMBER 1961

Dear Tilde,

Happy Christmas to you! We are in Hawthorn! For the purposes of play, Owen now has a big front garden behind a big safe fence with a big fat tree to climb, and I have private use of a light-filled room where I have set up a desk and my papers. The room is next to the 'nursery' (this is a small antechamber connected to our bedroom, where Owen sleeps). We have a little Xmas tree that shimmers amongst all our unpacked boxes, and are feeling delightfully, frugally festive.

Thank you for your account of M's wedding. Did my platter arrive unbroken? I assume it did. Or perhaps you would not tell me if it didn't. Never mind. My platter is the least of their concerns, or yours.

Jo is resuming management of La Coccinella in Little Collins Street. It will be a step up from 123 – which turned out, upon finalisation of the sale, to make us a nice little profit.

I encourage Jo in his ventures, because he seems to have a business head on him. God knows where he got such skills. Again, I say, I trust him. Isn't that a fabulous thing to say about one's husband? It makes me almost content to be a wife.

Meanwhile, I have had another rash of rejections. I think it is wise to describe them as a rash: it helps me see them as a temporary disfigurement rather than a permanent affliction. I had thought these last poems were un-rejectable. I really did. I've compared them to others being published – I do believe I'm knowledgeable about this, I believe I can identify what is good and what is not – and I really felt they stood up well. The crafting was good, the metaphors new and fresh, the ideas contemporary. So it was trying to have them come back to me, like barbed little boomerangs, accompanied by slight comments that told me nothing beyond 'no'.

Actually, it is more than trying, getting these letters. It is crushing. It makes me feel that, no matter how very hard I try, the world doesn't want what I have to offer.

But I am also enough accustomed to it to know that in a few days, the hurt will rub off and I'll feel back to myself again. I'll spring back, as they say.

In my daring moments, Tilde, I have thought I will hawk my writing on street corners. On a soapbox. I will be thought a religious preacher, no doubt, and will bring disgrace upon my family. I will self-finance a run of chapbooks and keep them under my bed; if they do not sell, I can line a ceiling with them. (Yes, insulation is my fallback plan!)

Would you buy a book of poetry, I ask, if some bolshie female waved it in your face as you passed her in the street? Well, you might be curious enough to look … would you? (I have gone so far as to wonder what colour to make my imaginary chapbook. Red, I have heard, is more attention-grabbing in shops.)

Happy happy, merry merry and all of that!

Veda x

† † †

7 FEBRUARY 1962

Dear Tilde,

You're very good and kind and loyal. You always were. I never understand those women who say they are not friends with their sisters. I feel I have never had a friend but a sister! And now I feel positively Rossetti-like …

The refurbished 'La Coccinella' (not sure why I put that in inverted commas) is close to opening. I am needed to play maitre d' and must leave Owen in the hands of Ornella while I do so. Ornella makes me nervous. I can't help suspecting she will thwart me in some way or other, undermine me. She has never liked me. But she's too damned convenient to do away with, I'm afraid. However, Owen is a lamb, and is good with anyone – only difficult with me. And what can I do? Who do I put first in the end: Jo or Owen? The needs of my husband or the needs of my child? That, it seems to me, is the greatest conflict in a woman's life, if truth be known. Or so it seems right now, when they both demand my attention so.

Hmmmmmm. Advice sorely needed, gratefully received.

Meanwhile ... I have met an interesting and possibly advantageous character who might avail me of new opportunities. Not sure. (Narrow your eyes when I say such things.) Mr Barrington Knox runs the bookshop across from the restaurant on Little Collins. Sells a lot of poetry – modernist imports mainly. He is a frequenter of the Savage Club, where he hobnobs with doctors and lawyers and bankers and gets them investing in his projects – one of which is an annual poetry and art magazine called Strident. It's not Meanjin, but I like what I've seen of it. He wants to read my work. Eeeek. I feel like a deer trapped in headlights. Paralysed. I will slip a wad of 'em under his door and run like 'the wind'.

Give me a moment: sudden nappy mishap. My laundry is the deep pit of hell ...

Where was I? My new friend, Knox.

He's a barrel of a man – drinks whisky, eats beef, takes cream. Large moustaches. Wears fur. Has a darling wife named Edith, the size of a sparrow, who is always rearranging books on shelves and smiling. I like her. I like him, I think. He has gusto. They are very good with Owen. Let me put him on the floor while I talk, without getting agitated about him touching things. They love books it seems, but they're not so precious about them that a small child is a threat. So I have been going in to their bookshop regularly and talking poetry with them.

Very different conversations to the ones I have with Parish. There's lots of laughter, and usually a sherry bottle passed around, and occasionally the little bell on the door will tinkle and some poor interloper will come in actually wanting to browse and buy and will be utterly discomposed by the sight of us, lounging on the floor with our shoes off, using the bookshelves to prop our ashtrays and drinks on. (The painter John Brack popped in last week! That sobered us up.) Anyway, in one particularly animated conversation, I got to telling them about my own poetry. (I can't seem to help myself from spilling the beans.) So, as above: poems will get slipped under their door. All I have to lose is a convenient, peaceable bookshop relationship. I should read the newspapers more anyway …

Will let you know the outcome, if there is one. In the meantime, send my love to Frank.

x Veda

25 MARCH 1962

Dear Tilde,

Well, the child talks! We have fourteen words now counted: opsicle (popsicle), toast, mamma, dadda, engine, ball, dog, milk (pronounced 'moolk'), banana, chip, car, book, rooster, and, unaccountably, cucumber!

Phew for that! He is and will be turning into a real person, it seems. I must say, I was starting to wonder … He will come to the word 'no' pretty soon, I imagine, and I will be thinking back wistfully to the days of gibberish. His father is gratified that nearly half his words are foodstuffs. For my part, I am particularly proud of the word 'cucumber' which he utters with great delicacy and refinement: 'Too-tumber!'

Owen has coped well enough with Ornella while I have been helping out at La Coccinella. I will do it only another week or so and then Jo will be properly on his feet and charming and seating guests and popping corks and folding napkins himself. He thinks I ought to be home, and he's no doubt right. In fact, I don't really know why he needed me in the first place – except that wives provide a sort of stabilising influence, attest to their husband's respectability etc. Anyway, it's been tiring for me who must be up at the crack of dawn dandling a baby and making infant-friendly stodge for breakfast.

You are, no doubt, hankering after details of my latest poetry exploits. Yes, indeed, who would not be? Such a grand story, such heights and troughs!

Well, Mr Barrington Knox read my little offering and 'really quite liked' it, selecting two or three (he is not sure which) for inclusion in the next issue of Strident at a payment of TBC. Edith is hysterical with excitement. I don't know whether to like her more for her enthusiasm or less. So long as her husband respects her opinion, I suppose all is well. Still, it has strained the friendship somewhat and the sherry libations are a little more measured, a little more businesslike. There's much more stroking of Knox's moustaches (him, as he thinks) and quiet, serious talk. Still, unlike at the Parishes', my status as a poet is at least taken seriously. Two (or three!) poems for real publication, Tilde!! I don't care if I don't earn a cent!

I should not be so complaining of Mr Parish, of course. He has been of immeasurable help to Jo, especially with a new business undertaking they are talking of. It is he who really gets behind us. (By us, I mean Jo. But you know that …)

Love Veda x

† † †

20 APRIL 1962

Dear Tilde,

Susan Mavis asks to be remembered to you. Do you remember Susan? She is now Mrs Gordon Bridie, and lives in Malvern, and, it seems to me, has a life of solid-gold luxury. She came to dinner after seeing *My Fair Lady* at Her Majesty's Theatre and was most surprised to find me at the helm of the newest, most fashionable restaurant in Melbourne. She herself, she says, is a practising watercolourist. (She does not call herself <u>an artist</u>, so I imagine she must be a painter of decorative wall-hangings for spare rooms, nicely framed in neat little gilt frames.) Anyway, she is now wife of Gordon Bridie, architectural historian and founder of the Melbourne Gallery. Old money, but good taste. She was dressed in the most beautiful Hal Ludlow gown, still has her perfect button nose, and elegant figure. Gorgeous, maddening creature. No children. She said this in a sad little whisper, so I am guessing this is not from a lack of trying. Gordon-Bridie is a patrician gent, thirty years older than her, but affable, gracious – like a fat old uncle who spoils you terribly and pays your school fees. Liked him immensely. She is still <u>exactly</u> as we knew her at school:

still capable of flexing a claw when you least expect it. I told her you were fantastically happy, had simply a glut of children, including one absolutely beautiful daughter just married (that was churlish, was it not?). And she told me about her house in Malvern, holiday house in Portsea, and the 'lovely little flat' they have just purchased in Nice. Grrrr. Anyway, she is now properly remembered to you, and I should be perfectly happy to meet with her again, now I know the score.

Send me a lovely gossipy letter about you and yours, will you? I am home on my own much of the time now, having finished at the restaurant. I wasn't needed anymore – well, I was needed more by Owen. But after the excitements of the late-night world, I'm rather ruined for going to parks and talking to other mothers, pushing swings and making sure children aren't clouted in the face by flying see-saws … it is tedious beyond description. I entertain Owen by popping him on the grass in the front garden with some dirt and a spoon and some water and saucepans and letting him get as muddy as he can, while I gaze and potter and write a word or two, and snatch poisonous plants out of his grip. (It is a fabulously lush garden, just brimming with poisonous flora.)

What I'm saying, in my usual longwinded way, is I'm missing the company of a working life, and I need to live vicariously through you and your busy flock of childer and tireless rounds of country life, good works, tea parties, sheep auctions, etc. & etc.

Love Veda x

18 MAY 1962

Dear Tilde,

Am feeling very odd, not myself at all. This afternoon I had a personal visit from Mrs Parish, with an objective that has left me in a very strange state. I hardly know what to think. I feel like, having journeyed through an unexpected tunnel, I have come out into a landscape I no longer know.

She phoned me on Monday, and informed me she was in town the next day and would like to take me to tea. Could she pick me up in the car at 11:30? (Well, I would once have thought she could take me anywhere in that car. It is about the most luxurious thing I have ever travelled in – I told her myself. I said, Should I die a rich woman, Mrs Parish, I would be buried in that vehicle.)

She came at 11:30 and drove Owen and me to tea rooms in Glenferrie. Owen was meek as a lamb all the way there. For his good behaviour, he got an enormous chocolate éclair that he made short work of, and warm milk in a cup. I had nothing because I've got so damned fat, just coffee. Mrs Parish had a scone and weak tea.

Mrs Parish was ill at ease the whole time: very serious, and embarrassed, and speaking so low it was hard to hear her. She had a proposition to put to me, she finally said. Well, the proposition came from her husband actually, but he thought it right the two of us talk it over as women, it being women's business – at which point, Tilde, my antennae went all a-quiver – and she could see it might work for me, it might be helpful, well, she hoped it might be helpful for me, for my writing ... So, here was the thing: they like us very much, Jo and I. They love Owen as if he were their own. They have much more money than they need, and no children. So, what they proposed was to invest in Owen's future: they would open a Trust Fund, and into it deposit an amount every month until he was twenty-one, if we would agree to allow them to become his legal 'guardians'.

Well, Tilde, lucky I had only ordered coffee because I suddenly lost all appetite. 'Guardians?' I said. 'And what do you mean by guardians?' Here she became all pink and unhappy and said, 'We would like him to be, in some formal way, a part of our family.'

I've never seen a woman wince so many times in a single conversation, Tilde. Still, I could tell that, in spite of her discomfort, and in spite of her husband putting her up to it, there is a desperation in her – that this is something she wants as well. Not necessarily for reasons that are bad or dishonest or mercenary ... God knows I have little enough writing time – on that, she's correct. So I restrained my sense of offence, and asked for details. She wants, she said – they want – merely to act as de facto 'uncle and aunt' to Owen. To have him on weekends and holidays. To give him some of the advantages they can offer: a really good education, good connections, country air, holidays abroad.

Tilde, I don't know how I feel about this. At the time, I was so angry it was all I could do to keep my seat. I thought: they think I'm not a good enough mother. But afterwards, in the car home, my heart went out to her. Just looking at her in the driver's seat, her stooped back, spidery grey hair – I began to feel sorry for her. She must be getting on for fifty. Stuck for life with a man who, despite his intelligence, is not warm, is not loving ... I thought of her in that big cold quiet house, and I couldn't help imagining how much joy a child's voice would bring ...

We took our leave from the car and I imagine she probably sobbed all the way home. I certainly did when I got inside.

I haven't even told Jo yet. What should I do? I am all crinkled up with pain and empathy. (And yet, there is a part of me ... Well, the truth is, I can't help thinking of all the writing time it would buy me.)

Write me wisely!

Love Veda x

† † †

5 JUNE 1962

Dear Tilde,

I'm looking at Owen right now as I write, and I am putting him in his nicest warm jacket and the only pants without mends or stains, and sending him off to the Parishes' for the weekend.

While he's gone, I will work on a new poem that is threatening to become something of an epic – a long poem, structured in many stanzas, mainly free verse (though there is of course no such thing – I am with Mr T.S. Eliot on this). I have my desk set up, with a lamp on a coiled metal neck that I can adjust to suit, and a pile of books to refer to (*Aurora Leigh* on top). A desk with a nice polished surface, and several drawers for my pencils, and notebooks, and bits of paper, and pins, and photographs, and glasses. It is the nicest workspace I have ever had. And yet I have no inclination to sit down and work there. No inclination whatsoever. All I can think of is the car coming for Owen at noon. What sort of a mother? Though Owen annoys me, and tires me, and exasperates me to my core, he is my very own little love.

Jo says it is normal for a mother to think like this and it would be strange if I did not. However, he's practical about the arrangement: it will mean, he says, that Owen will have all the things in life he did not. It will give me time to work. My parents live too far away have a proper relationship with Owen and so he has no grandparents to speak of. Yet I know there is another unspoken consideration at play. Jo is talking of leasing a small shopfront next to La Coccinella, and setting it up as a gallery … specialising in prints and works on paper, I believe. Mr Parish is to be his principal advisor and investor – he is pivotal to the whole scheme.

So, in other words, I am trapped.

You are right when you say that mothers get too caught up in their children. You are probably right too when you say that, when I have had more children, I will be less anxious. But I am not sure I will have more children. And Owen is so small. And what sort of a mother gives her child away to another woman? I feel sure that, were I to confide in anyone other than you – if I were to tell any woman of this arrangement – I would become a very suspect creature indeed.

And yet, there is another part of me that feels guiltily, horribly relieved. Because for two days I will be spared the grizzling, the whingeing, the feeding, the playing, the interruptions, the soiled clothes and the soiled floor and the soiled table, the crying – the endless endless crying – when I just want to slam the door on the room but must sit and rock and pat and soothe and meanwhile the clock ticking ticking ticking …

Must go. I think I hear the car. Wretched thing. I now consider it a kind of hearse.

Veda x

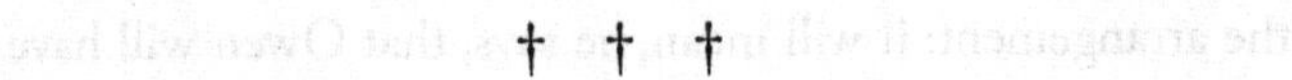

PART 2

CREATIVE BONES

FEMINIST COLLECTIVE 1985

Julia Graham-Hammond wore a brown pants suit that seemed to be made of plastic. It wasn't – it was some other sheer, rifling material, entirely professional. It squeaked when she moved in her seat.

'You're not a writer, are you, Mr Ferrugia?' she said, screwing up her nose in a way that suggested being a *writer* was really being a *pain in the arse*, and that we would get along much better if I weren't one.

I shook my head. I was twenty-five years old. As a child, I'd briefly thought I wanted to be a writer, but such ideas had long since evaporated.

'No, I'm not a writer,' I told Julia. She had ordered a pink wine I had never tasted before. It was tart, stringent, went straight to my head.

'Originally,' said Julia, carving a morsel off her veal scallopine, 'I had wondered if it might be suitable for *you* to write a foreword to the poems. The child's perspective. You know.' She put a forkful to her mouth. 'Not entirely in keeping with our agenda as a feminist press, you being a man and all, but the *relationship* is interesting, the mother–child relationship, I mean – it's a relationship that deserves to be put back at the centre of things ... But then I thought, well, this needs to be ... it *has* to have the force of scholarship behind it. Hence Emily Platz. She has a reputation as a feminist literary theorist, lots of people interested in what she has to say.' She smiled and chewed and put her hand up to her mouth as she spoke. 'I'm sorry, I'm sort of thinking my thoughts out loud. I'm such a *fan* of your mother!'

'Well, I don't think I could write a foreword anyway,' I said. 'Because I wouldn't have a clue what to say.'

'I suppose you could start with why you sent us the poems?' Julia said. She was like a bird, a smart one, beady-eyed. She put her hand across the table to me, but there was too much clutter in the way; her thumb connected briefly with my wrist.

'I had to do something with them. I'm no judge of poetry but, you know, if they were good – as you seem to think they *are* – I would feel a bit of an arsehole if I left them to …' I was going to say 'the rats and mildew' but fished around and came up with '…obscurity.'

'Ah.' She looked at me quizzically. 'I understand.' She withdrew her hand and clasped it with the other under her chin. 'And the letters? Do you have any thoughts on them? *I* was thinking, a companion volume. I think it's best to keep the two texts separate, you know, intact. Necessary to each other, but … separate.'

I must have looked horrified because Julia's face changed and she made a pained expression as though she'd said exactly the wrong thing and wished she could take it back.

'We don't have to talk about the letters now! I have this terrible habit of saying things as they come into my head. I'm always going too far.' She smiled broadly and resumed her attack on her meat. I'd never seen a woman eat meat with such relish.

'It's okay,' I said, 'but I'm not sure it's a great idea to publish the letters. You know, my father's still alive, for one thing …'

She nodded, but it wasn't a nod of agreement.

After lunch, back in her office, Julia sighed and sat down behind a desk piled high with proofs held together by rubber bands. She was about thirty, I guessed. She seemed incredibly old and incredibly sophisticated. But her office reminded me of the feminist collective office at university: dominated by a corkboard covered with slogans, a facsimile of the face of Virginia Woolf (yes, I knew who it was), book cover mock-ups with names like 'My Body, My Church' and 'Incursions into Femininity'. On the wall was a strange naïve horse painting by a local artist called Jenny Watson and a delicate paper collage by someone called Elizabeth Gower.

'Want to meet me for a drink this evening, Owen?' Julia said, apparently flippantly. 'There's a very interesting lecture on at Trades Hall. They have a great bar there. I'm obliged to go. Speaker's a friend of mine. Well, acquaintance.' She laughed a burly laugh that was out of keeping with her slightly prim good looks. 'Might be interesting for you. It's a feminist lecture.' I didn't say anything. She laughed again, gathered up some papers and thrust them at me. 'Here. Early proofs. *Veda Gray*.'

I sat in a chair and leafed through the proofs of Mother's book while Julia rearranged things on her desk and listened to messages on her answering machine. Mother's poems were alien to me. I didn't know if I liked them or not. I was a discerning reader, I thought – like other young 'educated' men of my time, I had read a little Proust and a little Joyce and probably too much Hemingway – but I didn't know whether my mother's poetry was any good, or whether Julia and her press were making a big mistake they'd later regret. The poems seemed to me to be about things poetry shouldn't bother itself with. Small things. Domestic things. I flicked through the proofs, noticing a misplaced comma, a hyphen where an en-dash ought to have been, an inconsistency in spellings, and pointed them out to Julia. She was impressed. 'Owen! Do you want work? I need a proofreader.'

But I stood her up at Trades Hall. Because I could. And because Mr Parish and Carlito had taught me the power of doing such things.

NONNO'S WILL, 1960

When Nonno died, he left everything to Papa. Everything. The house in Coburg was quarantined for Nonna's use until she died, and then it would become Papa's. The savings in Nonno's savings account: Papa's. La Coccinella: Papa's. Ornella, you got nothing. A girl would get married. Of course she would. After that, she would be her husband's responsibility. And there was Carlito, waiting in the wings.

But Papa could not run both 123 *and* La Coccinella. It was too big a job. So he sold 123, and took Rosa to work with him at La Coccinella.

Papa was twenty-five. He felt like a seasoned old man. He had money in the bank and he had his first child on the way.

Yes, I was about to be born to my shapeshifting mother, with her impenetrable moods, and my pint-sized father, altogether too small to ever get a proper hold on. And, in between, you, Ornella: smelling like perfume and pork fat, and entirely visible, from the very beginning.

Why is that? Why are you visible in a way that Mother isn't. I think it's because, as you have so often said, with relish: 'Owen, I don't have a creative bone in my body!'

ARMIDALE

At the end of 1963, Mother took me to Armidale, New South Wales, for Christmas. We went on the train. I had never been on a train journey longer than Hawthorn station to Flinders Street. Papa didn't come with us. We took sandwiches and drinks and Mother had a novel to read and I had a satchel full of toys and crayons.

We changed trains in Sydney. I could later say, at school, that I had been to Sydney. But I'd only been to the station. I wouldn't go to Sydney for years – not until Julia launched Mother's book in Glebe, in 1986, where it sold out on the night and we had to send someone in a taxi to get more from the warehouse.

We arrived in Armidale late in the afternoon, and it was still hot. Then night came. Suddenly. And it was suddenly cold. I grizzled for my jacket but Mother paid no attention. Her shadow was long and stretched out on the platform and I think she thought we were forgotten. I sucked the hem of her dress while we waited. I was not a baby anymore, but I still sucked on things and my favourite thing to suck on was damp beach towels. They were nice and sea-salty. But Mother's clothes were not nice and sea-salty. For one thing, Mother didn't sweat. I don't recall Mother ever sweating. Papa: he streamed with perspiration, but Mother was always cool as a *tutumber*.

We were not, of course, forgotten on the Armidale station platform. We were picked up in an FJ Holden ute by Mother's father, who was my *grandfather*. He got out of the car with big, heavy old-man's steps, said, 'Hello, love' and hoisted our luggage into the boot. His stomach was round and hard like a very large beachball. I was to call him 'Gramp'. In the car, through the passenger window, which Gramp wound down to halfway, I could smell water and dust in the air. It was a soft smell like wet soil and it made me realise I was far away from Papa, who had lifted me up that morning at Spencer Street station and called me 'my big beautiful boy' and told me to look after my mother. Afterwards my little summer jacket had been hooked up strangely under my armpits and Mother got cross. Gramp took one hand off the steering wheel and, without taking his eyes from the road, passed me and Mother a very dead packet of Lifesavers with crumbly silver foil. Mother recovered one for me and one for herself and passed them back. 'Same old you!' she said to her father, and I saw him turn his face to smile at her.

Mother's whole body changed when she saw the house. She sat up. She poked me in the ribs and said: 'Look Owen, look where Mother grew up!' She was almost pressing her face against the window. It was a big, dry wooden house. The roof was red like a storybook roof and from a distance, it looked like a squashed red hat. There were two more squashed hats, to the right of the house – bigger than the house, and flatter, grey in colour. Mother pointed to the distance. 'These are the Tablelands,' Mother said to me in a happy hushed voice, reaching for my hand, and I imagined the Tablelands as a series of great big dining tables with yellow tablecloths, covered in flat men's hats.

Mother's parents, my grandparents, were a pair. They fitted together. Gramp was grey-black and burnt like a gypsy; Grandmother was pink and white. They were salt and pepper shakers in a cruet set. Not like Mother and Papa, who came from entirely different crockery drawers.

On the verandah, Grandmother hugged me in a hot floral hug. She hugged Mother too, but with a little after-sigh that made Mother go immediately stiff. Mother's sister Jane came behind Grandmother. She hugged me too. Cousin Marigold and her husband hugged me. Auntie Tilde and Uncle Frank hugged me. Hannah, Aunt Tilde's freckly little daughter, did not hug me. She was thirteen and skinny as a piece of string. Skinny like a giraffe. She paid me no attention at all and I immediately, desperately, wanted her attention.

They ran Merinos, Mother had told me. I didn't know what a Merino was, but by the end of the visit I knew it was a *kind of sheep*. On the wall in the sitting room was a picture of Gramp's Prize Merino of 1952 with curly horns and big slabs of wool hanging in pieces across its back. It looked laden down with wool. It must have been a great relief, I thought, to get rid of all that wool. There was probably a skinny little sheep underneath that wanted to *gambol*. Gramp had the soft hands of a sheep farmer. 'Feel them,' he said and they were soapy and smooth.

Grandmother had crinkled white hair that reminded me of sheep's wool. Everything was *sheep sheep sheep* here: we sat in the kitchen and Gramp told Mother, ticking them off on his fingers like a shopping list: '1500 merino ewe hoggets, 560 border Leicester-merino cross, 200 first cross ewe lambs ...' Mother clapped her hands softly as though he were singing her a song.

In Armidale, Mother came into focus, Ornella. I could see her properly for the first time. She was a real person: of average height, with clear skin, symmetrical features and golden hair. Her eyes were grey, but sparkly too. When she moved it was with a nimble grace I hadn't seen before. She tripped happily about her parents' kitchen, picking up a cup, putting a jar in a cupboard. At home, she had two ways of being: *uptight* or *sloppy*. She either moved with great deliberation or she slumped. Both states of being were disturbing to me. Both were unhappy. Now, in Armidale, she put an apron on, tying it at the back and smoothing it at the front. She pushed her hair back from her face and fastened it with two pins. For the dishes, Grandmother had a little wire basket with a piece of Velvet soap in it. Mother held this under the hot tap and the bubbles bubbled out over her wrists.

At home, Papa always did the dishes. At the end of the night or before he left for work. Mother couldn't bear dishes. They depressed her, she said. She said she took one look at them and felt life was not worth living. (She said this frequently in fact: 'Life is not worth living' until one day I climbed up onto her chest and put my hand in her mouth to stop her.) Now she plunged her hands into the dishwater and happily clinked dishes in the rack for her niece to dry. She smiled tolerantly when Gramp teased her that she'd 'make someone a good wife one day' and when she finished the dishes she flicked him with the tea-towel.

'I'm so blessed to be the mother of daughters,' Grandmother sighed. 'When I've got all my daughters around, I don't need any help. I don't want anyone else in my kitchen!' Mother, hands dripping, came and put a kiss on Grandmother's crinkly head and Grandmother made a fuss about hot water dripping on her skirt.

I had never seen Mother so happy. She had a crisp outline in her shirt, a proper profile when she turned to look out the window. She was pretty and young and she had a good figure and a clever brain. *She was not a hog or a frog; she was not a cow or a sow; she was not even a witch or a bitch; she was* beautiful *and she was my mother*! That night I lay in the dark in a twin bed next to hers, with the covers tucked tight across my chest. I could hear Mother breathing next to me in her own bed, I could see her shape beneath the blanket, and I felt one hundred per cent happy. Why oh why had Mother ever left these kind *Merino people* who so obviously made her happy?

It became apparent at dinner later in the week.

It was Sunday. We'd been in the Tablelands for four days. We'd had Christmas dinner. And we'd gone visiting on Boxing Day. Mother's mood was still heightened. She laughed and clapped her hands and made Gramp open a bottle of wine for Sunday dinner, which, it was clear, was something they only did on special occasions. Gramp promenaded around the table with the bottle and everyone had a little, just to be sociable. Except Grandmother, who put her hand over her glass.

Mother filled hers to the brim. When Gramp said grace – a thing I'd never heard before – Mother said it along with him in a voice that was not quite right: a little too loud, a little too sing-song. I saw Grandmother's shoulder twitch. I saw her look at Gramp, and then at Jane.

And now, again, in a good way, Mother was being *different* to how she was at home. At home, she was testy about food. She pushed things around her plate and chewed them too long. She didn't like the 'feeling', she told Papa, of the food going into her, making her filled-up and sluggish. 'I like to have space left over,' she said. She could never be a true partner in Papa's love affair with food, because while capable of *sampling*, she was not capable of *savouring*. So now it was strange to see her tucking in to the tortured grey meal Grandmother had prepared: the tired chicken; the floury potato; the overcooked peas and undercooked pumpkin. Everyone at the table made sounds of appreciation but even I, at not-quite three years old, had a palate that rejected this fare. I'd been reared on delectable morsels provided by my father, fresh fruit from Nonna's garden, splendid leftovers from La Coccinella. Even Mother, otherwise out of tune with such things as *complementary flavours*, would pick figs from the fig tree in the back garden and serve them with cheese and walnuts on a plate after dinner.

I had never experienced a 'Sunday roast' before. I did not like it, but Mother's niece Hannah kept plugging my mouth with meat every time I accidentally opened it.

'Have you got all your teeth, O-yo?' Hannah said, putting her finger in my mouth and rooting around. I wished Hannah would keep her finger in my mouth forever, but she whisked it away and wiped it on a napkin (we called them 'serviettes' at home, but Grandmother's brow wrinkled when Mother used this word so I knew 'serviette' was not a wholesome word to use). Hannah plugged my mouth with food again. But this time it did not go down well. I spluttered. Aunt Tilde passed me a *napkin* but not in time and the lump of meat came out directly onto my plate. Mother glanced at it, and laughed and said, 'He seems to struggle sometimes with the swallowing function. What do you think, Frank? You're the amateur physician round here. Should I be worried?'

Uncle Frank put down his fork to exercise himself on the subject. 'The infant swallowing function …' he began, 'or should I say the gag reflex …' but Aunt Tilde nudged him in the ribs and he stopped. *Gag reflexes*, I understood, were like *serviettes*.

Mother had finished eating, and now she tipped her neck back, disposing of her wine, and got her cigarette case out.

Grandmother cleared her throat. 'Veda,' she said. 'We don't smoke at the table here. You know that.'

'Oh yes,' said Mother breezily. 'But I'm a married woman now, Mother.' She clicked her lighter open and lit her cigarette. Grandmother said nothing but she and Jane looked at each other again.

I think Mother's wine was not the first glass of wine she'd had that day. I'd smelt wine on her breath when she put me in the bath at five o'clock. I already knew the smell of wine. It was like ripe fruit that had sat in the bowl too long.

Aunt Tilde watched Mother across the table and then turned to Grandmother. 'Just one cigarette, Mother,' she said. 'Can we get Veda an ashtray?'

But Grandmother wouldn't get Mother an ashtray. There was silence for a bit, then Gramp announced that 'if Veda's smoking', he was 'darn well getting my pipe then'.

Once Gramp had safely left the room, the knives came out. That was how Mother described it later anyway, on the train home. Aunt Jane narrowed her eyes. She put her elbows on the table. Mother had told me elbows on tables were not a good thing in the Tablelands, but Jane didn't seem to know this. It seemed Aunt Jane owned the table once she got her elbows on it. She looked long and hard at Mother, and my cousin Hannah stopped putting food in my mouth. 'While Dad's out of the room, Veda,' said Jane, smiling a not-real smile. 'We've all been wondering why *exactly* you came here. Now. After all this time.'

Mother was un-fussed. She put her head to the side, as though she were thinking, and took a long drag on her cigarette. 'Because our mother wants to be surrounded by her daughters,' she finally said. She smiled at Grandmother. 'And because I want you all to get to know Owen.' There was an inch of Riesling left in the bottle in the centre of the table, and Mother reached over and took it.

Jane continued: 'But you're a married woman now, Veda. What does your husband think about you coming all this way without him? Coming all this way on your own? Mum and I have wondered ... Is something wrong?'

'Oh Jane,' said Mother. 'Not every man is a New England farmer's son. Nice though they are and, certainly, good husband material should one manage to *net one*. I don't need my husband's permission to go where I bloody well like.'

'Veda, there's no swearing at my table either,' Grandmother said.

Mother ignored her. 'Why are you worried, Jane? Do you think I come back with the aim of corrupting some nice farm boy?' She puffed rudely on her cigarette – somehow the cigarette made her both rude and superior to Jane. 'Only they're not nice farm boys, *most of them, ya see* ...'

'I don't see that's relevant to anything, and it's not what I meant ...'

Gramp, trotting back into the room with his tin and matches, said brightly: 'Well, Philip Greengrass just got married, you know, Veda. Lovely girl from Hillgrove. She's been to the university.' His face was gleaming – possibly in anticipation of the pipe. I looked up at Hannah, but all I could see was a bulb of snot in her nose, hanging unattended, slightly shocking in a person so nearly grown-up.

'Oh,' said Mother. 'Lucky Philip. New England University.' The ash had grown long on her cigarette and Tilde got up and fetched an ashtray from the sideboard.

Gramp nodded, not understanding her tone.

But Mother was looking at Jane, not at Gramp, and her eyes had a hard gleam in them, like a particular marble I had, a tombola with a spiral of plankton in its centre. 'You should look into it for yourself, Jane, the university. You might get your own husband. Then you won't have to exercise yourself about *mine*.'

Jane had gone red.

'I don't know why you have to be so nasty,' Jane said.

Grandmother got up and started collecting plates.

'Yes, come now, Veda,' said Tilde, and put her hand across the table towards Mother.

Mother's eyes flashed. 'It's not my fault, Jane, that you're stuck here at home with our parents …'

Jane was red like a tomato.

'You're being obnoxious, Veda,' said Grandmother. 'Utterly obnoxious. You're behaving like a drunk. The fact is you've married a man we know nothing about …'

'And don't use the word *university* with us, Veda,' Jane piped up. 'We all know the state of your university studies …'

Mother bore this with calm and drank the last of her wine.

'Come now, come now, everyone,' said Gramp. (He had just got his pipe packed, for god's sake.) 'Let's forget all this …'

But Grandmother was the person Mother had learned her coldness from, I suddenly understood. Mother took a mouthful of Riesling and Grandmother watched it go down her throat, three gulps of the Adam's apple.

'Someone needs to say it,' said Grandmother softly and clearly. 'And I'm going to.' She looked up at Mother. 'Fact is, in my day, there were names for girls like you, Veda, and they were *not* nice names …'

Mother nearly choked on her wine, in hilarity or outrage, I am not sure, because at this point, I was collected by Tilde, as was Hannah, and swept out of the room.

It was straight up the stairs and into bed in the tightly tucked single bed. The door was closed, the sounds muffled. All I could hear distinctly was the clock ticking on the bedside table.

And the little side-lamp buzzing a dangerous electrical buzz, like wasps approaching.

Tilde sat with me a few minutes, eyes on the door, ears monitoring the dining room. Then she patted me and left, switching off the bedside lamp so darkness came all at once as though, by virtue of turning off a light, other things, other problems, ceased to exist. I wondered whether Hannah was allowed to keep the light on in her room.

Downstairs the rising and falling of voices continued, occasionally too loud. At one point, something crashed, followed by an outbreak of sobs, but I could not tell who was who: Mother and her sisters all sounded the same. I whimpered. Not long after, Hannah opened my door and came into the bed with me, cuddling me hard, smelling of unwashed teeth, whispering, 'O-yo, Poor little O-yo. What a poor little lamb you are.'

The next morning things were different. Everyone was careful around each other at breakfast and didn't say much. 'Pass the eggs.' 'Pass the toast.' 'Milk?' Mother did not get up til nearly noon, which seemed to confirm there was something bad in her. After breakfast Gramp took me to the shearing shed. He put a piece of wool in my hand and I rubbed it and held it against my cheek. 'You're a good little man, Owen,' he said. He took me back to the house on his big, solid shoulders. His head was a ledge for my hands; his hands were stirrups for my feet. He put me up so high, I could see mountains and rooftops and birds' nests in the highest parts of the trees. I felt safe.

When we got back to the house, Mother was up and had our bags packed.

INIMICAL TIMES

The next months and years pile up on one another. In my memory, things happened quickly. Images appear and disappear; objects too, and sounds. There is the sweet, dumb face of Nonna as she becomes frail and ill and confused. There is the twisty stool at La Coccinella where Papa sat me to watch him work. There is Mother's alliance with the Knoxes, all fur and sherry and buttery afternoon light. There's the compost heap at Coburg: sharp and flyblown and brooding. There is the upright figure of Mrs Parish and the toy-laden bed at Park Orchards. There is Paddy Cow, my little pet calf, bought as a runt, big-eyed as a cartoon character, soft as a blanket.

There's Papa's manic energy as he comes and goes, increasingly excited by his projects, but perhaps a little forgetful of Mother. Papa loves Mother, he tells her he loves her, but he doesn't spend much time with her anymore; with us. When I look back at photographs, I see what Papa thought he had: a beautiful blonde pin-up wife who, unknown to the photographer, had the added bonus of *brains*.

There is no absolute way of photographing brains, Ornella. Sometimes brains are visible in a person's eyes – a certain spark or gleam of vitality or quickness. Even in the most studiously composed images, Mother's brains definitely got in the way of beauty. There was a crease in her brow long before the age at which creases naturally appear.

Veda Gray, says Julia, had the ambition but not the resources to further it. She had the intelligence but not the requisite belief in her intelligence. She had the talent, but not the right temperament. She had the talent (so says Julia) but not the right sex. Emily Platz says: 'Veda Gray lived in inimical times.'

TYPES OF LOVE

Mother was working on a book. Papa told me this in a hushed voice so I knew to creep around her, not to disturb her. I didn't like this *working on a book*: it made Mother even less comprehensible to me. This *book* sent me away to the Parishes, where the toys were good but the floor was cold and the food had no sugar or salt. This *book* made Mother a hunched-over shape at a desk with smoke rising from her elbow. She took long sleeps. She smelt sweet and sticky in that way I had become accustomed to, and she would switch abruptly from ignoring me to shooing me out of the room to gathering me up and kissing me and saying: 'Poor poor Owen! Poor darling O-yo, Mummy's such a bad old Mummy ...' And then she might drop me and become despondent again.

How could I know what to be, with a mother like that?

If I interrupted at the wrong time, saying I was hungry, she could be joyous – 'Darling O-yo! Let Mummy feed her darling O-yo!' – or murderous, thrusting a hastily peeled banana at me as though the act of getting up and collecting it from the fruit bowl had extinguished an irretrievable moment. I slunk away. I talked to my Matchbox cars and drove them over cliffs. I made her pictures of things she might like, like red flowers and purple dresses on pretty women with yellow hair.

Sometimes she talked to me like a grown-up: 'I don't know

why I force myself to sit here like this, Owen, at my desk, trying to squeeze out words. I'd be better off in a typing pool.' 'Mummy's problem is concentration. Professionals damn well shut out the world and they concentrate. Yes, that's it ...' Or sometimes she'd say, 'Oh bugger it' and she'd pack a picnic and we'd eat it in the front garden and I would explore behind the ferns, and peel the bark off the paperbark tree in the street, thinking she was watching me all the time, until I'd notice she was scribbling in her little book, after all, and would become cross with me when I stubbed my toe.

It was different at your house, Ornella. At your house things were messy, things were sometimes even chaotic, but you yourself were reliable. For instance: you were irritable. You were always irritable. Your irritability was utterly predictable. I could rely on it. Also: your rules were *rules*. There was no playing in your bedroom or in Nonna's bedroom. There was no pulling up of edible produce from the vegetable garden. I could play in the front garden but not climb the tree. I had to have a nap for three-quarters of an hour after lunch. If I was good, I got pannacotta when I got up.

Mother, however, had no rules. Or she'd try and put rules in place but would dispense with them completely whenever she felt like it and let me do what I pleased.

To use the vocabulary of art (which I *know you know*, Ornella, and I know you haven't forgotten – just the other day you spat the word *chiaroscuro* at me, out of nowhere, just as you were having your pudding), Mother's love for me was an ever-changing canvas, while yours was a solid, geometric affair. A big square love, Mondrian-like, primary-coloured.

It did not change or wrinkle or forget its purpose. The only square of love that was not reliably perpendicular was that which you had for Carlito, which was pulled out of shape by the demands he made upon basic geometry.

It was different again at the Parishes' house. There, everything was under control, but it was a dark baroque control. It was the control of meals on the table at precisely six, because any later would make Mr Parish angry. It was the control of having always the same bread with the same hard crust, because Mr Parish would only eat this bread. It was the control of classical music on the stereo – never anything but classical music, because anything else Mr Parish found *appalling*. Once Mrs Parish had been caught playing *free jazz*, and Mr Parish had broken the record across his knee. I was there, I saw it, Ornella. Free jazz was like abstract art, I think.

Mrs Parish had a different type of love again. A delicate, hands-off love that seemed not quite solid enough to withstand life's difficulties: a wind through the open window might desiccate it. It was, I guess you'd say, *impressionist*.

And, finally, Papa's love. Though fluid in form, it was always composed of the same material. In that, it was reliable. Like plasticine or clay, it might be worked and reworked into different shapes but was always, essentially, plasticine or clay. Papa might become a successful man – a restaurateur, an entrepeneur, a chef, an art collector – but all those people were made of the same material as the young man under the bridge with rope in the loops of his trousers. Papa was always vulnerable, and vulnerability drove him. When he got home late in the evening, before doing anything else, he came to my bedroom and picked me out of my bed. Mother argued, said it woke me. But it didn't. He cradled me and he put my face up to his so I could smell the soap and the herbs and maybe the wine. And when he placed me back in bed, whatever his vulnerability, there was nothing left of mine. I was asleep on a Papa-smelling boat.

WILLIAM BOOTH MEMORIAL HOME FOR DESTITUTE AND ALCOHOLIC MEN

Money came to Papa easily, but he was wretched about it, and every week when Rosa totted up the takings and found that this week's profits exceeded last week's, Papa suffered. His gallery, Works on Paper, had its inaugural show – an up-and-coming watercolourist by the name of Herbert Dickinson. The pictures sold well. There were reviews. After costs, a small profit was taken. Papa felt terrible for making so much money. Mother said, why not give a percentage to charity? 'Why not donate to polio,' she said. 'To help those poor children, with their bodies in those hideous contraptions. Poor little chits. They could use your money!'

But donating money to an anonymous cause, no matter how virtuous, was not sufficient for Papa. It required nothing of him: nothing of his spirit, nothing of his time, nothing of his heart. He could not atone for success with a mere donation. He couldn't buy his way to moral comfort.

Papa read in the newspaper that his former Fitzroy neighbours were being 'removed' from their cottages. 'Forcibly removed,' said the newspapers. Whelan the Wrecker was laying waste to the derelict houses of Fitzroy. The poor were under attack. They were no longer permitted to live in the communal conditions of poverty. The Housing Commission was going to build high-rise towers in the place of their former homes.

I remember those high-rise towers going up. I didn't think it was sad, I was excited by it. My ambition in life was to live on the top floor of the Carlton commission flats. You could lean out from the balcony and touch the birds. The traffic below would be so tiny it would look like ants. You could tie a red balloon to the balcony and watch it bob around in the wind. I told you this, Ornella, and you smacked me round the head and told me I was an idiot. 'Owen,' you said, 'those flats have no balconies.'

Papa kept on making money. It was as if money could not help but be attracted to him. He did what he did, and the result: money! Who would've thought that *food* and *art* could produce such effortless profits. He contacted the Citizens' Welfare Service and spoke to an unhelpful young woman.

'Our focus,' she said, 'is on helping those unemployed people who are looking for work. We provide support in cases of marital disharmony. We rehouse the deserving poor ...'

Papa said he wanted to help the poor, deserving or not. The woman tittered and said, 'Maybe you should set up a soup kitchen?'

Papa went away. He walked home to Hawthorn, all the way down Victoria Parade, past the abbatoir, through Richmond, along the façade of Vickers Ruolt, thinking about what she'd said – how it might be done, where it might be done, and *what sort of soup*?

He thought all these thoughts but it took the fire at the William Booth Memorial Home for him to do anything.

The William Booth Memorial Home, at 462 Little Lonsdale Street, housed more than a hundred homeless men, in small cubicles kitted out in cyclone mesh and packed close across five floors. Rooms cost next to nothing, and soup and bread could be had for a penny. Despite the cold of Melbourne winters, heaters were banned. But on 13 August 1966, Vincent Fox, a former chemist down on his luck, came home to his room at the William Booth, turned on his prohibited heater and, in the process of passing out for the night, knocked it over. When the smoke was detected and the door kicked open, the rush of oxygen made for a conflagration. The fire consumed the third and fourth floors of the building. Twelve men died of asphyxiation in the shower room, having made the wrong turn for the stairs. Another eighteen died in their sleep – or in the process of escaping, no one was ever sure.

Fifteen of the bodies were never claimed. They were men of no concern. Men from under bridges. War veterans. Pensioners. Invalids. Alcoholics. *Derros*. There was no one to miss them. There was no one even to identify them. Papa studied the photograph in the *Herald* as he drank his coffee on the Sunday morning after the fire: fifteen anonymous coffins laid out with flowers in the Salvo's City Temple in Bourke Street. If he closed his eyes he could see the water lapping at the pylons again; the grey bird that pecked in the grass; a blade of glass, sheer and sharp …

Atonement was a solitary pursuit. Papa got up, put on his

hat, and took the tram to Lonsdale Street, where he found the William Booth building blackened and cordoned-off, the lost inhabitants still milling around.

Then Papa went back to La Coccinella and made an inventory of his stock. He took out the largest pot he had. He fetched a second pot and a third. He took out a dozen jars of tomato sauce. He took up a sack of spaghetti. He cut handfuls from a side of ham. He pitted olives with the cherry-pitter so fast the stones pinged against the tiled wall. The smell of ham and onions rose in the pan, the tomato sauce sizzled. He threw in oregano and salt and sugar. He threw in white wine. He boiled the water and brought the spaghetti to al dente.

Les Preston ran a transport company and had an Italian wife. He drove people from Melbourne to the Peninsula and back in his Ford Zephyr. In fact, he was always pestering Papa to let him take Mother and me to the seaside for the day. But it was not the Zephyr Papa was now thinking of. Les also owned a 1955 De Soto van, size of a milk-truck. He rang Les and by 5 pm they were passing out bowls to god-knows-how-many homeless men in Little Lonsdale Street.

Afterwards the men lit cigarettes and talked quietly. Then they bundled up what stuff they had and left, having timidly returned their bowls. They went to find bridges, or wind-protected corners, or places of camouflage in parks. They didn't need to thank Papa. On the contrary, the robust thanks of the Salvos embarrassed him. And when Papa said he'd be back the next day, little Major Trent Paulie, in his soot-stained black and red uniform, the Blood and Fire crest bright on his Army hat, almost choked up. Then he gave Papa the Salvation Army salute with his right hand. 'Hallelujah,' he said. 'Sir, you are a true citizen of heaven.'

Papa went home slowly, happily. The light was pink. The tops of the trees were tremulous against the sky. He had done a good thing.

POLLY WAFFLE

On one particular cold winter's day, Mother bundled me up and took me on the tram to Knox Books. I must've been five or six. If my memories before have a dream-like intensity, from this age – the age when my memories really kicked in – they are painfully sharp. Like sun that pierces the eyes after you emerge from a dark room. Mother peers down at me, a vast shadow against a backdrop of light, tying the strings of an itchy woollen hat under my chin. I'm ensconced in puffy woollen articles till I look like the Michelin man; even my little hands are bound up in mittens. I have claws instead of digits.

We are going to the Knoxes, and Mother is in a state. A letter arrived in the post. It was a short letter. I saw it over her shoulder, though I didn't get the chance to read it. (I could read by this time.) Three lines. Lots of space. A scrawling signature. It was the fourth letter of this kind that had come in a fortnight. Mother screwed the thing up and threw it across the room. She sat on the sofa with her arms crossed. And then she put her face in a sofa cushion and made several short yelps. I tried to climb up next to her, but she refused to make room for me. 'Mother!' I said. I could feel the rage and hurt emanate from her. It was like a pulse. It came into my body and made my blood run to the same beat. I didn't want to feel her pulse like that. I wished my own pulse would take over.

I played dumbly on the carpet until Mother sat up and took the cushion from her head and shook her hair out. 'Stupid, *stupid* me,' she said. She punched the cushion. 'Mother is a *stupid* woman, Owen.' She caught a glance of herself in the mirror across the room and clenched her teeth. She thrust her jaw forward and flared her nostrils, as though making herself ugly might help her feel better. Then she seemed to change her mind. She set her back straight and started doing up her cardigan. 'Come, Owen,' she said.

Then we were on the tram, making our way into the city.

Barrington Knox was surprised to see Mother; he had been on his way out, I could tell – he had his fur coat on. He gave his wife Edith a quick look and she began fussing around us. Mother was fighting back angry tears, like when she broke something by accident that she really liked.

'Get the tea on,' said Mr Knox. 'I'll take Owen out for an ice cream while you ladies sort things out.'

I didn't want an ice cream. It was freezing cold. Hadn't he noticed this? But Mr Knox got my little claw hand in his big bear hand and out we went, onto Collins Street, blowy and bare.

'Have to drop something off quickly, O-yo,' he said.

My hand had completely disappeared into the floppy furcuff of his coat. I hesitated. He looked down at me and yanked my hand gently. 'Then it's straight to ices, alright? Let your mother get her hair on.'

He steered me down the street, round a corner, and into a small dirty shop with the words 'Mintie & Sons' on the window. I thought for a moment this was the lolly shop, but it was no such thing. There was a brownish quality about the room we entered; a brownish quality about the receptionist who took the envelope Mr Knox handed her and looked slightly downwards at him over her glasses before emptying it and counting the contents. Greasy note after greasy note ran through her thin, witchy fingers. I could imagine Mr Knox making fun of those witchy fingers later, when the sherry bottle was open. 'Crone fingers,' he'd call them. 'Medieval. Hasn't she heard of *hand-cream*?'

'Mr *Knox*,' said the receptionist finally, like a school teacher, cocking her head. He was such a big, confident man, it seemed wrong that a woman at a desk might use this tone with him.

'It's not all here, you know that, don't you?'

'Marilyn,' said Mr Knox. 'Have a word, won't you? It's a bloody awful winter. Spring sales'll be up. I'll be good for it. Trust me.'

Marilyn made a disapproving little mouth and indicated the frosted glass window behind her. 'He won't like it, you know. He's got people after your place.' She opened a drawer in her desk and divided the money into what were presumably differentiated sub-drawers deep inside. I wanted to see them. I peered over the edge of her desk. She shut the drawer. She was no sucker for children. 'I hope you're keeping track of payments so you know where you're up to.'

Mr Knox nodded. 'Edith has it all under control.'

Marilyn began writing a receipt in a square carbon-duplicating book that mesmerised me: the purple carbon that she placed like a thin tongue between pages; the transmission of her curly hand from original to lilac duplicate. '*I'm* keeping a running total if you ever need a reminder,' she said. 'You are in my Debits Book, Mr Knox.' She ripped along dotted lines and passed him the original. 'Make sure you don't get in too *deep*!'

Having suffered this schoolmarmish rebuke, Mr Knox nodded sheepishly, made a good show of folding the receipt carefully so she could see how responsible he was and slid it into his wallet. 'Thank you, Marilyn,' he said. 'You are a gem!'

Then we were out, back to the street and my promised ice cream, and any forbearance or humility I had witnessed in Barrington Knox was immediately transformed into resounding good cheer. There was something like a jaunt in his step.

There were no ice-cream shops nearby, we soon discovered. But Mr Knox got hold of a Polly Waffle in a dingy tobacconist's, and, having never before eaten such a strange concoction of marshmallow, chocolate and sweetened cardboard, I did not return to sentience until the treat was devoured and my fingers licked clean (mittens lost forever somehow in the process, thank god).

We were back in the bookshop. Mother was sipping tea. Mr Knox decanted whisky from a flat bottle with a label into a cut-glass bottle without a label. He said: 'Put a good spoon of sugar into it, Veda, and a dose of this. Edith, have we biscuits?'

I was forgotten, on the floor, with crayons and colouring books, a copy of *The Tawny Scrawny Lion* and, the most fabulous book I'd ever seen in my life, *Where the Wild Things Are*, which Mr Knox had just got in from America and which was selling, he said, 'like hotcakes, god bless Mr Sendak!'

Mother was nursing her cup like an invalid. 'I'm sorry. I don't know why I'm letting myself get so upset about it all. It's just another rejection. I know to expect them.'

'Nonsense,' said Mr Knox. 'The whole thing is a bloody boys' club. I know it. I've dealt with them. They think because they've been to some crummy Antipodean university, they're the educated elite. Change your name to something masculine – John Stonnington, *Wolfgang Mannheim* – and they'll be begging to publish you.'

Mother snorted. 'I don't think anyone would believe a man had written my poems. Too many brooms and cupboards and bits and pieces from jewellery boxes.'

'I think you give men too much credit,' said Mr Knox. 'We're not that clever, Veda.'

Mrs Knox nodded and passed Mother a Monte Carlo. 'Absolutely true, darling.'

'It goes without saying,' Mr Knox continued, 'that I will put you in every issue of *Strident* that goes to press, Veda. Hand on heart. I have all conviction in you, you know that.' Mrs Knox nodded again. 'You're very talented, Veda. Don't let these form letters get you down.'

'Still, you've got to harden up. Rejection is part of the territory. Start building some armour, a thick skin.' Mr Knox looked for a moment curiously simian, as though he might beat his chest. 'A woman's got to be twice as good as a man to succeed, you know. Twice as strong.'

'Though it's precisely Veda's *thin* skin,' corrected Mrs Knox, 'that makes her the poet she is. You can't give up your sensitivity either, Veda.'

Mr Knox dipped his Monte Carlo into his tea and sucked it. 'Well, no. Try for a balance, Veda. Or bypass these little provincial twats and send your work directly overseas.'

'I wouldn't have the courage!' said Mother.

What did she mean, she wouldn't have the courage? I couldn't believe how small and forlorn she looked, my relentlessly shapeshifting mother.

'What have you got to lose?' said Mr Knox.

'*Nothing* to lose!' chimed Mrs Knox.

Mr Knox sat back in his chair. 'Look, Veda, if I had the time and didn't have to make money, I'd bloody sort it for you. Believe me, I would.'

'You're very good to me, both of you,' said Mother again. 'It's just ... it just seems so impossible for me to get anything in print. I always thought the work was in the writing, but now I see that the true work comes *after* the writing. And it's not the sort of work I'm good at. I feel deadened by this process of pushing myself forward.'

'It's not in women's nature,' said Mrs Knox.

'I thought it was in mine. I used to be brave. I used to be tough as old leather.'

Mrs Knox leaned towards Mother. 'Veda,' she said. 'You *are* brave. Don't give up because a couple of silly editors don't know a poem of originality when they see it.'

'You've got to get the ear of that Parish chap,' Barrington said. 'For god's sake, he's got every literary connection in the country. If anyone can bloody well get you introduced to the right people, it's him.'

Mother went red. She poured herself another drink. 'I just

can't,' she said. 'I tried once and I can't a second time. It feels ridiculous to be making a fuss in the first place. I feel ridiculous for letting this matter so much … I don't know, I feel a kind of … paralysis.'

'Get your husband to talk to him,' said Mrs Knox.

Mr Knox nodded. Mrs Knox smiled. I looked at the wild things *gnashing* their teeth and *rolling* their eyes and felt seasick. Maybe it was the Polly Waffle, but it seemed to come directly from the story. Or maybe it came from Mother. I could see her. She looked green, smiling wanly at Mrs Knox: she looked seasick too. She looked scared.

Mother took Mr Knox's advice and had a conversation with Papa. She decided to cook him a special dinner. The days when Mother could just bring up a subject with Papa were over; she had to make special efforts now, she had to put on a special show. So you came over and you brought your overnight bag, Ornella. You were wearing the green dress you had made yourself from a Simplicity pattern. You had pinned up all your hair like Mary Poppins. You will say you never wore such a hairstyle, but you did, and if you'd had a carpet bag and a parrot-headed umbrella, you would've convinced every child in Melbourne who'd been to the Odeon that you were Mary Poppins, in the flesh. You got me into my pyjamas in five seconds flat.

When you stayed with us, you slept in the narrow cane bed in the enclosed verandah, where the walls were thin and the outside world felt very close. The swish of wind and trees was both near and far. It made you feel cosy, like you were in the hull of a ship.

That night you bathed me and read to me and snuggled next to me in the bed and smacked my fingers when I kept turning the reading light on and off. I lay there, cocooned inside your arm, and you read *The Man with the Golden Gun* till you fell asleep.

Mother had cooked for Papa, something Mother did less and less these days. Papa had taken a night off. This also was rare. Now that he was working with the Salvation Army, as well as running the restaurant, as well as running his Works on Paper gallery, we rarely saw him. There were homeless men who depended on him for their survival. He said this, astonished, to Mother, when she complained.

'Yes, only—' said Mother.

'But Veda!'

Papa wished he had two or three or perhaps even four carbon copies of himself so he could spread his love properly around and make it fill every necessary corner. I understood this. I knew it when he came late to say goodnight to me. 'Sorry I'm so late, O-yo,' he said. 'Little tacker.'

Men didn't say 'I love you' in those days. They said, 'little tacker,' and 'bruiser' and 'muscles'.

Mother had lit candles and set the table with a tablecloth. I don't recall what she cooked. Mother's cooking comes to me without precision, like Mother herself. Something baked, perhaps slightly overdone. She probably didn't eat. She probably smoked cigarettes and drank the wine she'd got from The Whitehorse Inn on the corner of Barton Street and Burwood Road, and watched Papa as he forked her bland offering into his mouth. He would've played his part. 'Darling,' he would've said, 'this is *delicious*!' Then he would've pushed his plate away and lit a cigarette too.

Beside me, in the cane bed that I had insisted on accompanying you into, you snored your wet whistling snore, Ornella. But I was awake, and I could hear the buzz of Mother and Papa talking at the table. I heard the voices rise and fall like the voices in the Tablelands. I didn't trust that rising and falling. Soon a glass would break or a cry would crack the air. There were bronze velveteen curtains draping the arch in the hallway. They were held to the wall by ropes of what I imagined to be braided hair. They were perfect for hiding in.

'I doubt myself terribly,' Mother was saying. 'I feel so completely alone with it all.' She had one elbow in the other, propping up her cigarette hand. She looked like Lauren Bacall. I had watched *The Big Sleep* and *How To Marry a Millionaire*.

'You're a genius, darling!' said Papa. 'My genius poet.'

'Will you read them?'

Papa put his cigarette in the ashtray. 'Darling … What do I know about poetry? I wouldn't know what to say …'

'But you don't have to *say anything*. You can just read them. *You just have to read them*.'

Papa felt dumb, I knew it. He knew, ahead of time, that however he responded to Mother's poems, it would be the wrong way. I knew this feeling. I put a bit of the velvet curtains in my mouth and sucked them, but there was only dust.

'Veda, I don't understand these things. I go with my guts, and they're sometimes wrong. I'm not educated. If I didn't have Parish to guide me, I'd be making a big fool of myself with the gallery. Don't make me *read poetry*. I'm your stupid money-making husband. Let me just bring home the bacon and let you be brilliant.'

Mother looked at him levelly. 'I'm not brilliant, Jo.'

Papa looked at her and sighed.

Her voice rose a notch. 'I'm *not brilliant*. I need help.'

'Well, can't Knox help you? Hasn't he helped you already?'

'Yes, but—' I heard Mother's note of frustration. 'But Knox *runs a bookshop*. He is a retailer who occasionally puts out a magazine. He has rent to pay and stock to sell. I need to find a *publisher* for a book. A proper publisher. And I just, well, I can't ask Mr Parish ... I need *you* to ask him. I need you to *give him my manuscript*.'

Papa relaxed, all of a sudden. I saw his body go soft in the middle. He poured some red wine into his glass and resumed his cigarette. 'Darling, no problem. Easy peasy. Course I'll talk to Parish. He'll find you a publisher. He'll find you the best publisher. Darling, *dar*ling!' He moved his chair round to Mother's side of the table and put his arm around her. '*Ve*da. Why didn't you bring this up before?' Mother looked gracious, imperious, but I knew she was just tired.

I retreated from the curtains. I didn't want to see the rest. I got back in the bed with you, Ornella, but you were dead to the world, not even snoring. Your arm went over me like a robot's arm.

ATTENTIVE PLACEMENT

Papa started taking me to work with him once a week. You started having me in Coburg overnight. The Parishes had me in the gaps. I didn't like it. I had to have a bag all the time that went between places with me. I had to have a different routine, a different kind of dinner, a different toothbrush at each house.

'Mother needs it this way for a bit,' said Papa. 'You have to be a big boy and understand.'

I was a big boy, I did understand: everything was arranged to give Mother time and space to work on her poems. But I didn't get in her way. I knew how to play by myself and watch TV by myself. If I wasn't there, she'd be alone all day long. She'd go mad. She'd even said it to me: 'I'd go mad,' she'd said, 'if it wasn't for you, O-yo'. So why was I the problem that had to go away to different houses with different dinnertimes, and no TV, and toys that were so new they weren't even soft yet? It made me want to kick things I loved: like my meccano and the tin telephones Aunt Tilde sent down from the Tablelands. It made me want to kick the things that would crack and get dented and maybe even hurt my foot. It made me want to bash things.

And whenever I got home from Papa's or your place or the Parishes, Mother was not working anyway. She was staring into space or drinking wine on the couch with a record on. Once Papa and I got home and we couldn't even find her for a whole hour, until we searched in the back garden, right down at the neighbour's fence, and she was asleep on a patch of grass that was still warm from the sun, a teacup next to her with yellow stuff in it.

On Sundays, Papa took me to the restaurant, where he made big stews full of meat and vegetables for the homeless men. He called it *minestrone*, and at the end he added pasta shells. I wished the pasta-makers made seahorses and starfish as well as shells. Papa gave me pasta dough and I cut out my own shapes, but they ended up looking like cups or bowls, or essentially, shells anyway. He threw them in the broth.

Les Preston came at five o'clock to load the van. Les was an ex-boxer. His muscles were hard, but old, shrunken down like an apple core. He'd left school, like Papa, at thirteen, served in New Guinea, seen atrocities. He was tough. But though he said he looked like a 'fucking fairy' buttering bread or ladling soup alongside Papa and me at the Salvos, sometimes his eyes got teary, or he clouted Papa on the back a little too hard, like he really wanted to hug him, or he went over and shared a smoke with one of the men with dirty faces and bad teeth. He made rings for his granddaughters out of ten-cent coins.

I liked being with these two small, hard men as they fed the other hard men: men with tacky eyes and red noses, stinking trousers and crazed voices; conmen and gamblers and *shadows of their former selves*. They all got fed. Once Papa even cooked them roast pork. He got a deal at the Vic Market. He made gravy and apple sauce and roast potatoes and peas. Major Paulie shoved the roasting trays in the gargantuan ovens at the Salvos kitchen to heat them up and get the skin crunchy. The men chewed on the crackling, and the ones without teeth sucked it.

Afterwards, back at La Coccinella, there was always a lot of washing up to do. Rosa had started to come in on Sundays too. Then we'd all eat together and I'd eat with them, and we'd smile and laugh, and Les would head off in the van and Papa would put Rosa on the St Kilda tram and we'd catch the Mont Albert. Lazy old Sunday-night tram. Took ages to come – was that it, cresting at the top of the hill, or was it just a Herald van returning home? Papa would read out of the papers to me with his legs crossed. Mostly it was crime reports, but sometimes there were other stories: *Two women chain themselves to Brisbane bar to protest men-only service* – 'Why the hell they'd wanna go in the bar for!?' said Papa. *Police raid the Austral bookshop in Melbourne and seize copies of* Lady Chatterley's Lover. *Thea Astley wins the Miles Franklin Award for Literature.*

'Darn it, O-yo,' said Papa, lowering the paper onto his lap. 'Haven't mentioned Mama's book to Parish yet.'

He folded the paper into a wedge and smacked my thigh with it.

'Papa's gonna be in the doghouse, son,' he said.

I didn't know what the doghouse was because we didn't have a dog, but I was nervous about getting home now and wished the tram-ride would just go on and on. All the way to the end of the line. To the magical place that was *Mont Albert*. I imagined a snow-covered mountain and tobogganing. Perhaps a chalet, or even a cosy sick-room like Heidi had in Frankfurt.

'Darn it,' said Papa again. 'God-darn it.'

Usually on the weekends now, I went to the Parishes. I had got used to their house: my room, my toys, the flat brown tiles that lined the low-slung house. But it was cold there. Even in summer it was cold. 'Mr Parish built this house by hand,' Mrs Parish told me. I imagined Mr Parish slathering mortar on bricks, checking the spirit level, trowelling off the excess. He was good at building things. 'Gave up cigarette-smoking and built this house by himself with all the extra time he had.'

Mrs Parish put her own hands out in a small marvelling gesture. She wore a straight brown skirt and a plain-coloured cardigan; occasionally she swapped her plain-coloured cardigan for a gold spangly one, if there were guests. Sometimes she wore pearls. Her straight up-and-down clothes gave her the appearance of height and also a certain unclimbable rectitude, like a straight brown tree with smooth bark and not very many lower branches.

Mr Parish, gregarious and generous outside his home, was different inside it. All day long, he hurt Mrs Parish with words and silences till I imagined her pitted in minute dings like a car I once saw after a hailstorm. 'Would you like grapefruit, dear?' Mrs Parish would ask at breakfast, holding out the serrated teaspoon and jar of sugar. Mr Parish would keep reading his newspaper, or his book, or his magazine, and not answer. Quietly, Mrs Parish would lean over and place before him the neatly segmented grapefruit on its blue plate. She would pour his coffee, butter his toast, put his marmalade to the side (because he liked to apply this himself), and all of the time he would ignore her till, pushing the finished plates aside, he would stretch, look at me, say, 'Buck up, soldier! It's not the end of the world!', chuck me under the chin and go wherever he went for the rest of the day. Mrs Parish would then clean up. At lunch it would be similar. And at dinner, similar or worse, because then Mr Parish would drink and alcohol made him difficult.

In his absence, Mrs Parish inhabited long, quiet regular days. After breakfast, she would go walking: a solid hike if she could manage it – she had stamina, pushing through the bush in her gymkhana pants. She even once or twice put me up on her shoulders, a manoeuvre that required her to squat down, position me, and then come up in two goes like a weightlifter performing a clean and jerk. She was not as solid a mount as Gramp was, but she made good progress through the bush with me up there. She hung onto my leg with one hand and picked specimens from the bush with the other. It was steep walking around their house. It was hard. She was fit. Sometimes I held bits of wattle for her, or bits of heath, trying to keep them neat and intact in my sweaty scrunched-up fist. Back at the house, after her tense and conversation-less lunch with Mr Parish, she read to me: *Flat Stanley, James and the Giant Peach, Five Children and It.* We made ourselves comfortable in what she called 'the sitting room', which had a Chesterfield lounge suite and a large hungry fireplace that we never lit during the day. She didn't make me have naps like you did, Ornella, but if I fell asleep, she draped a blanket over me and took up a seat by the window where she spent the latter hours of the afternoon studying perilously boring books about *dried flowers*, arranging her own in differently shaped earthenware pots and vases, trimming, secateuring, splitting, shaping. It was for this she collected plants on our morning walks. When she had finished, she had almost always made something lovely out of what had looked to me like dried leaves, dirt-encrusted sticks, tiny shallow-coloured blossoms, *nothing much*.

If Mother got hold of a bunch of flowers (and Papa did buy them for her, regularly, guiltily), she clipped the string off and jammed the whole lot straight into a vase. She had a ceramic 'basket' with holes in it that you could wedge flower-stems into, and another receptacle made of oozy green sponge that performed the same function. But if the process involved cutting, trimming, attentive placement of any kind, Mother would not bother. So it was very curious to me, the way Mrs Parish thought and reflected and removed from and added to and straightened and bent her flower arrangements. While she worked, she became quite still and, though I thought her extremely old, almost young looking. Her nose was very straight, I noticed, and when you looked at her in profile, nothing was too big or too small. When her hair hung a little loosely on her neck at the back, when it came out of its pins, she looked like an old-fashioned picture illustrating a particular feminine virtue: *Charity in Repose*, *Honour at Home*, *The Noble Gentlewoman*. Mother had these, hung on the walls where her desk was.

Mr Parish spent the days in his study if he was at home. He had frequent lunches in town with painters and businessmen and editors and he talked about his 'club' sometimes and berated me because Papa wouldn't go there with him. 'Bloody foolish bloody socialist,' he said, but fondly, because for whatever reason – and I never knew why – he loved Papa. 'Don't let your father indoctrinate you, Owen! Let him run himself ragged with charity, but you listen to me: I help the poor in a much more meaningful way than your father does. Once a year I write them a *big bloody cheque*!' Then he would put out his glass and Mrs Parish would fill it with more Scotch and soda.

Another time, he mused, slightly drunkenly: 'There should be a charity for poets, Owen. They need all the help they can get.' This was after we'd had a large, evil-smelling man called Raymond Sermon over for lunch. Mr Parish called him 'Ray' and Mrs Parish called him 'Mr Sermon'. He wolfed his food down, drained his glass multiple times, had three servings of pineapple upside-down cake and then went to sleep for two hours on the Chesterfield. When awake and in good form, Ray Sermon held forth on everything from the retired prime minister Bob Menzies to the proper way to set up a gin still in one's backyard. And though he looked like nothing so much as a pig farmer (or what I imagined a pig farmer to look like), he had a way of speaking that transfixed me. 'Unforgiveable muck again in *Foment* this month, Parish,' he said. 'I could take a tray of words and trip over it and come up with better.' Or: "There's about as much talent in *Meanjin* these days as there are daisies in a combine harvester. More entertainment had in a commie on a donkey. Give me a flying windmill and an idiot and I'll come up with better.'

I had no idea what he was talking about, and I saw Mrs Parish wince more than once, but he certainly spoke in a way no one else I'd ever known did. 'Who's this curious little truckbuster?' he once said of me, and I smiled nervously.

'Is Mr Sermon a poet?' I asked Mr Parish after he'd gone. The enormous fireplace was booming its wood and flame, reddening our faces, warming the tiled floor. Mrs Parish was intent in a corner with a book.

'He is,' said Mr Parish, rolling port around in a small glass and staring into the fire. 'Another impoverished gentleman of the pen. Sells his poems like peanuts to any taker. Poor bloody bastard.'

'My Mother's a poet,' I ventured. It came out timorously. It didn't have the declarative force I would have liked it to have. I also knew, in the way that children intuitively know these things, that Mother would be horrified I had blurted this out. But I also knew it needed to be said. I noticed Mrs Parish's face lift and become alert to our conversation.

'Indeed,' said Mr Parish, still looking into the fire. 'So I have heard.' He rolled the port around in its glass again before putting it to his mouth. 'Lucky she has a husband.'

OF ALL THE DAYS, THE BEST

But of all the days, the best were the days with you, Ornella! I'm not even sure why they were the best. The house in Coburg – you said it yourself – was *going to the dogs*. Things were always breaking there, even though it was not a very old house. Curtain rails came down when you pulled the curtains open in the mornings, nearly hit you on the head, *such a fright, O-yo!;* the back-gate jammed in cold weather and so did the back-door; the silicon on the bathroom basin had come loose and the pedestal wobbled when you brushed your teeth. These were all fairly ordinary handyman jobs – Nonno would've fixed them in two seconds flat. Papa might've come round and repaired a thing or two in his temporary hold-it-together-till-you-can-get-a-tradesman way but you refused to ask him. Your boyfriend Carlito waved his hand, said, 'Sure, Ornella, no problems, I'll do it' and never did a thing. You berated yourself because, actually, you didn't want to have to rely on a man, but you didn't know how to use a drill or a saw or even (really) a paintbrush. And having never been taught to use tools, you were scared of them. They made you stupid. You didn't know how to handle them with conviction. It was like when a stray tennis ball rolled to your feet in a park and you had to throw it back, across a distance. You'd lift your arm, prepare for a fulsome arc, but lack the confidence to pull it off: the ball would drop short, land yards away from its intended destination … *Stupid girl's throw* – so weak, so limp, so unsure of itself. *Why didn't Nonno teach you these skills?* You couldn't fix stuff, and you couldn't ask, and so the house began to disintegrate around you.

Nor was Nonna there to keep things going in the garden. Nonna was now resident at the Donna Vincenzo Home for the Elderly in Parkville. In her absence, the garden had also *gone to the dogs*.

But I loved it. I loved the ravaged back yard with its desiccated twine and rotten wood and all those dead plants. You would put the hose on, Ornella, and leave me out there, without my clothes, to get black with mud, to fish slaters and worms out of the ground to keep in pots and jars.

But you were sad because Nonna was no longer at home. And ultimately you had to sell the house, because the Donna Vincenzo Home for the Elderly was *molto caro*. And when you visited Nonna, she cried because she still knew you, but she wasn't sure where from and she wasn't sure how to get on and off the bed – which foot, and why that way, and where did the arm go to support the torso? Her legs were fat and stiff and her kidneys were leaking protein and blood. Nonna held your hand like a baby and called you 'Nella, Nella,' and sometimes 'Mamma' so that you couldn't visit her without falling a little bit apart afterwards.

Meanwhile, I traversed the increasingly derelict rooms of Coburg on my rusted blue tricycle. I spilled my drinks and pulled up pieces of lino (they came up with such a satisfying *crack*!). You didn't care. We made cake and left the flour on the bench. We let egg set on the cooktop. We never made a single bed and sometimes we would eat dinner watching the black-and-white TV propped on your dressing table. If Nonna had become *derelict* (yes, you sometimes used this word by mistake), there was no point in keeping house to please her. And so you performed only the absolute necessities of maintenance – once, when you put me in the bath, you gave me a sponge and made me clean the shower screen while I was in there.

But I rarely slept by myself. I slept in your bed with your black curly hair in my face, and your smell of almonds and lemon juice, pork and perfume. 'Oh my God, O-yo,' you said one morning after we had had a feast of chocolate cannolis for dinner the night before, 'I have a stomach like a fat puppy-dog. How'm I gonna fit into my dress?'

Your stomach was a whole two inches sticking-out. You were slightly knock-kneed. When we slept, I coiled inside the curve of your body like a baby snake, warming myself on your blood.

Carlito was the only problem in our arrangement. He was your fiancé now. Sometimes he would come over at dinner-time, and at midnight he would still be there. What was he doing? I was getting too tired to stay awake but I had to keep my eyes peeled in case he tried to sit you on his lap. Or put his hand inside your clothes – as if I couldn't see! And if he didn't go home, I would have to sleep in Nonna's old room, which was filled with clocks and Virgin Marys and had a bed like a horned beast, made out of gold-and-cream painted wood.

I was six years old and Carlito was my enemy. He called me 'Onion' and thought it a big joke. He made a show of shaking my hand, but gripping it so tight I had to eventually say 'Ow' and make him let go. I huddled under the too-heavy quilts in Nonna's bedroom, overseen by wooden asps and apples, and heard Carlito grunting in the other room, pulling out at the last minute in strict Italian style, forever denying you a shotgun wedding, Ornella. It sounded like he was going to the toilet.

And in the morning, what were you doing, frying up meat and eggs for him at seven o'clock, in your dressing gown? I see his fat square jaw working away at a bacon rind, slurping coffee, chewing egg, everything in his mouth at once because he was so frantic to get it all down, as if someone might whip the plate out of his reach and deny him his due. Then he'd promise you he'd return after work, but he wouldn't. And you'd sit up all night, watching television in a state of agitation, bolting to the door at every stray noise. This was how he kept you in thrall, Ornella. Even I understood this, at my tender age: the male power of abstaining. Of promising and not delivering. Of *saying* love but not *doing* love. I nestled into your lap and your hand roamed over me, really wanting Carlito, but making do. I didn't mind. I understood.

DOLOMITES #2

Rosa had been making sketches for a new mural on the walls of La Coccinella – an up-close Dolomites, this time, not the panoramic expanse of 123: 'More intimate,' she said. 'So you feel you are really *there*!'

It was intimate alright. Rosa's new Dolomites mural had a severe perspective that made you feel like you were travelling up a treacherously steep mountain path, possibly to your doom. Heaps of snow lay underfoot; the first green tufts of spring poked from ledges in the rockface. The optical illusion was almost terrifying. When I first laid eyes on it, it made me dizzy. Up high, in a narrow V, the sky shone wan and yellow.

This was no mere tourist attraction. No Renoir grouping of crystal glasses and boating hats at a table. No maps, grapes, grains, or livestock with bells around their necks. Rosa's mural did not, this time, lend itself to easy ingestion of bolognese and a soft red table wine. She had created something awe-ful. She knew it. She herself was a little silent at its unveiling, a little shocked by her own creation. She sought me out, as if what she had to say were too precious for the ear of an adult: 'Look, Owen,' she whispered in my ear. 'I think this one is special.' When the small gathering clapped, it was long, appreciative applause. Mr Parish whistled. The papers visited again and this time, in the photograph, printed in speckled black and white, Rosa looked much more dignified, gazing up and slightly combatively at her artwork, as though she were equal to it and responsible for it. As though what she had created were no mere accident.

Also present at the unveiling of *Dolomites II* were several of the artists who had exhibited at Papa's gallery, Works on Paper. Jim Carlyle. Arthur Bellows. Pavel Zly. And a young blonde woman named Muriel Green.

Muriel was not an artist. Papa and Mr Parish employed Muriel three and a half days a week to supervise Works on Paper, answer the phone, relay enquiries. She studied Fine Arts at the Royal Melbourne Institute of Technology, and had previously worked at the National Gallery of Victoria. She was able to talk very convincingly about art and artists and colour and limited editions and German Expressionism. She had absolutely no artistic ambitions of her own, which made her the perfect candidate for the job. She had what was then described (after Marilyn) as a 'bobbed nose' and (after Ann Margret) a 'sex-kitten hairdo' and was just plump enough for men to want to take good fleshy handfuls of her while pretending to respect her intelligence.

Muriel was *very good at selling art*. It wasn't just her sex appeal or even her art education: she had a natural instinct for the vulnerabilities and vanities of the art collector. She could detect a buyer from among the milling and merely interested. Once detected, she could read him. (And it was always *him*.) The businessman who needs reassurance about appreciation in value. The undecided aesthete who wants to buy but can't choose, and needs to be talked logically through the possibilities. The stamp collector who needs one of everything, but most of all needs a patient ear to work out what is missing. The impoverished would-be collector who needs to be convinced he can get by without food and gas for a month. Mr Parish actually referred to her as 'Kitten' – not to her face, behind her back – and said he kept his fingers crossed she wouldn't *fall in love any day soon* ...

I understood what he meant because *I* was in love with Kitten straight away. If I were a grown man, I would have given her flowers and perfume and talked her into marrying me. That was what men did. But Mr Parish was also wrong, because I didn't think women were the ones who *fell* in love. I couldn't imagine Mother ever falling in love with Papa, or Mrs Parish falling in love with Mr Parish. Falling in love was something men did: they fell *head over heels* and then a woman couldn't get away until she finally said *yes*. That was how marriages got done.

On the night of Rosa's second Dolomites instalment, I witnessed Kitten and Mr Parish in the back courtyard at La Coccinella. A rickety wrought-iron table and chair stood on uneven bricks and candlelight came from a wax stump in a red glass. It was hot inside the gallery: early April, but hot. Mrs Parish had not been in attendance. She had 'headaches,' said Mr Parish – 'Bloody change of life'. Kitten was in the courtyard smoking a cigarette and pulling jasmine from her cardigan where it had got tangled. Her teased blonde hair had come loose at the fringe – a hank of yellow fell across her line of vision. I could see she was itchy and irritable, and that something in the evening's proceedings had maybe made her feel less vital than she had anticipated. She had this feeling sometimes – she had told me herself, she confided in me about these things: an intense, agitated disgruntlement that her mother had always ascribed to *that time of the month*, but Kitten ascribed much more generally to *being female.* She pulled the bit of jasmine creeper cleanly off her now-burled cashmere cardigan and swore and crunched the cigarette butt to bits beneath her foot.

I remained unseen in the shadows on a rusted trike that Papa kept parked in the bushes, in case I was bored when visiting. It was then that Mr Parish emerged, without signal, from the darkness along the side of the building. With barely a crunch of autumn leaf, his compact form silvered across the courtyard. Kitten's disgruntlement went away – you could feel it ebb from the garden. She had *been found* after all!

'Muri-el!' said James Parish warningly. 'Have you been hiding from me?'

Kitten clawed back her loose blonde lock and put one foot up against the wall. 'You,' she said, 'have been otherwise engaged.'

I had never seen Kitten pout. She was generally quite straightforward and, unlike other adults, gave me lollies without using them to get promises out of me. But now she was using a voice I hadn't heard before, and didn't trust. And it surprised me that Mr Parish trusted it.

'I'm *very* hungry and tired,' she went on, 'and perhaps *you* had a good meal made by your wife before you got here but I've been all day at the gallery and I haven't had a bite to eat. Makes a girl cranky!' She pouted again. 'Are you taking me out to dinner?'

Mr Parish did something now that I couldn't see, and Kitten squealed, and then laughed, and he murmured something low-pitch down her neck.

'Well, if we can get out without being *seen* …' Kitten said.

But Mr Parish was still absorbed in the neck of her blouse and, though Kitten was still laughing, she was also batting him off.

'I want my steak, James,' she said. 'A girl needs a good meal. Steak with mushrooms and cream ... Now how do we get out of here? Is there a back gate?'

There was a back gate, and Mr Parish located it. As Kitten ducked through, I saw his hand dive to the back of her skirt and she squealed again and smacked him and laughed and said, 'Oh no, you don't!' and then they were gone – a faint titter and screech in the air outside that could've been anybody.

I rolled back and forth on my trike over the uneven bricks and wondered about this, Ornella, and if it was somehow connected to Mother and Papa, and to you and Carlito, though not to Rosa, and not, strangely, to Mrs Parish. I didn't understand why someone playful and young who always had Minties in her handbag would want to eat a steak dinner with someone old and boring like Mr Parish.

'He's famous,' you said to me once, scoffing, like being famous was a stupid thing to be. 'He can do whatever he likes.'

10 JULY 1966

Dear Tilde,

Oh Tilde, Owen is in the hospital. You won't believe what happened.

Sunday night, I made soup to take next door to my elderly neighbour. I had just taken the soup off the stove and was carrying it in my big blue pot. I'd made an apple pie too, and Owen was carrying that on a plate. Well, we set out all right, but Owen stumbled and dropped his pie and so I put the soup-pot down on the ground to help him. But the pot went down on something not flat, on stones or rubble or something, and it tipped – so fast, Tilde! – and the hot soup went all over Owen's legs. I rushed him straight to the garden tap and ran cold water on his legs. And then I made a cold bath and held him in it for a whole half-hour – you have no idea how hard it was to keep my nerve, he just screamed and screamed. I'm not even sure how I knew to keep him in the water that long, but they said at the hospital it was the best thing I could have done. Thank god! But oh Tilde, he is wrapped from knee to ankle in bandages, and they had to give him morphine to get him to sleep.

I am utterly wretched. What sort of a mother am I? I should give him up entirely to the Parishes.

He is in the hospital by himself for at least the next two nights. And when I go in, he doesn't even want me. It's like he knows that I'm a failure, Tilde. And perhaps it is my fault, because I'd had a drink, I'd had a couple of sherries, before I got the pot off the stove, you know.

Send me something, darling Tilde, to make me feel better.

Veda x

† † †

21 JULY 1966

Dear Tilde,

Thank you so much for your telegram.

Owen is now home, tottering around quite happily. They've assured me at the Children's that the burns are mild and will not scar because of my 'quick-thinking' with the cold water, but that is not sufficient to ease my conscience.

Owen and I have been quietly recuperating at home. I don't think I deserve sherry-drinking and literary self-congratulation for some time, so I have been avoiding the Knoxes, though Edith writ me a kind little note. Mr and Mrs Parish too have been very restrained and kind, though I am sure a part of them is thinking: thank goodness the child has a pair of reliable guardians now! Mrs Parish bought Owen three lovely books, and has promised there will be more next time he goes to theirs.

So I am feeling chagrined and grateful and regretful all at once. I have written three horrible poems that I have immediately torn up, and have now set myself to child-safing the house – Jo laughs at me, but I'm sure he wouldn't if he were responsible for these bandaged legs. They are a constant reprimand, reminding me that perhaps I should've stuck to my childhood conviction: 'No Children For Me!' I'm not sure how I knew at the age of seven that I would be an appalling mother, but I did you know, Tilde. I could never even look after a doll properly.

Strident comes out next month, with two of my poems in it: 'Slumber' and 'Entitled'. There is an event to mark the publication at the bookshop, with all contributors invited. I will go, of course, but the whole thing seems somewhat of an ordeal right now.

Don't worry about me, though. I will recover. I'm not about to go into a slump, I promise you. But I wish I could see my older, wiser, more practical sister: she makes me feel a little less stupid in the world.

Love Veda x

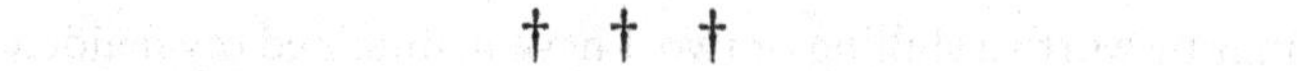

1 SEPTEMBER 1966

Dear Tilde,

I'm sorry to hear about Mother. Is there anything I can do?

Jane is no doubt keeping everything running smoothly while Mother's laid up. Send her my love, won't you.

I have inserted into this letter the latest photograph of Owen. This is a portrait shot we had made in a studio and I think it is fairly good, as far as such things go. Captures his spirit, generally speaking, his joie de vivre (he is joyful, you know, it's a constant surprise that a human creature could be so reliably bloody joyful). He is as blonde as a little wheat germ: hair, eyebrows, eyelashes, the whole lot. I know his looks will darken as he gets older, so I wanted to capture this particular angelically blonde phase. Show Mother, won't you? She never asks for any information or pictures. I suppose she has enough grandchildren, what with all of yours. Owen is a belated and somewhat superfluous addition. Meanwhile, the bandages are off, Tilde, and there is a mark the size of a penny on one shin, and that is all. I feel I have been thrown a rather large Get Out of Jail Free card.

On other topics: I suppose you have noticed that this two-sheet missive is accompanied by a slim journal with the name Strident in yellow and red across the top? Have you also noticed, beneath the masthead, somewhat smaller, but near the top (purely on account of alphabetical order) the name 'Veda Gray'? You have? Well, yes, I have included a copy of my real-life publishing debut. Put it away safely! One day it may be worth a shilling or two. I have maintained my maiden name for publication purposes because, for goodness' sake, I don't want to be mobbed in the streets!

Read the poems. Say nothing if you don't like them, and shower me with praise if you do. There will be more I hope, so long as Knox keeps his business sense about him and doesn't go bust (I have never seen a man give away his wares so generously. Someone merely has to mention a vague interest in modern poetry, and Knox is piling them up with 'super' examples.)

The launch was great fun in the end. A small group of devotees and contributors, tea and cake and wine, a speech by Knox, lots of sales and autographs splashed across title pages. (I must come up with a better flourish. Something utterly unreadable. My signature looks like it did in the fifth form.)

Love Veda x

† † †

25 NOVEMBER 1966

Dear Tilde,

It is like some kind of blessed nor'westerly, getting a letter from you!

When you write of your daily activities, I find myself wanting to stomp around among your hens, collecting eggs and sprinkling chook feed, and picking your bee-infested lavender.

For my part, I'm feeling dead on my feet at the end of the day, though I don't seem to actually do much. I remember working at Goodwin's and having enough energy at the end of the working day to write, read, go out, socialise, stay up late. Then I'd be up in the morning, and off I'd go again … Perhaps it is that I have a lack of structure. There is something to be said for structure. It puts you on automatic like a washing machine. (Which I now have, in a purpose-built laundry. A Hoover Keymatic – It tends to jump across the floor occasionally, in thrall to its lumpy, unbalanced contents, but it does not destroy them, and they seem to come out cleaner than they went in.)

Truthfully, my nerves are so a-jangle by the basic things of life sometimes. It rises up in me, in my chest and stomach, a kind of rage without an object – I don't know where it comes from, Tilde. I have nothing to be angry about. I wonder if this is all part of the character flaw our mother used to speak about. 'You will never be happy with anything,' she said, 'It is not in your nature to be satisfied.' I am beginning to think perhaps she was right. You know I can't even bear to get out of bed sometimes because I know there is only cleaning up to do. And an empty house, with dust collecting ... I had not properly realised that you do not need to create mess for there to be cleaning to do.

I'm quite alright when I get going. I put a record on and clean and wipe and soak and scrub and can almost even enjoy it. I stand back (yes, I really do this, Tilde!) and admire my washing hanging on the line because it makes me feel I have accomplished something. The problem with housework, generally speaking, is that it feels so meaningless. No one notices it or praises it. And no one really cares what sort of a house we live in anyway. No one comes to see us, except Ornella. So then, for whom am I dusting and sponging and polishing? For Jo, who comes in the door at eleven, takes a cursory look at the place, and falls asleep on the bed until morning, still dressed? No. For the neighbours? The only neighbour who speaks to me is Mrs Mathers next door and she is in an old woman's unravelling world and completely disregarding of small details like dust, mould, rubbish. Were I a better woman, I would be over at hers doing her housework as well as my own. (That is what you would do, I bet!)

Perhaps I will become the sort of woman other women mutter about, who doesn't clean her house sufficiently and comes to the letterbox in a dirty dressing-gown. I will let my hedges grow over the footpath and won't rake up my leaves. Furthermore, I will learn an off-putting squawk I will deliver when passersby look at me too curiously.

At least I have now the school run to keep me tidy. It is structure of a sort.

It seems this letter has become one long, unseemly lament.

Well, I hope you find in it something to make you chuckle.

Think of me as you chuckle, won't you, and write soon.

Love Veda x

† † †

13 DEC 1966

Dear Tilde,

Edith got hold of a book by an American woman, that has made a great storm in America in recent years, and looks at all the things that have been bothering me about my life. It discusses the trap that has been laid for us women who spend our days alone in our houses with only our chores and our children to keep us company. I will send you my copy if you are interested – it is much underlined and annotated in the margins, but still readable I hope. (Though I am not sure I am quite ready to give it up ... it has become something like a friend.)

You will consider me on my way to becoming some kind of female chauvinist. I am no such thing. But it's interesting to see that perhaps I am not completely mad, that other women have a similar sense of frustration and loneliness.

These are all things I would not mention to anyone else, so keep them under your hat, won't you?

I keep thinking of my fourth form English teacher. 'Genius!' she wrote, on my essay about Shakespeare's sonnets. 'You have a gift, Veda!'

Well, I wish she never told me this, it has been absolutely no help in my life.

What good is genius? I don't believe there is any such thing, anyway: genius is an idea men made up. It has nothing to do with women.

Silly old suffragette spinsters at that school, they never taught us how to make peace with our limitations. They didn't teach compromise cooking cleaning conciliating or caring. They didn't teach disappointment and they didn't teach hurt. I have had to learn those things all by myself.

I have been toying with calling my first collection of poetry 'The Housewife's Lament'. Only then nobody but housewives will buy it. That is the shame – only housewives listen to housewives and no one cares what housewives think.

(Farmer's wives, though – that is something completely different.)

Love Veda x

24 DEC 1966

Dear Tilde,
Well, I know I am not preserving turns, writing before I've had an answer from you, but as nobody is home here, and as I've just (finally!) got something positive in the mail from a publisher, I'm writing anyway. Bear with me. If you ever have a similar need to write out of turn, be sure and do so.

So: a publishing house, name of 'Vellum Press', is 'interested in the poems I have sent and would like to read the rest of the collection'! John Honey (editor-in-chief) was particularly taken by my 'urbane and dry commentary on the reality of a woman's life in contemporary Australia'. He wonders why he has never come across my work before in print. Hip, hip, hooray! All is well in this little writing room! Children might blot my copy, spill drink on my desk, crunch biscuit crumbs in the margins of my notebooks – but all is well! Husbands might go on frying and scoring and peeling and pureeing, I blow them kisses, for all is well! Mothers might shake heads and think the worst, but daughters have proved they are not fools after all!

Yes. I know. I am getting ahead of myself, but I don't care. I want to enjoy this feeling while I can. I'm going to spend the whole afternoon writing because this letter assures me that I am <u>not stupid</u> for doing so. It's very hard, you see, to keep on writing without positive criticism. Poetry-writing is a 'dubious activity', especially for a woman. (I put quotes around this because I made it up, and it has a certain ring to it, don't you think?) Poetry is a 'dubious activity' because: a) it does not make money for anyone – or very rarely (unless you are Mr P), b) it has no use, in a practical sense, in the world, and c) it takes up time a woman could be using to scrub out the bathtub or do an extra load of whites. Furthermore, to really clinch the matter, your average Australian would always choose a <u>rural gazette</u> over a book of poems.

This country is indeed 'the Arabian desert of the human mind'. (That's A.D. Hope, you know.) 'A landscape lost in its thoughts.' I mangle the quote possibly ... though I'm not sure Australia <u>is</u> lost in its thoughts. It seems to me Australia does not think enough! Or it thinks silently, stoically, like Father does, but is endlessly unforthcoming, doubtful of its originality ...

In poetry I can say the things I'd like to say but otherwise can't. I can't really say the political things – one has to come at it from an angle. It can't be literal. And I have to pretend much of the time that I'm not a woman, because the female sensibility is considered a little <u>on the nose</u> (you know what I mean: not tough enough, too sentimental). But I can explore things through a sort of code when I write poetry. Most of the time I'm not even sure myself what I am saying; it's as though there's a background part of my brain at work: my reptile brain. Though sometimes there are moments of brightness in it too: flashes of sun, something coming from the pen like an electric shock.

So, there's hope for me yet. I am refreshed and ready to work. Write soon of your own triumphs, large or small. Send latest recipes for jam, clippings from newspapers about agricultural news and local gossip, piano compositions in A minor, knitting patterns for superior winter scarves. All of it interests me at this moment!

Love Veda x

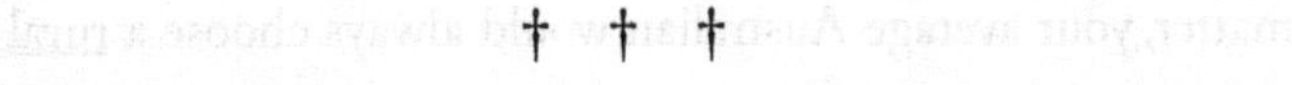

20 JAN 1967

Dear Tilde,

Listen to this:

On Wednesday last, Jo was putting up the latest exhibition by an artist called Frank Healy – abstract blots and shapes and lines; it was not clear whether the images were landscapes or strange writing characters from an ancient civilisation. Anyway, I said to Jo: 'Gosh, doesn't it remind you of Egyptian symbols, those blobs and shapes and wedges. It's like hieroglyphics!' No response. Twenty minutes later, witness the arrival of James Parish, and this is what I hear come out of Jo's mouth: 'It really is fabulous stuff, James. Reminds me of hieroglyphs!'

Well, knock me down with a feather, Tilde!

Thing is – and this really is the thing – <u>I don't even think he was aware of it!</u>

I begin to think I have no purpose of my own. Am I just my husband's echo? (Or, more aptly, is he mine?) I started out an exotic creature he couldn't tear himself away from, and I've ended up an empty, dry-sucked shell useful for sending an echo out across the landscape. Is this some age-old secret that men know and women don't?: they get us by way of ruse, a conspiracy of flattery and attention that quickly evaporates once their object is attained.

I feel vaguely traitorous when I speak of this, because Jo is not bad or unkind. He is a good man and, probably, better than most. But he is neglectful. He will let me die like an old plant for want of water. And then he will be inordinately sad. I almost feel a comforting revenge as I write and imagine that.

It does seem that loving him has not paid off like I thought it would, Tilde. I find it has saddled me with a version of myself that I had nothing to do with. How exactly did that happen? I wish he would be a little bit more part of the family. It feels like Owen and I are the family, and Jo is some kind of satellite who orbits us from a distance. The restaurant requires long, late hours. He sleeps through the mornings and is then up and shaved and off. I know this is the way of men, and this is the contract – bringing in the money etc., home fires tended – but I do not believe the arrangement is conducive to conjugal happiness.

Is it like this for you? Does Frank talk to you, in depth and about things other than rotary hoes and sheep feed? Does he listen? Or does he just assume that everything's alright?

I know it's prying of me, but if you let me know your own experiences, I might have better material with which to judge my expectations – whether I'm being fair or not, or complaining over nothing.

Owen gets bigger and bigger and has no teeth in the front and guzzles chocolate milk as though he is determined to get his bones as full of calcium and sugar as possible. He is a joy and an annoyance and, sometimes I think, my only real friend.

Love Veda x

10 FEBRUARY 1967

Dear Tilde,

I am very glad to hear Frank is, as I expected, the model husband – though I also suspect you to be the model wife, which makes everything easier on everyone. If only I had inherited some of your calm and measure. What was mother's comforting saying? That I always go 'headlong into catastrophe'. Well, it is very apt. As a child, it threw me into such sterling company as Anne Shirley and Katy of Ohio. But as an adult I discover it is something that the Annes and the Katys have long outgrown and only Veda has stayed true to. And perhaps

I was never as lovable as Anne or Katy in the first place.

Jo is taking me out, as a present, to cheer me up. We're going to the theatre, would you believe? He is making me dress up – has even sent me into town to go shopping – and has taken the Saturday night off, and we are going to the Palais Theatre to see Eartha Kitt (do you know her?) and are then going dancing. (God forgive me, can I even remember how?)

It all sounds fun, doesn't it? But I couldn't even be bothered trying anything on in Georges this afternoon. It seemed too much effort. I should've taken a girlfriend so we could have encouraged one another to make purchases and then gone and had lunch in the Myers caf. But then I realised I didn't have anyone to take. Once upon a time, Mrs Parish would've been a good practical, critical companion on such an excursion. She has style – well, a very conservative style, but she knows quality when she sees it. But I don't feel I can call on her for such expediencies as friendship – our relationship is of a different nature now. Edith Knox doesn't care a fig for fashion and would adore any old thing I held up to her to admire. Mrs Gordon Bridie ... No, Susan looks so brilliant in everything herself that I really couldn't spend an afternoon playing second fiddle to her. Besides, I'm not on close enough terms with her.

So, actually, I needed you. And without you, I went but I didn't buy anything and Jo got rather cross with me when he came home and I had nothing to show.

Bring on the cooler weather. It's been an appalling summer, and no sign of letting up yet. The heat has been too much for me this year, Tilde. I am on the point of melting.

Love Veda x

† † †

27 FEB 1967

Dear Tilde,
Before I talk about my own problems, as I do so regularly and predictably, I will respond properly and brightly to your last related offerings. Regarding the loss of your lambs: I don't know how you bear that aspect of the farmer's life. I remember worrying myself sick alongside Father when prices fell or foxes marauded or frosts happened when frosts were supposed to be long over. I feel my stomach do a little downwards flip even now, like a dying fish on a pier.

But you ask about the progress of my poetry collection ... I feel my heart begin to flip like said dying fish. The situation is as follows: Having tweaked all my poems into what I thought were perfect little kernels of truth and sent them off (long ago, it seems now), I have just received a letter from my assigned editor at Vellum telling me he would like me to rework the following ... according to the following editorial comments ... and would like to cut blah, blah and blah ... and he wonders about the logic of the sequencing ... and feels an 'emotional resonance is lacking' in some of them and, presumably, could I please put one in? Well, how does one insert 'emotional resonance' into one's poems – without, that is, pressing them into a kind of abject service? Would they like more obvious emotion, is that what they want? I loathe these vague requirements and suspect that fulfilling them will result in a book of poems I cannot bring myself to read.

They also believe the poems are not sufficient in number

to comprise 'a collection' – they think I need twice as many – the word they used was 'flimsy'. They believe publishing it in its current 'flimsy' form will do a disservice to the work and to the reputation of the publishing house.

I am so bloody tired!

Owen grows his hair long like a little blonde beatnik.

Veda x

† † †

14 APRIL 1967

Dear Tilde,

I have a temper and a big mouth. When you get to the end of this letter, you will wish I was in restraints of some kind. Yes, I think I require restraints – ones that do up at the back perhaps.

Things don't go as I'd like. Knox says Vellum are as good as any other publisher, but then I consulted Mr Parish on the same question. 'Vellum Press!' he said. 'Lot of rubbish. Don't mix yourself up with that lot, they don't know what they're doing.' But he had no advice and offered no alternative. We were at dinner. He said what he had to say and then turned back to talk to Jo about Fred Williams, who is going to show at Works On Paper in November – it represents a coup for the gallery.

So I sat there drinking my wine and feeling the tepid water leaking down upon my enthusiasms. Mrs Parish – 'June' as I now call her – smiled and at one point even squeezed my shoulder as she passed me doing something or other, putting out cutlery. She is good to have in my life, I realise now.

A modest and kind person. On a Friday, she picks Owen up from school and often has him the whole weekend. Sometimes I feel tempted to pack a little bag of my own and go off with the two of them. I want her to cook me a meal and read to me and put me to bed. However, I don't think her husband is very good to her. Just a hunch, as the Americans say. I can see it in the way he talks to her – one suspects his disrespect (and he is disrespectful, as you will see below) is a manifestation of some kind of guilt.

Perhaps it was his disrespect, or perhaps it was his dismissal of Vellum Press, and by extension me, that made me behave so badly in his house.

Yes, I did, Tilde, abominably.

As I said, we were there for dinner. There was an absolute storm outside, but I'd got Owen off to sleep, and the fire was blazing and the house (finally – it is all sort of brick or tiled floor, freezing cold!) was warm and cosy. June had set the table with care. She has a set of lovely hand-printed linen napkins with floral designs. Her crockery is all glazed earthenware and she has lovely crystal wine glasses. Everything's very expensive, I can tell. And well chosen. And the centrepiece of the table, an arrangement of native flowers and leaves in a tall rectangular vase. I saw all these details and they made me appreciate the attention she brings to everything she does. And I thought, Gosh, she must have inner resources that I know nothing about, a whole and complete inner life that only shows itself in these beautifully constructed details she creates about her.

The food was arranged with equal meticulousness and style: Chilli Bourbon Meatballs with Grape Jelly, arranged three on a plate, on bamboo skewers stripped at the top and tied into interesting knots. Yes, really! Her Beef Bourguignon was utterly gorgeous, strewn with parsley, melting with carrots and mushrooms. I ate sparingly but really, I could've shovelled two helpings down, which says something for me. Meanwhile, the men just kept eating and talking – about Fred Williams, about profit margins, about the forthcoming American art exhibition (which they were disparaging before they'd even seen it). They seemed not to have noticed the effort June had gone to. I raised my glass to her secretly as the cutlery scraped away on the plates. But then, listening to the men, all of a sudden I lost my temper. Maybe it's the book I've been reading, the one Edith sent me, but I said: 'For god's sake, gentlemen, could we make a proper bloody toast to June for this fabulous dinner?'

Jo put his glass in the air at once and said she'd better not open a restaurant because he'd be in serious trouble. Mr Parish was obviously not in the mood because he ignored me and kept talking to Jo. June collected the plates, and I got up to help, and we rinsed them at the sink. Then she got another bottle of wine from the cellar and brought it to the table. Mr Parish looked at it and nodded and she uncorked it and poured it and the men talked on and June and I started a little quiet conversation about Owen and how excited he is to be in Grade 2. Then all at once, we were arrested in our talk by what I can only describe as an expostulation. Mr Parish was spitting bits of wine out through his teeth into his wine glass and looking apoplectic. 'Jesus June,' he shouted. 'There's cork in this wine!'

June got up, swift as anything, apologised profusely and, rushing over to the kitchen, poured the offensive beverage down the sink. Opened another bottle. Got her husband a napkin (to spit into more genteelly). Rushed around to check neither Jo nor I had an atom's worth of misplaced cork bobbing around in our dregs.

Mr Parish had recovered by this time. 'I've told you,' he said to June (patiently now), 'not to use that corkscrew. It strips the cork. There's a perfectly good new one I bought you and I don't understand why you continue to persevere with the old one.' He smiled through teeth at me and Jo. 'Darling.'

Well, I accepted this as him making amends, but I was probably a bit tipsy now and I was feeling quite cross about everything.

We went on. We ate dessert. They talked about Fred Williams and Fred Cress and Donald Friend. Mr Parish put on his glasses and got some slides from his library and he and Jo held them up to the overhead light. He returned to the library and came back with a book of prints. Each print was protected with waxy tissue paper. They drew back the tissue-paper and inspected the originals.

'How are you progressing?' June asked me, quietly, in a little air pocket in the room protected from the attentions of men. 'With your book? Are you making headway?'

I told her, very briefly. She sighed a little and nodded as if she knew all about it. 'It's very difficult, isn't it?' she said. 'But you must go on, you know. You really must.' She gripped my hand in her own, surprisingly firm hand and said: 'You would never forgive yourself if you stopped.'

'What are you talking about, you women?' Mr Parish now said. Or something along those lines. He had gone all bird-eyed, like he had spotted a lush little worm below. Two lush little worms. 'Are you discussing us and our latest transgressions?'

'Not at all,' I said. 'We were discussing ourselves.'

'Well, there's a minefield!' he said. And laughed. 'Or a desert.'

June had got up, was collecting bowls again.

'A minefield, definitely!' said Jo. He winked at me. It was an ill-timed wink. And, continuing his ill-timing, he went on to say: 'So what do you think of my wife, James? She's going to become a published poet. What do you say to that?'

'I congratulate her,' said James. 'It's no easy thing.' He leaned over to raise a belated toast. His eyes connected with mine and I wish they hadn't because I saw in them a sort of amusement that made me feel instantly stupid and violent.

'Did you manage to read them, James?' I said. I knew he had a copy. Jo had given him one, ages ago.

'Of course I've read them, Veda,' he said. 'I read them a long time ago, when you first left me that package ...'

I blushed at the memory of that, Tilde – that ambitious, ludicrous batch of poems I'd left with him years ago.

'No, I mean the latest. Jo gave you a copy of my manuscript. Oh, months ago ...'

'I'm not sure what you're talking about,' he said. 'Jo has not given me any manuscript.'

I raised my head at this and looked across the table, and I could see, from Jo's pleading red face, that this was indeed the truth. (He had promised me, Tilde! Why hadn't he followed through?)

Mr Parish didn't notice my alarm. 'I will do my best to look at the manuscript if you get a copy to me. Certainly. There was some originality in that first lot of poems. Didn't say anything then. Thought it best you find your own paces. No good to drench a young poet in praise – but you're onto something. You're not an imposter. It wasn't all derivative.'

Well, that's pretty ample praise from Mr James Parish, but unfortunately I didn't really register it at the time. I'll admit, Tilde, I had a few under the belt (might a woman say that? I was in fact wearing a belt if that helps) and all I could think was: Jo didn't even give him the manuscript!

Jo reached across the table. 'Veda,' he said. 'I'm sorry darling, I just kept forgetting ... I don't know why. I was so busy, Veda ...' I could see he was trying to keep my lid on so I didn't explode.

But I did explode, Tilde. All the wine, and the resentments of the evening – they overcame me. I felt myself rise up like some sea-creature from the depths of the ocean. Jo got out of his seat, fearing the worst, saying: 'Veda, Veda. Bloody hell! Just stop for a second ...'

But I couldn't stop. I picked up my full glass of red wine and I threw it at him. Across June's beautiful table linen, across the front of Jo's shirt and Mr Parish's grey jacket, and across the book of original limited edition prints Mr Parish had open in front of him.

Yes, Tilde, red wine.

And then I was properly ashamed. Straight away. Immediately. I shrank immediately to nothing. Mr Parish called me a 'fucking idiot!' Mrs Parish ran for salt, vinegar, water. The table setting, the shirt, the jacket ... these were all forgivable. But not the book of prints, Tilde. Not the book of prints.

I will not report on the rest of that evening. Suffice to say, Jo and I left. Mrs Parish presumably dropped Owen at school this morning; I will pick him up at half-past three. Beyond that there has been no word. Jo phoned half an hour ago to say he will stay at Ornella's until I 'feel better'.

I am being rightly punished. I have wept and wept, but now I am cold, like stone. I am a stone-cold statue and, of course, that's what I should've been in the first place, and none of this would ever have happened.

Write to me.

Veda x

† † †

24 APRIL 1967

Dear Tilde,

No, don't come. Of course I'm alright. I'm just under a period of probation – you know what I mean. Jo has locked the liquor cabinet (a move I suspect you approve), which I'm sure is all very responsible. I concur with you entirely: if I had not had anything to drink, I would have kept my temper. But you really don't have to worry. Owen is at Ornella's tonight and tomorrow with the Parishes. For my part, I'm just very tired and am sleeping a lot and thinking about my poems. Will write to you properly again very soon and love you and everything else. And thank you for reserving judgement of me, yet again.

Veda x

PS. No, of course I don't want money to pay for the prints.

† † †

7 JUNE 1967

Dear Tilde,

'A distinctive Australian poetry,' says my silly little Scots editor at Vellum, 'needs, at its heart, an engagement with the particularities of Australia.'

I do not know how to make sense of this comment. Is it a statement, an exhortation, a criticism? How would you take it? Is my life not rich with 'particularities' and is it not 'Australian'? Next time, I am going to send into the world some of my absurdist nonsense:

I am not a Nationalist
Nor Poltergeist
Nor Pugilist
Nor bloody weekend Cubilist…
So spare the bloody Bugle-ist

The critique I receive is such abominable nonsense that I may as well meet it in kind.

Now my publisher is telling me they'd like me to build up more of a 'publishing history' before they 'collect' my poems – they need to be able to quote all the journals my work has been printed in, so that my collection is verified by the world at large. John Honey, the chief editor, says to be patient: they are 'building me'. But he's not editing the poems himself – I wish he was because I rather like him, but instead he's put this vicious little Scotsman onto me, who's got the secateurs onto all my poems, trimmed everything which implies 'female' to the reader. (There was one verse in which the word 'bosoms' rose up, but it has been cut down like a scandalous pair of knickers on the line. 'Bosoms' might only ever be discussed in the context of sisterly friendships. 'Bosoms, Brassieres, and Bunyips' – there's a particularised engagement with Australia for you, sister!)

The days are gone when a poet had the ear of a king. Not anymore. Nope. (How's that for an Americanism? Haven't you heard the kids saying it? "Nope. Nope. Nope." Whitman is over: there's only one Walt now.)

Hark! I hear a key in a door! A scratching of husbands and small children. Quick, hide these painful scribblings. What will the neighbours think?

G'bye g'bye g'bye, darling Tilde, till next time.

VEDA xxxxx

PART 3

SNOW WHITE IN THE FOREST WITH THE APPLE

LOVE-LETTER: 1987

You don't know a book until you're inside it. This, Julia has said to me many times. You cannot dip into a manuscript and know the book. You cannot read a passage here and a passage there. A book, unlike a painting, cannot be immediately apprehended. Unlike a meal, a book cannot be appreciated at the first mouthful. A book only unfurls itself across time.

But a book of poetry is different, Julia says. It is not like a painting, or a novel, or a meal, and yet, it isn't a commitment of time either; it is not real estate (how poets wish it were!); nor does it have to survive in the memory alone. A poem can be taken in very quickly, says Julia, but it can last a lifetime. It can be gone back to, over and over again, and bring a different response each time. 'It doesn't matter,' says Julia, 'if only one image captures you. Or one line.' She takes off her glasses and looks at me sternly. 'We have forgotten how to read poetry, I think. We're frightened by it.'

After pretending she was glad that I had no writerly aspirations, she decided, in the wake of Mother's success, that she'd better just make sure she wasn't missing an intergenerational talent. 'Bring something to me, Owen,' she said at the end of our first date. I had stood her up at Trades Hall but went sheepishly back to her office and told her I'd got the day wrong. I was temperamentally incapable of being cruel. 'Bring me something. Let me see what you can write! I may not be able to publish it myself, of course, but if it's any good, I can forward it on to the right people ...' She smiled. She was five years older than me. It seemed a lifetime.

I spent the first month of our *courtship* furiously writing, albeit only to impress Julia. An experimental, fragmentary novel, heavily influenced by Raymond Queneau, whom I was reading at the time, about a family that thought they were alive but in fact were not. I got 20,000 words down, which I left on her desk one afternoon before going and getting drunk at the nearest pub. Julia didn't read it in my presence, nor even mention it for some time, but eventually, when we were out for dinner (that was mainly what we did in those days), she took off her glasses, very businesslike, and said: 'That manuscript of yours. It's a good premise. But completely derivative. Sort of limply so, to tell you the truth. You don't mind me saying that, do you?' She rammed her fork into her food and chewed merrily. 'I don't think you're a writer, Owen. I'm sure you could be if you put lots of time and effort into it. But not in terms of natural talent ...' She took another bite of whatever it was: lamb, beef. 'This meat is so tender!'

Firstly, I felt a childish pang of embarrassment, humiliation. I felt myself blush. What an idiot, with my derivative French-inspired absurdist nonsense! And then the relief came: *Oh, thank god, now I don't have to write the bloody thing!* 'You couldn't make a publisher money, Owen,' Julia said, smiling affectionately at me. 'But you're an absolute darling for trying your hand at it. I will tuck this manuscript away and treat it as a *love-letter*. You are the first man to write me a proper literary love-letter! I won't forget it.'

And she didn't.

Did Papa ever write Mother a love-letter, I wondered. I have found scraps of poems, birthday cards. Mother wasn't much good at birthday cards. 'Dear O-yo, Happy Birthday, Love Mother'. I found: 'Sorry about last night etc love Jo x' on the back of an envelope. I found 'his pretty ears in sleep; his straw-coloured hair; his tulip mouth' in her handwriting but it is torn off something else, something bigger, something I won't ever read the whole of.

Did Papa ever write Mother a love-letter?

Did Mother ever write one?

Did they love each other?

PADDY COW – 1968

I remember, Ornella, all the different driveways from this time. The tree-roots and tyre troughs of the Parishes' dangerously steep driveway, Papa zig-zagging left to right in first gear. Arriving safely in their garage required acceleration and a kind of mad confidence. In wet weather, the wheels spun.

Your driveway in Coburg was a gentle ascent and drop, buoyed by the good suspension on the EH Holden Papa bought from Les Preston. The Holden did not so much stop as *come to a rest*. The concrete in your driveway was smooth too, perfect for playing ball or for practising in roller skates. I missed Coburg when it was sold. When you moved into your house in Richmond, Papa had to reverse in and out several times to get the car straight in the narrow driveway and then there was barely any space to open the doors. In Richmond, everything pressed too close to everything else. You couldn't even roll a ball on the floor. It felt like a ball rolling on the floor might put a dent in something.

Our house in Hawthorn had a driveway made of stubby bricks, and the car made a *pit-a-pit-a* sound when we turned in to it, as though we'd just got a flat tyre. A ball, once bounced, would ricochet from the bricks into unpredictable places. You could stub your toe if you weren't wearing shoes.

To and fro and to and fro: I spent a lot of time in the car and I was not sure any night where I was going and where I might wake up. I was confused sometimes when I opened my eyes: if I wanted Mother, you were there; if I wanted you, Mrs Parish was there. Things got cleaned up and changed around between visits, so if I'd put something down I couldn't expect it to still be there when I came back two days, three days later.

I still use the word *home* about Hawthorn, the place where Mother was. But other times, when I thought about *home*, the whole thing made me angry. It made me rip up pictures I was working on because *home* was a place that kept changing locations. I ripped up my own drawings to spite them, all these adults throwing the word *home* around like it didn't matter. I'd rip up something they thought was 'great' and 'fabulous' just to show them that them that I could do it. *Take that!* I wanted to say. You like this? Well, I can *wreck it*!

You didn't care much about my drawings that I ripped up, Ornella, but Mrs Parish was mortified. She collected the pieces and tried to put them back together with sticky tape. When I ripped up my pictures, it hurt her, physically, like I had cut myself on the arm on purpose or pulled hair out of my head. Mother thought it was funny. She laughed. 'He's having a little rage!' she said. She laughed so hard once that I picked up my glass of orange juice and poured it over my head. I don't know why. Except there was nothing else I could do. I had no other weapons. I sat there, dripping with orange juice and fuming, and Mother was cross because it meant she had to stop what she was doing and run me a bath and wash my hair.

All the adults were *trying so hard* and *doing so much for me*. You said I was luckier than other kids because I was not stuck all the time in one boring place and I got so many birthday presents.

But I was angry. I wanted to kick the footy after school with George Zigouras and Callum Webster. I wanted to practise with the stumps and ball and cricket bat that Father Christmas brought me. I wanted to try out Callum's glider. I wanted to be part of the neighbourhood. Instead, I kicked the football by myself at Park Orchards. I hit a tennis ball against Ornella's neighbour's fence with my cricket bat until the lady who lived there came out and said to stop it cause I was giving her a headache.

I didn't have after-school friends, but at the Parishes' I had Paddy Cow.

Even now I don't really know what a paddy cow is – is it related to rice paddies? Or is it supposed to be 'poddy cow'? Whatever it is, that is what Mrs Parish called the sweet brown-and-white calf that wandered the Park Orchard 'paddocks' with a little bit of rope hanging from her neck. She had been given to Mrs Parish by a local who didn't want her. She came at half-size, a runt who needed feeding with a bottle and teet. Mrs Parish adored her. She was just like Wilbur in *Charlotte's Web*, she said. Only she wasn't a pig. Mrs Parish cuddled her like a baby and gave her treats from the kitchen – wet spinach, pieces of orange. Even Mr Parish loved Paddy Cow and scratched her on the side of her neck to make her happy. Her big brown eyes were wise and solemn and faintly mischievous. Mrs Parish called them 'moony'. She was as gentle as a lamb – she was as gentle as a *calf.* Sometimes, waking up early and holding back the bedroom curtains to see the sun coming up, Paddy Cow would be there, snuffling steam at the glass and tilting her head. Waiting for me to wake up. She made up for my lack of schoolmates.

Mother was not welcome at the Parishes anymore. Mrs Parish sighed when I asked her about this. She put her hand on my head, and said, 'It's all a big silly mistake, Owen' and then steered me into the lounge room and put the telly on so I could watch Skippy or Mr Squiggle – both shows that I had long grown out of. I asked Mr Parish the same question, summoning all my courage. I took a deep breath. 'Why isn't Mother allowed to come here anymore?'

Mr Parish was putting on his work boots, preparing to fix some fences. Writing and thinking about poetry seemed to take up most of Mother's time, but Mr Parish accomplished the same thing in a couple of hours, every morning in his study. The rest of the time he got about on the property fixing things and tending fruit-trees and making fire breaks and crafting new and interesting pathways through the bush. When Mrs Parish called him for lunch, he bounded up the steep driveway as though he were taking the stairs three at a time.

'Why can't Mother come here anymore?' I asked.

He looked up at me, not sternly so much as seriously – as though I were worthy of knowing, of being told the truth.

It made me feel strange to be taken seriously like this. It made me feel like I was part of the grown-ups' story, rather than just the kid character, separate, on the outskirts. 'We are your guardians, Owen,' Mr Parish said. He yanked his boot onto his foot, and then the other. 'We became your guardians because your mother needed help, and your father – well, a father is not a mother, is he? Your father works all day, all night.' He touched my hair. 'Any time your mother is ready, she is welcome to come back here.'

He asked me if I wanted to come and work with him on the fences, but I didn't want to, and I said No, and he seemed relieved.

In the lounge room, Mrs Parish had naughtily lit the fire, and there was a citrus smell as she peeled off twigs from a stick of lemon-scented gum.

'Come on, Owen,' she said. 'Let's make a bouquet you can take home for your mother.'

PIE CHART

I guess you could say you were my *primary carer*, Ornella. If I look at it in terms of a pie-chart. We were learning pie charts at school. We started by dividing up the different countries our parents came from. Britain was the biggest part of the pie chart, then Italy, then Greece. We learnt a song in Greek and how to count to ten in Italian. My primary school was the local state school and it was halfway between your house and Mother and Papa's house. Mr Parish hadn't wanted me to go to Hawthorn West State School No. 293. He wanted me to go to Christ Church School, which was at the other end of Bridge Road, 'just as easy to get to, for god's sake,' he said, 'and I'll pay, of course.' But it didn't happen. I don't know why. Was it you, Ornella? Did you say no?

Hawthorn West sat up on a hill, with rich kids living on one side and poor kids on the other. The rich kids lived in big Victorian houses in streets with names like Shakespeare Grove, houses that backed on to the Yarra River with bona-fide Aboriginal canoe trees in their backyards. The poor kids lived in single-fronted terraces with party walls and concrete backyards, or way up high in commission flats in Richmond. The rich kids remained at our school till second or third grade and then went off in caps and long socks to the private schools that netted the Hawthorn side of the river – or to schools like Christ Church. Goodbye, we waved: the poor kids and the commission flat kids and immigrant kids and sons of bus drivers and restaurant owners. Off they went to their separate realm. We never saw each other again. Never.

'There's no class in Australia,' you said, Ornella. Didn't you know you were working class? Carlito did. It was what made him angry all the time.

But you were too busy doing your nursing training at the Royal Melbourne Hospital to think about *class*. Nonna's house in Coburg had been sold. Papa had taken the money and bought our house in Hawthorn for $36,000 ('much too much!' said Mother). He kept helping you with your bills and with your rent. But you were learning hospital tucks and catheter-insertion and fluid-drainage and instrument cleaning and cardiogram-reading and expert patient-transfer. You could do *phlebotomy*. Not to mention hand-holding and reassurance-giving. Did you think you might get yourself a nice middle-class doctor, Ornella? But then Carlito married you, all of a sudden. He married you with little ceremony and very few relatives. No fuss. It was sprung upon us: a quick jaunt up the aisle and into a waiting car and it was over. And then Carlito was fully moved in, for ever and ever, and I just had to *suck it up*, as they say nowadays.

I was glad you worked at the Royal Melbourne and not at the *Iron Ear Hospital.* You had once threatened to take me to the Iron Ear Hospital when I put candlewax in my ear-hole. I was scared of the Iron Ear Hospital. I had learned about medieval torture from a book Carlito had brought home from the Richmond library. Iron was a frightening medieval product that brooked no escape. 'The Iron Lung,' I told you, muddling my references, 'crushes its victim's bones one at a time, until they are dead and their heart has stopped beating forever.'

You put on your nurse's smock and support stockings and washed your hands extra well with Salvol so you could really feel the germs come off and said, 'Don't be stupid, Owen. Where do you get your imagination?' Then you walked me to the Eye and Ear Hospital at a snickety pace I could barely keep up with, and they got the lump of wax out quick smart, without even hurting.

Carlito slept through the mornings and left the coffee you made him to go cold next to the bed. I heard you gloatingly tell the neighbour from Number 6 that he was your husband. You had a big fat ring, like an ugly blister, on your finger. It looked like it was going to go bust or get jammed in a door somehow.

LEGACY

Yes, Ornella, you are quite right: better to forget childhood altogether. You have forgotten yours entirely now. And you have kept nothing to remind you.

After Nonna died, you threw out the photo albums: *Ornella, Sandringham: 1943; Tootgarook: 1948; Bronte Beach: 1951*. There you were: wrapped in a towel in Nonno's lap. Testing the waves with a cautious toe. 'Look at these, Owen!' you said wondrously and then you threw the lot of them in the rubbish. I watched, astonished. 'Nup, nup, nup. Don' wan' it …' The whole time crying, rubbing your nose, re-tying the elastic band in your hair. You kept two photographs in the end: Nonno and Nonna on their wedding day, trussed into uncomfortable suits; yourself as a baby in a christening gown: black-haired and beady-eyed, fists raised.

Nonna lived a long time in the Donna Vincenzo. Brains get holes, like ink blots, that spread. They turn up white on brain scans: I imagine it like coral bleaching. Nonna's white coral spread and spread till her only mechanism that worked was her thumbs. She couldn't speak or show that she knew you, but she could be adamant, nevertheless, with her thumbs, using them to punch out long-forgotten messages in the palms of hands or on the arms of chairs. 'Mama,' you said, and stroked her hair, and brushed it, and put bobby pins in it. Then one day, she died, just like that: no warning. You were on a night shift. You didn't find out until you got home at 7 am and saw the note Carlito had written: 'Your mother died.' I guess there was no gentle way of putting it. You went straight to the nursing home and saw her still, quiet body, covered by its white cotton blanket, and you got to put a kiss on her forehead.

But you weren't there when she died and you never forgave yourself. You'd seen people die often enough in the hospital. You'd put drip buckets under their bodies on the way down to the morgue. You knew about it. It was *no big deal.* But they weren't your mother.

And then, after her funeral, after everything, there it was: the money she'd creamed off the housekeeping for thirty years, *invested in shares,* for godssake. Enough money to buy the house in Richmond you were renting. Plus some to go in the bank. Her gift to you. A mother's legacy trimmed off a son's rights. You walked over that bridge with me to school the next day and said, 'Those kids who get picked up in them cars, Owen, don't you worry about them. One day, you'll have a better car than every single one of 'em.' You pulled your cardigan so it sat more neatly over your pointy tits and held your head high. Your Roman nose was straighter than ever, a precise and noble nose that gave you dignity. 'Is that your mother?' asked Callum, awed. 'Yes,' I said. 'That's her.' And then I laughed at his round eyes and punched him in the ribs and said: 'Sucked in!'

On Wednesday and Thursday nights I went to my real Mother's, I went to Veda's. I tried out calling her 'Veda' instead of 'Mother'. I tried really hard for a week. I thought she would like it. I thought it would make us grown-up friends, and she would listen to me more. But she didn't like it. 'O-yo,' she said, 'There are lots of people who can call me Veda, but only one who can call me Mother, and that's you.' I wasn't sure if this marked me out in a good way or a bad way. I was relieved not to have to keep calling her Veda (it was hard to remember), but it had made me sound modern, I thought. There was a kid at school who called his parents Helen and Bruce and it made him sound more grown-up than the rest of us. But Helen still looked like a normal mother and she made cupcakes for the school fete, and Bruce did after-school soccer training with the boys on Wednesday nights. Veda didn't do things like that. I was glad she didn't, and I was disappointed she didn't. That's how it was: I was spared and I was ashamed, both at the same time. It made me want to kick dust at pigeons eating crumbs on the way home from school, or wrench loose bits off people's fences, or whack my cricket bat against a gate where a dog barked.

Mother had recreated herself again recently. She was trying to entertain me. She was trying to win me back with her fun fun fun self. She had become an egg-and-bacon-frying, over-talkative, late-night *crazy woman*. Reckless. And embarrassing. She would wire up tin-can telephones, or regale me with enormous impossible jigsaw puzzles, or begin a combative game of Chinese checkers – she was exhausting. She let me stay up late. She would *make me* stay up late. I really just wanted dinner, bath and bed at 8 o'clock. In truth, I liked her most when she fell asleep on the couch with the television on and her scraped-egg plate in front of her. Then I would prop myself next to her and watch the black-and-white transmission: *Pick-a-Box* and *Bandstand* and *Homicide*. If Papa got home and I was still awake, I would pretend to be asleep, so it looked like Mother and I were out-and-out TV-watching *addicts*, so obsessed by the flickering TV that we couldn't bear to relocate to our bedrooms. Mother's arm over me was a big hot drooping weight, but I let her leave it there; Papa would transfer me to the cool sheets of my bed and help Mother to hers. I liked this thing of Papa looking after us. I liked him coming home to set things right.

When I went to the restaurant with Papa on Sundays, I drew. Rosa brought me paper offcuts, different kinds of art paper: thick, crinkly strips that absorbed waterpaints and ink; canvas-y paper that was like fabric, with fibres and small lumps that a pencil could capsize on; sheer, smooth polished paper on which my textas ran beautifully; chalky paper that was perfect for black fineliner. Rosa sat near me and peeled things, cracked things, pitted things, now and then glancing up at my prowess. It was a slow, gentle day, Sunday: quiet preparation for the Salvos meal in the late afternoon. The kitchen belched and steamed stew vapours; meat melted off shank bones; celery fell to liquid, carrots to butter. Everything was cloaked in a perfume of food: Rosa said she'd rather smell like Papa's lamb shank stew than Chanel No.5. We snorted it up into our nostrils and laughed.

Most times, I'd stay behind in the restaurant with Rosa when Papa and Les delivered the food and doled it out to the homeless men. When Papa and Les returned, they'd be a bit drunk, happy and pleased with themselves, part of a *brotherhood of men*.

Rosa and I co-existed like old friends these days, usually without much conversation. Sometimes she'd sing in a crackly high old woman's voice that embarrassed me. I kicked the chair leg in time with my foot to disguise my discomfort.

Rosa's face was heavy and dog-like when she concentrated, even when she sang, but when she looked up and smiled, her clean square teeth glistened in her mouth and her cheeks bloomed with dimples like a girl's.

'Why do you work here?' I asked her one day. The men had gone. I was drawing a dinosaur – with black marker first, and then I was going to colour it in with broken pieces of Conte crayon. It had a body like a surfboard, covered in leaf-shaped scales. Actually, it looked like a pineapple.

'Need money,' said Rosa. She was grating cheese standing up, her shirt cuffs rolled back.

'Well,' I said. I added a tail on my dinosaur. The tail was small and dinky, like Eeyore's. 'You could work in the gallery.'

'Psssht, what?'

'You're an artist, Rosa,' I said.

'Yes, so why do I want to sit at a desk talking on a telephone all day? You think artists are good at that?'

'No. But you could talk to people about art. That's what Kitten does.'

'Si, Signore.' She turned the cheese block to a different angle.

'If you're an artist …' I said, feeling my way, 'why do you have to work at all, Rosa? Mr Parish is a poet. That's a kind of artist. *He* doesn't have to work.'

'Mr Parish got good luck on his side. And family money. And he's famous. Right from the beginning, bang! Mr Parish make an impact. They all talking about his work, he's a genius.'

'Why don't you have a show at Papa's gallery and make money?'

Rosa stopped. Her face was a little red. She scraped a heap of cheese from the table into a bowl and rolled down her shirtsleeves. 'Haven't been asked,' she said. 'Anyway, I paint on canvas. Or walls. I don't make my works *on paper*, Owen.'

'Yes you do. That's why you brought this paper for me. You said it's your scraps. You said, Here Owen, here's my paper scraps!'

Rosa rubbed her nose with the back of her wrist. 'I use paper for practice. For working out a picture. I use canvas for *real*. Or walls.' She sighed and came over to me. She put the cheese and the bowl down and sat down next to me. 'You know what I heard last week, Owen?' she said.

I shook my head.

'I heard they painted over my mural.'

'No, they didn't!' I said. I pointed to the wall: there it was: the narrow path between the mountains, the tiny V of sun in the distance, the little scraggy billy-goat ghost in the evening light.

'No, not this one: my first mural, in your papa's first restaurant,' Rosa said. 'You don't remember it. You were too little. You were probably not even born!'

I nodded furiously. 'I do remember!' I said.

She smiled. 'Well, my friend told me they painted over it. The new people running the place. Bam, bam, white paint over the top.'

'Why?'

'I dunno, Owen. Things change. They running a different kind of restaurant there now. Maybe it got faded. Maybe it didn't suit.'

'Damn!' I said. This was a word I had heard a lot lately. I used it now to test it. Rosa didn't flinch.

'Yep,' she said. 'Damn is right. You know what really makes *my blood boil*?'

I shook my head.

'I didn't get photographs.' She shook her head in disbelief. She lifted her hand as though she wanted to smack herself. 'I didn't get any photographs, Owen. Just got the one from the newspaper, that's all there is. Dumb, huh?' She clicked her fingers. 'Now it's gone. Bam, bam, white paint, finished!'

I clucked my tongue in sorrow. I began to add a small baby dinosaur to my picture; it was hanging off the mother dinosaur's neck by the teeth. 'Will you do another wall, Rosa?'

Rosa thought for a while, sadly, and then brightened. 'I will do your bedroom wall, Owen. What you want on it?' She glanced at my drawing. 'Dinosaurs?'

I wasn't sure I could live in a bedroom with dinosaurs. 'Maybe … flowers,' I said.

'What, like a garden?'

'Yes, or just flowers. On their own. You know, like Mrs Parish's …'

'You want me to do flowers on your bedroom wall?'

I hadn't thought about it, but now that she said it, I knew that's exactly what I wanted: flowers, a whole lot of them, maybe even with Paddy Cow in the centre, a dandelion in her mouth. I would ask Mr Parish if Rosa could make a mural in my bedroom. Mrs Parish would love it.

'Yep,' I said. 'I want flowers on my bedroom wall.'

'*Concordo. Consideralo fatto*!' Rosa said, whipping bowl,

grater and cheese from the table. 'Let me know what they say!' She turned towards the kitchen and then turned back. 'But Owen: you know, I love working here. I love your Papa's restaurant. I wouldn't work anywhere else. He's a good man, your Papa.'

I nodded. I knew that.

No one explained why I only stayed with Mother on Wednesday and Thursday nights now; no one talked about it. Or maybe you all talked about it when I wasn't there. Did you? Somewhere, outside of my hearing, it had been decided that Mother couldn't be trusted with me anymore, except in a limited way. This was on account of several things, and Mother throwing red wine at Mr Parish and Papa was only one of them. That was a 'warning sign'. I heard you say that to Carlito: 'It was a warning sign, Carlito.'

Papa said it had to do with the night he came home and Mother had fallen asleep with the electric radiator on. The satin trim of her blanket was touching the orange radiator bar and had begun to smoulder. 'Five more minutes!' said Papa, smacking his hand on his forehead like Nonno would have done. 'Five more *bloody* minutes, and the whole thing would've gone up.'

'She might have woken up,' I said. 'She might have smelled the smoke, you know, Papa. She's got a good sense of smell. She smells things going off in the fridge ...'

Papa just sighed a frustrated sigh, wrapped the radiator up in its cord and threw it into the bin. 'She gets cold, she can use a *bloody second blanket*.'

But he'd also stopped trusting the gas stove, the front door, the back gate, the hot water tap, and the kettle. 'I know about the back gate and the front gate!' I said. 'I know about the taps, and the kettle. You can trust me, Papa. I can look after Mother. I know about electricity, and I know where the keys get kept and what number to ring for emergencies!' I felt desperate. I didn't want Mother to be a bad mother who couldn't look after her kids. There was another boy at school like this: he came sometimes with a bruise in his eye, or nits in his hair. Mother was not like this. *Mother was not like this!* But Papa shook his head. Mother was limited to Wednesday and Thursday nights.

Mother, too, must have suffered over this because I remember Barrington Knox campaigning on her behalf. He turned up at the restaurant one Saturday in the lull between lunch and dinner service. Tracy, our new waitress, was folding napkins and filling the pepper grinders, writing specials on the chalkboard in curly writing. I'm not even sure why I was there, as Saturday was not my usual day. Mr Parish was there too, maybe he'd brought me. I was in the kitchen with Rosa and the kitchenhand. Rosa had given me a lettuce heart and I was on the floor with my legs crossed, eating it like an apple. The kitchen rose above me in a din of white tiles and simmering pots.

I heard Barrington Knox come in; I knew it was him because he was so heavy-footed: he couldn't disguise how big he was. He was like an old draught-horse in his fur coat. I stole out to listen.

'Mr Ferrugia,' he said to Papa. Mr Knox didn't know Papa very well. He was Mother's friend. They shook hands.

'Mr Knox,' said Papa. 'Nice to see you. How's the shop?'

'Sit down,' said Mr Parish, proffering a chair, amused by Mr Knox, who was like a character Toulouse Lautrec might have sketched, in Paris, in the 1890s.

Mr Knox inclined his head. 'No, no,' he said. 'I'm just here for a moment. Just have something quick I need to say and then I'm off.'

'Is Veda alright?' said Papa.

'Yes,' said Mr Knox. 'It's nothing like that. I just promised her I'd have a word ...' He lowered his voice and I couldn't hear him now, but I knew he was talking about Mother, and about me. He leant down to Papa, and Papa lifted his head. Rosa, oblivious, turned up the radio behind me and the kitchenhand began to whistle.

Then 'What a *bloody* nerve!' I heard Mr Parish say. Papa had put his head in his hands.

I was listening alertly now.

'I'm relating what she's said to me, that's all,' Barrington Knox continued, ignoring Mr Parish, 'and I'm doing so because I wouldn't forgive myself if I didn't. I have a lot of respect for your wife.'

'The man knows his own wife!' said Mr Parish. 'By god, if you came to me telling me how to deal with my wife ...'

'It's alright,' said Papa. He got up, pushed his chair in, and turned to the kitchen. 'Rosa, can you look after the restaurant tonight,' he called out. Papa didn't even wait for Rosa's reply. He packed me up; we caught the tram; we arrived home at quarter to six. When we came inside the front door, Papa put his arms around Mother and kissed her, and Mother sobbed.

'I didn't mean to make you unhappy!' Papa said. He thrust some flowers at her. She took them and put her arms around him.

Papa loved Mother. I would write it on a wall and put a big heart around it and an arrow through it and '4 eva' inside. Just like they did at school, the big kids. On desks. Scratched into the wood with their compasses, so no one could ever erase it.

BEEHIVE

But Wednesday and Thursday nights continued as they had. Maybe Mother didn't really want them to change. And pretty soon Mother made another mistake, even bigger than the radiator. Mother made a mistake of 'monumental proportions'. It was 'the final straw', you said. 'It was the straw that broke the camel's back'.

But the way I remember it, Mother's mistake wasn't so bad – grown-ups make things worse than they actually are. Mother's mistake was just a mistake.

It was a weeknight, a Wednesday or Thursday. Papa was at the restaurant as usual. Mother had looked in the cupboards and come out muttering like Old Mother Hubbard, and then had a bright idea. 'I know, O-yo,' she said. 'Let's go to the Beehive.'

You could have a half-price meal and drink at the Beehive on a Thursday night. Mother and I had gone there before and eaten in the Ladies' Lounge. I liked walking down Barkers Road and feeling the cars zip up fast beside us in the dark. It was spooky and dangerous and our breath came out in puffs of steam. They had crumbed cutlets on the menu at the Beehive, and Mother always got a steak with vegetables and gravy, and we talked like grown-ups. I could almost pretend I was Papa and Mother was my wife.

That night it was empty in the Ladies' Lounge except for us. I could tell Mother found it a little lonely. 'Don't worry, Mother,' I said. 'I'll look after you,' and she smiled. She drank wine and I drank Fanta. From the other side of the wall, from the bar, we could hear outbursts of laughter, loud groans and cheers of triumph – maybe they were playing darts or billiards? I knew those games were men's games that got played in pubs. Another pair of women came into the Ladies' Lounge. They nodded at us and sat down: an old woman in a blue dress, and an even older one in purple. They both ordered lemonade.

Mother was agitated. She cut her meat into tinier and tinier portions and rubbed it in the gravy and never seemed to quite get it into her mouth. She took another swig of wine. A shout and a portion of a song started up in the bar and I saw her eyes swivel towards it crossly.

'Do you know something, Owen?' she said, putting her cutlery down and wiping her mouth with a napkin. 'Can I tell you something important?'

I nodded. Though I already knew that what I thought was important and what she thought was important were two quite different things.

Mother took a breath. 'Owen. What I want to tell you is this: *You are lucky to have been born a boy and not a girl.*'

I shrugged. I didn't have a lot of time for girls, that was true. I certainly didn't want to be one. She was right: I was lucky.

'Do you understand what I'm saying to you, Owen?' she insisted. The waitress came and put our bowl of chips on the table; Mother sat back and smiled tightly, and then leaned forward again when the waitress had gone. 'Do you understand? There are all sorts of things boys can do in their lives that girls *can't*.'

'Yes,' I said, setting to with the knife and fork on my cutlet, though it would've been easier just to pick it up in my hand. 'I know. Girls are *not* lucky. They don't run fast. They don't throw balls far. They like dumb things.' I felt bad for a moment, as though I'd insulted Mother. I thought for things that Mother could do that would make her feel better. 'But they can have babies,' I said. 'When they're grown-ups.'

Mother narrowed her eyes at me and leaned so far over her plate her silver chain was dangling in her gravy. Her eyes had a dangerous glitter in them: the tiger's-eye glitter that changed them from grey into a different, more violent colour. 'Did you know, O-yo, that in our country, if a woman and a man do the *same job*, the woman gets less money than the man? *Did you know that?*'

This didn't mean much to me, so I shrugged again and picked up my cutlet.

'It's true!' she said. 'Do you think that's fair, Owen? Do you think so?'

'Well,' I said. I was not going to be able to eat my cutlet in peace so I put it aside and turned my thoughts to her question. 'Do you mean that, if I washed Papa's car for pocket-money,' I was proceeding cautiously, I didn't trust Mother's mood, 'he'd pay me more than if a girl did it?'

'Yes!' said Mother.

'So. If that girl Michelle who lives down our street – if Papa asked *her* to wash his car, he would pay her less than he would pay me?'

'May-belle,' said Mother. '*May-belle* is her name.'

I was irritated. 'No, Mother, her name's Michelle!'

'That's exactly right!' Mother stabbed a cigarette in the ashtray and flicked open her lighter as she picked up another one. She had pushed her plate away. 'Papa would pay Michelle *less* than she would pay you!' She lit and sucked. The smoke came out over my cutlet and peas.

'What if ...' I said, thinking hard, 'Michelle did a really good job. Like, a better job than me. A really really *great job* at cleaning the car?'

'Same thing,' said Mother, puffing heartily. 'Wouldn't matter.'

I thought this over and it did seem unfair. I tried to understand how it related to Mother, who didn't work, so far as I understood the concept of work. I didn't really believe Papa would pay a girl less than a boy. Papa was fair to Rosa. He wouldn't pay her less because she was a girl. I experimented with a thought: 'So, Mother,' I said. 'When you have your book of poems in the shops, will you get paid less money than a man poet?'

'Yes!' said Mother furiously. 'Yes, that's exactly right, Owen. Publishers pay women poets less money than they pay men poets. It doesn't matter what *area of endeavour* ...'

I tried another thought experiment: 'Maybe people like the poems of the men better?'

She laughed an ugly laugh. 'Listen, Owen: this week in the news there was a story about a woman, here in Melbourne, who was so angry about women being paid less than men that you know what she did? *She chained herself to a building*! Imagine that, Owen! She chained herself to a building and the policemen had to cut her free!'

I felt a bit sick to hear that. I put a chip in my mouth to disguise my sick feeling. 'But you're not going to do that, Mother?' I said. 'About not being paid enough for your book of poems?'

'Me?' she said. 'Oh god Owen, I haven't got the courage to do something like that! I wish I did. I beg and plead with my publishers like a *pathetic mouse* ... I do whatever they say, and it makes no difference.' She drew heavily on her cigarette, right to the end where the cork filter started. 'Where is my book, for instance? They've been saying they'll publish the bloody thing for nearly a year now.' She put her cigarette out. I was glad. The cigarette smell made my food taste bad. 'Fact is, your mother is a *coward*, Owen. If I had any gumption, I'd withdraw my book altogether and send it somewhere else. But I've invested so much bloody time doing what they ask ...'

The thought of Mother being a coward was upsetting. She was strange and changeable and erratic, but she was not a coward; she was not a *mouse*. It was stupid to imagine her as a mouse. She was the least mouse-like person I had ever known. But she seemed to like saying mean things about herself. She kept putting herself into mousetraps. She kept snapping herself shut with mean ideas about herself.

'You're not a coward!' I said. 'And your book will sell *millions and millions*!'

She ignored me. 'You know what else, Owen?' she said. 'You hear all those men in the bar next door?'

I nodded, still upset.

'Well, do you realise that women are *banned* from going into that bar?'

I shrugged again: why would women want to go in that shouty bar full of stinking men?

'Women are *not permitted* to just step through that door and have a drink at the bar. How's that, Owen?'

'But you can have a drink in here,' I said, 'with me.' I pointed to her wine glass. 'And you like wine. And men drink beer.'

'Women drink beer too!' she said. I didn't understand how we were somehow having an argument. She leaned forward at me again.

'Recently, I heard of some women, O-yo – a group of women in Ringwood – who got sick of their husbands staying out late at the pub every night while they stayed at home with their babies. So you know what they did? They stormed the bar! With their babies in their prams! What do you think of that?' She leaned back again with her arms crossed.

I didn't know what to think of it. All I could imagine was the babies crying. And then maybe the men getting cross. I imagined the women all dragging the men home, and the babies crying, and the men getting cross.

'I have a mind,' said Mother, still with the dangerous glint in her eyes, 'to just *go in there* and order a beer. What do you think, Owen? Then you'd know I wasn't a coward.'

A ripple of panic invaded my chest. 'I don't think you're a coward!' I said.

'I *am* a coward. I always have been.' Mother straightened her back. She took her handbag off the chair-arm and fossicked for her purse, pulled some notes out and put them on the table. 'Here,' she said. 'Give that to the waitress. There should be enough for ice cream. I'll be back in fifteen minutes.'

'Can't I come?' I said. 'I'll just go behind you. No one will notice me.'

'Not possible.' She pushed back her chair and swung her handbag over her shoulder. 'Just order your chocolate sundae. Sit here.' She bent down to me, warningly. 'Sit here, and *don't move* until I get back.'

And then she went, across the threshold, into the yellow, smoky light of the bar. The door opened on its springs, the bar talk rushed out, the door swung shut again and she was gone.

I pushed away my cutlet. I didn't even strip off the crunchy stuff from the bone with my teeth. I didn't want the chips, or the ice cream sundae. But I ordered the sundae anyway, and by the time it came, I had started to feel alright again. It was peaceful in the Ladies Lounge by myself. There was an open fire burning. There was candlelight, soft and warm. The two elderly women diners looked at me when they got up to leave and spoke to the waitress. The waitress came over with cutlery and napkins in her hands. 'Where's your mum?' she asked. 'Oh, she's just nicked out for a bit,' I said. The waitress seemed satisfied and disappeared into the kitchen. She came back with some paper and coloured pencils, which she put in front of me, smiling.

I drew. I drew a frog having its blood sucked by a piranha. I drew a robot with a pet dinosaur robot. I drew a freckled kid with vampire teeth. I drew a medieval castle surrounded by dragons and archers. I ate scoops of melting chocolate syrup and ice cream in between pictures. Occasionally I thought I could hear a loud laugh from the bar that sounded like my mother, so I wasn't worried; I knew she was in there, just on the other side of the wall.

At some point, the lights in the Ladies' Lounge dimmed and I grew tired. I didn't know if fifteen minutes had passed or not, but it was hard to keep my eyes open. The fireplace was sucking up my oxygen. I drew an astronaut gasping for oxygen. The drawing of the oxygen-deprived astronaut kept me awake for another two minutes and then I slid from the chair onto the Ladies' Lounge floor, asleep.

Papa says the Hotel rang him. I don't remember. I don't remember being discovered at closing when the waitress was putting chairs upside down on the tables for the cleaner. I don't remember telling the publican of the Beehive the name of Papa's restaurant. The publican rang Papa at La Coccinella and Papa caught a taxi to the Beehive. He arrived furious, and his fury was what properly woke me up. Papa had me under his arm. He was furious and Mother was nowhere to be seen. Papa had made the taxi wait outside. It had its lights on, and it was raining. The smeary lights and the windscreen wipers and the swoosh of car tyres on Barkers Road. Papa said, 'Where the *fuck* is my wife?' He said it loudly, to the taxi driver, and to the world, and then he bundled me into the car and we went home.

Mother was already there.

PAYING DUES

Mother was under house arrest again. But nothing bad had happened to me! I said this to everyone, because I didn't understand why everyone was so upset. *Nothing bad had happened to me!* Mother hadn't left me in an alleyway, or in the aisle of a supermarket, or under the swing-set at a deserted park. She'd left me somewhere safe and warm where people would find me. Hadn't she? *I* didn't feel betrayed by Mother.

Luckily for Mother, someone she knew had been in the bar that night: her old nemesis from the solicitor's office, Mr Franck. He had watched her curiously from a distance all night. Mother would have liked to have said he was 'watching over her', but she knew him well enough to know he was doing no such thing. He was entertaining himself, biding his time. He did, however, collect her from the bar stool when she was clearly *on her last legs*, made her tell him her address, and, surprisingly, deposited her safely home. She had forgotten about me, it was true. 'But really, O-yo,' she said, 'I'd forgotten about myself as well. And that was the best thing of all.'

I had strange dreams for some time after this. I dreamt I was trying to sleep in a sleeping bag tied to a 'No Standing' pole in Lygon Street. I dreamt of coloured foam, doorbells and terrible wrong numbers. I dreamt of buildings in the distance, with the sun on them, that suddenly collapsed into the ground like sand.

I woke a lot in the night during that time. I woke and you had to come and get me back to sleep, Ornella, and that made Carlito mad. He could be nice, Carlito, I had found that out now. But more often he was mad.

Carlito had got a job in a shipping yard on the recommendation of his cousin. It happened overnight; Carlito became a stevedore, a wharfie. A transformation came over him. He became obsessive about his alarm clock; he memorised the train timetable so he could get to Victoria Dock on time every morning; he brought home *flowers*, and *bottles of Lambrusco*, and *marbles* or *Matchbox cars* for me. Loading and unloading: dirty, heavy, 'good honest' labour. He got his first paycheque and joined the Maritime Union of Australia.

Carlito had tried to set himself up in small business: selling sausage, importing patio tiles, doing handyman work. But now he said, 'Forget all that, Ornella. I'm gonna work for the man. You watch me, I'm gonna bring home the bacon.' And he did. Uncomplainingly and unexpectedly. And you brought home your share of the bacon, and between the two of you, and Nonna's 'gift', you nearly had the whole *pig*. If Papa ever offered you money now, you shook your head: 'No thank you, Jo, I have no need.'

You looked beautiful and scary in your nurse's outfit. Nurses had to be very clean and their uniforms had to be stiff and ironed. You dabbed bleach onto any single spot that got onto your uniform, and you soaked it, and after it was washed and dried, you went over it with the iron like it was a work of art.

There was a constant friction between Carlito's dustiness and your cleanness. You were opposites, you and Carlito; you attracted, like magnets. Some magnets are drawn to each other, and some will not touch no matter how much you push them together. Mrs Parish and Mr Parish were the not-touching kind. You and Carlito were the irresistible coming-together kind. Mother and Papa had a faint charge, like a fridge magnet that can't hold very many papers. All the notices fall off every time you open the door.

'MY BLUE'

Mrs Parish's floral arrangement was selected for an exhibition. She got notice of it in the post. She told me very quietly of this, facing the sink and peeling potatoes into it. 'My ikebana arrangement,' she said, 'will be shown in the 1968 Sogetsu Victoria exhibition.' It had been selected by the head and founder of Sogetsu Ikebana himself, Sofu Teshigahara.

'I put in my Blue, Owen,' she said, scraping away at the potatoes. 'My Blue, remember it?'

I did remember her Blue: her Blue had little spots of blue heath in it, pinpoints against blackened dried twigs that went upwards in the shape of a flame. It was beautiful and delicate and sad, like a burned out house with jewels gleaming up from the ruins. I, in fact, had given it its name. Had she forgotten that?

'My name will be in the catalogue. I have to provide a small quotation about my use of *unconventional* materials," she continued, her back quivering slightly. Then she let the last potato fall into the sink, and turned around to me, almost frightened. 'They will put it on display in Georges, Owen. *In Georges*!'

I didn't know what to say. 'In Georges!' I said.

'Oh Owen,' she said. 'I feel quite … exhilarated!' She put her hand on her chest. I saw there were tears in her eyes, but they weren't like Mother's tears, which were bitter and angry: they were clear, glad tears. 'Sofu Teshigahara is the *Picasso of flowers*! You know, I nearly didn't even bother getting photographs made ...'

'Mr Parish will be glad,' I said. I don't even know why I said this. It wasn't what I really thought. 'He'll be proud of you.'

'It was Rosa who encouraged me,' she said, and put the kettle on. 'If Rosa were here right now,' she said, 'I would open one of Mr Parish's bottles of champagne. Just like that! Without even asking him! I've got a mind to ring her on the telephone.'

This thought seemed to make her even happier. She went and put some jazz on the record player, changed into her gold twin-set and red lipstick, and poured herself some cooking sherry to drink with her tea. I drew her a card of congratulations, upon which I attempted a rendition of the winning work and an abbreviated 'Congrats' with kisses and stars. She put it on the mantelpiece, next to a framed photograph of Picasso, dog-eyed, bleary-jawed, that Mr Parish kept there.

I had thought Mrs Parish's *success in the field of floral arrangement,* as Mr Parish put it, might have been a good opportunity for my case for a bedroom mural of *Paddy Cow in the Garden*. But it was not to be. Mrs Parish had won on account of flowers, but flowers had not in themselves proven anything. Nor had Rosa. 'No, Owen,' Mr Parish said. 'There will be no Paddy Cow on your bedroom wall. Unless you draw her yourself, on paper, and we pin it up.' Though Mr Parish liked art on his walls, he did not like his walls to *become art*. Murals (he never dared to say this in front of Rosa) were *not art*. Walls in bedrooms were to be painted white and they were to stay painted white. 'And anyway, wouldn't you want something a little, well, *more boyish*, than flowers on your walls, Owen? You could have a medieval battle scene. Or something from *Arthur*.'

Maybe he would've given in to a proposal for a jungle. But a jungle was not a garden. I wanted Paddy Cow in a flower garden. A boy was not supposed to want gentle things like moony calves and carnations in his bedroom. But, like any child, I was scared of monsters under beds. I didn't want battle scenes and fortresses watching over me. I didn't want boa constrictors or aliens who took little children hostage and did experiments on them, or atomic bombs that blew up the whole world. The world had been formed by a Big Bang explosion; the universe was terrifying. Even a flower garden wasn't entirely safe. There was a *Lion in the Meadow*, after all – and a dragon came out of a matchbox to scare it away. I wanted to be safe. I didn't understand why Mr Parish couldn't understand this.

When I told Rosa I couldn't have a mural after all, she was nonplussed. 'Ah well,' she said and shrugged. 'You tried, huh?' I had expected her to be cross, but Rosa never got cross with Mr Parish – though Mother did, and even Papa occasionally, and Barrington Knox called him a 'mean little brute'. Mother said Rosa had rose-coloured glasses on when it came to Mr Parish.

'Without James Parish,' Rosa said, 'I would never be brave enough to make art. I would've just got married to a greengrocer.'

'That might be nice, Rosa,' I said. 'It might be nice to be married to a greengrocer.' We were in the kitchen at La Coccinella as usual; she was stirring something frothy in a pan and I was nibbling salami. 'You could get fruit and vegetables for free. My friend at school, his mum and dad have a stall at the Richmond Market. His name is George. They sell nearly every kind of vegetable.' I gulped back a bit of string with my meat. 'They have a doughnut van at the Richmond Market. Ten cents for three. You could've bought doughnuts for your kids.'

Rosa shrugged her head to the side. 'Kids, Owen. Look at me. Not cut out to be anyone's mother.'

'Don't you like kids?' I asked, astonished at this. 'Don't you *like* me?'

'Oh, yeah, I like *you*,' she said. 'But I wouldn't want to *live* with you. Washing your clothes, making your lunch, putting you in the bath, getting the pidocchi out of your hair ... pfft, *non grazie*!'

'Well, I wouldn't live with you either,' I said. 'You smell like paint most of the time. And when you don't smell like paint, you smell like ...'

I couldn't think of anything sufficiently disrespectful here, so I left it to linger. But I imagined being a kid of Rosa's: what would it be like? Would she be cross or happy? Would she cuddle you when you felt scared, or would she *snap you out of it*? Would she spend long hours painting paintings and forget to make dinner?

And then it occurred to me: maybe Mother was like Rosa. Maybe Mother was not cut out to be a mother. She hadn't had any more kids after me – maybe having me was *the straw that broke the camel's back*.

Maybe she didn't really want me around at all.

It made me sad to think this, because although I sometimes wished she were different, I couldn't imagine life without her. I didn't want not to be her son.

NICE LITTLE POEM

Meanwhile, at school, I had a success that I thought would make Mother really happy: I had won a *writing competition*.

A poster had been put up in the library, and the librarian had tapped me on the shoulder. 'You're good *with words*, Owen,' she said. I didn't quite know what she meant by this. 'Words', as I understood it, was when grown-ups had arguments. She beamed down at me. 'You're *very* good with words. I bet you could write a nice little poem!'

I liked the school librarian. She was tall and a little stooped and reminded me of Mrs Parish. She'd found me books I really liked when I was little, books like *Robert the Rose Horse* and *Sam the Firefly* and *A Fish Out of Water*. And, of course, Dr Seuss. All the same size books with the same kind of covers. All the same *good stories*. 'What would you like to write a poem about, do you think, Owen?'

I didn't need to think twice. 'Monkeys,' I said.

A week earlier, you had taken me to the Richmond Town Hall, Ornella, and there, I had waited in a queue to get my dose of the Sabin oral polio vaccine.

It was a long wait. The hall was cold and crowded. Everyone was tetchy. It took hours to inch towards the front of the queue. And that's when I heard the conversation about *Rhesus monkeys*.

It came from the boy ahead of me: a boy with outlandishly long hair, curling about his ears and down his neck and almost to his shoulders. I had never seen a boy with such long hair before. His mother looked strange too: she wore a yellow bead necklace that rested oddly on large, drooping bosoms under a roll-neck jumper.

'Mummy,' said the long-haired boy. 'How many Rhesus monkeys again?'

The mother shifted her hips and looked for something in her handbag. 'Oh, about 10,000.'

'And they all died? Every one of them?'

'Yes, darling. Or perhaps they were paralysed, I'm not sure. I can't remember exactly.' She pulled out a tissue and blew her nose. Her handbag had a leather tongue on it and a tribal face.

The boy was quiet and thoughtful. 'It must be awful for a monkey to be paralysed,' he said. 'They couldn't swing around or *anything*!'

'It must be awful for a *little boy* to be paralysed,' said the mother. 'Though it's sad for the monkey, that's true, darling.'

I nudged you. 'What are they talking about?' I pointed to the mother and son in front of us.

'What?' you said.

'Monkeys being paralysed.'

You looked momentarily befuddled and slightly cross.

'*Ree-zus monkeys*,' I said. 'Getting paralysed.'

'Oh,' you said. 'Yes, they did experiments on monkeys, Owen, to make the vaccine. That's what they're talking about. They had to experiment with the injection before they tried it on humans. You know, to make sure it was safe.'

'*Experiments on monkeys* ...?' I said.

'Yes. The scientists experimented on the monkeys and that's how they come up with the polio vaccine. No monkeys, no vaccine.' I must've looked appalled then, because you said:

'What? You think a monkey is more important than a *human being*, Owen?'

'No,' I said. 'I just don't think it's fair to the monkeys.'

'Look Owen.' You were putting on your hospital voice, which I always took to mean 'end of conversation'. (It often coincided with you looking at your watch.) 'My cousin Frank, right, he got polio when he was seven. 1952. Had to go in an iron lung for months. Never walked again. Never got to run and jump like you and grow strong bones. Has to go in a wheelchair now. You want that to happen to other kids, maybe to you?'

'No.'

You must've heard my lack of conviction, because you sighed and pretended to be patient. 'If they don't experiment on animals, Owen, human beings gonna keep dying of things. Those monkeys give their lives for a good reason. You want little kids to grow up crippled?'

'No,' I said again. I felt very glum. We were getting right close to the front of the line now. The curtains on the cubicle were open and I could see a white plastic spoon going into the mouth of a little blonde girl. Now it was the boy with long hair's turn. Despite his previous questions, he didn't seem fussed. He marched forward and opened his mouth like he was getting a lolly.

'Do they always have to die or get paralysed, the monkeys?' I said.

'No,' you said, very firmly. 'Sometimes they get cured and then they get sent home to live with a kind family, or to a zoo. That's what happens. Cross my heart.'

I didn't believe you, but I went forward anyway, and got my sweet spoonful and my lifelong immunity and felt guilty for the rest of the night.

I didn't tell them about the monkeys, but I did tell Barrington and Edith Knox about my ambitions for the Mary Martin Poetry Competition. I told them when Mother was not in the room, because I didn't want to make her feel like I was copying her. I was highly conscious, from what kids in my grade said, that copying was a very bad thing to do. The girls at school were always accusing each other: *Copycat from Ballarat, went to school and got the strap*. 'Mary Martin's,' I told the Knoxes, 'will give me a *book-hamper* if I win!'

Mr Knox swore mildly. Mrs Knox crinkled her mouth and eyes into what her husband called her 'persimmon frown'. Mother came back from the toilet and asked what the problem was.

'Max bloody Harris's bookshop,' said Mr Knox. 'Enticing future loyalty from the young with *book hampers*!'

Mother raised her eyebrows and didn't ask. But when she later saw me lying on the bookshop floor, labouring over my poem with a grey-lead, smudging the paper horribly as I crossed out and rubbed out, she became interested enough to ask what I was doing.

'I'm writing a poem,' I admitted unhappily. The rhymes weren't working. The lines kept getting too long and out of time.

'Oh,' said Mother. 'Good lord!' She raised her eyebrows at Mr and Mrs Knox but said no more. I took this to mean I had her approval. But I didn't ask her for help, and she didn't offer it. I was glad her book of poems hadn't been published yet, because then, if I won, everyone would say Mother had written the poem, not me.

But a funny thing happened while I was writing my poem: I became completely deaf to everything Mother and Mr and Mrs Knox were saying. They might've been talking about anything; they might've been arguing, or crying, or laughing hysterically: I just didn't notice. They ceased to exist. I fell deep into the land of my difficult, painful rhyme. And once I started, I couldn't stop, and that was the really annoying part about it. It was like an itch that you couldn't stop scratching once you got going. It was like a song playing round and round in your head. It was like a kind of medieval torture.

Monkeys crying, dead and dying,

Why must monkeys pay the cost?

Keep them alive, let them survive

Or their race will soon be lost.

That was as far as I had got. In my head I had the tune of 'Oh My Darling Clementine.' The poetry competition judges wouldn't know this, but it helped me write the poem and I thought I might mention it to them in my letter (the librarian said I had to write a 'cover letter'). Still, the poem was not quite right: for instance, I knew somehow that 'race' was wrong. I think it should have been 'species', but that didn't fit the pattern of the beats. This gave me grief for some time. Then I moved on to the second verse, which was even more difficult:

Crippled children, in the cauldron

Of a terrifying fate

We can save them, but don't enslave the

Rhesus monkeys, it's not too late…

And that was where I got stumped and the pencil got chewed and I realised that poetry-writing could make you get really MAD, like in Maths. It just wasn't *right*. The pattern didn't fit and you had to say some syllables really fast at the end to make the beats work.

I was grumpy for the rest of the evening. And even Papa's leftover lamb shank stew didn't help.

But the school librarian said it was: *Genius!* She said, 'All those internal rhymes, Owen! It's absolutely brilliant! *Children* and *cauldron*! Let's send it off right now. Make sure you tell them you're in Grade 4, Owen: I think that will impress them, alright!'

I could tell she wanted to hug me, so I stepped slightly away, and instead she retrieved her glasses from where they hung on a chain and went to find an envelope and a stamp.

'To Whom It May Concern at the Mary Martin Bookshop,' I wrote:

'Here is my entry for the poetry competition. It is a poem about the monkeys that got killed and paralysed for the polio vaccine. My name is Owen Ferrugia and I am in Grade 4 at Hawthorn West Primary School. I hope you like my poem because I would very much like to win a book hamper.'

Mrs Plumridge gave me a little nod of approval, then we sealed the envelope and I put it in the red letterbox on the corner of Bridge Road and Burnley Street on the way home.

I forgot about it for a while, and then one afternoon I was called to the headmaster's office. This was sufficiently terrifying for me to almost burst into tears. The headmaster's name was Mr Box, and, though everyone knew that girls didn't get the strap anymore at our school, boys still did. I racked my brain for something bad I had done. I had thrown a pear in the bin without even taking a bite. I had knocked my school milk over onto the bitumen and not owned up to it. I had ripped a piece of paper out of another kid's schoolbook because he'd done a mean picture of me on it.

'Owen Ferrugia,' said Mr Box. He had recently shaved off a black moustache and he looked more frightening without it than with. 'Sit down, sir,' he said. 'It seems congratulations are in order.'

While I squirmed, bug-eyed, in his too-big office chair, he fetched a document in a yellow manila envelope.

'Here you are, boy!' he said. 'You have won this poetry competition. Get your parents to take you down and retrieve your prize. We're going to announce it at assembly on Monday morning and give you your prize on the stage up there. Alright? So make sure you go and get the books or we'll have nothing to give you.'

I nodded because what else could I do and he handed over the manila envelope. Mrs Parish took me to Mary Martins on Saturday morning. I got my hamper (though I cannot remember a *single book* that was in it) and was fussed over by the bookshop staff. I then had my prize re-presented to me on Monday morning in the school hall and suffered all the same fuss all over again from the teachers. I was not, however, resented by my school friends for sticking my head so far up above the general field of poppies – none of them thought a *book hamper* was any sort of prize at all. George and Callum only read things about VFL.

Ornella said: 'You little brainbox!'

Mrs Parish said: 'Exceptional, Owen. Exceptional.'

Papa said: 'Damn you, Owen, I thought you were going to take after me and become a chef!'

Mother said: 'Chip off the old block, O-yo' and kissed me on the forehead.

I wanted Mother to be impressed by my win, but Mother was going through a phase of nonchalance now, accepting everything with a wave of the hand and a slight incline of the head. Like the queen. I didn't trust it. I knew it was not real, and that in her head a million things were gathering and exploding and biding their time. But everyone said she was 'much better' and 'doing really well' and 'Sometimes a person *needs* to get a fright ...' I believe it was you, mainly, saying all those things, Ornella. You put your head on one side when speaking of Mother. 'She's on the wagon,' you said, and I imagined Mother in a fringed suede jacket with a whip, standing up and spurring on the horses. She looked like Miss Jane in F-Troop.

On account of Mother's newfound serenity, I was, however, enjoying my Thursdays more than I had in a long time. I think Mother liked them too. She had stopped trying to be a Mother in the respectable normal way, or in the struggling slightly desperate way, and as a result things were much more relaxed and we were having much more fun. We were just incidental companions on summer holidays together.

'Oh, it's so boring trying to write,' she told me one day. 'You don't really want to be a poet, Owen, it's a stupid, terrible occupation.' We were sitting on the tram and she was smoking with the window open. It was hot, so it might've been the summer holidays 68/9. I was about to go into Grade 5.

'But I *want* to be a poet,' I said to her. (Actually, I wasn't sure. I was happy with my book-hamper, but the poem had been torture.)

'Do you?' she said.

'Yes!' I said, wanting to please her.

'Mmmmm,' she said. 'Well, it's very hard work,' and she sucked on her cigarette and looked out the window.

Darling, I had hoped she might say, *let me let you in on my poetry writing secrets. It's so easy when you know how!*

'My book will be published sometime in the next year,' she said. 'But I'm not happy with it.' She blew a little squawl of smoke into the tram carriage. 'I wanted something much better. Something all of a piece. Not ... this!'

I nodded sagely.

'It's impossible to match *my* intention with *their* expectation, so I have to do what I can. It's such a compromise. They're such nervous nellies. And they've wasted so much of my time already.' She stubbed her cigarette in the wooden windowsill and it sat there, squashed and upright, still fuming. She smiled a wan smile. 'Did Papa read your prize poem?'

Of course Papa had read my poem. Hadn't he?

'Ye-es,' I said.

She laughed a laugh I would recognise some years later when I saw Glenda Jackson play Elizabeth the First, opened her cigarette case and lit another cork-tipped Old Gold.

'Papa came to my school assembly,' I said, shoring myself up. 'He *saw* me get my prize. I read it *out loud*.'

Mother raised an eyebrow.

I became inexplicably cross. 'He's busy!' I rebuked her. 'He has to run the restaurant and ... and ... help the poor!'

Mother's eyes closed and opened dully, like Papa feeding the poor was something boring that we just had to put up with. 'Yes, he does,' she said. 'Yes, Owen, he does.'

I didn't speak to her all the rest of the way into the city. Of course Papa had *read my poem*! It was so *mean* of Mother to be mean about Papa. I wasn't going to talk to her all afternoon.

But when we got to the Knoxes I couldn't keep my resolve. 'Knox Books' had big clanging doors so the Knoxes would always hear if someone was coming in. They made their clanging sound as we entered. Mrs Knox looked up brightly from the counter and Mr Knox could be heard making his way back from the stockroom.

'Look, Mother!' I said. The shop floor had been re-arranged, and now, central to the room, was an enormous table, piled high with books of every stamp and colour – children's books, wildlife books, poetry, cookery, novels, novellas. A sign read 'Marked Down: 50% off *Everything* on this Table!'

Mrs Knox came over and kissed me and kissed Mother. Mother took off her gloves and flopped down in a chair in what they called the 'nook' – a cosy space behind the counter where there was a fireplace and a mantelpiece and a decanter, as well as several small clean glasses turned upside down.

Mother gestured at the book display. 'What's all this, Edith?' she said. 'Are you going out of business?' She poured herself a drink, and one each for Mrs and Mr Knox. She was not on the wagon, Ornella.

'It's a *clearance*, Veda,' said Mr Knox. He plonked an armful of paperbacks down on the floor. 'Making space for new stock.'

'God help us!' said Mother. 'A clearance! Do you have any puzzle-books for sale, Barrington? I'd quite like a *puzzle book*.'

I had been fossicking around on the clearance table ever since we'd come in and, yes, I'd found a good puzzle book with cross-words and trivia and word searches, 'crazy cartoons' and 'ridiculous riddles'. 'Look, Mother!' I said, holding it up. 'Only 10 cents!'

'Oh bloody hell! You've become a newsagency, Barrington!'

'We got a shipment,' said Mr Knox. He knocked his drink back. 'Bulk purchase. Just got to get rid of it all, nice and quick. There are some goodies in there, aren't there, Owen?'

I nodded. There *were* goodies, and I was putting a pile of them aside. I had the puzzlebook and one on worms and another on cave-people and one called *Black Beauty* that I had heard of before and which had very small print. 'You're going to need a credit account, Owen,' Mrs Knox said.

'God,' said Mother again. 'You'll be selling ballpoint pens soon!'

'Nothing wrong with a good Bic Crystal!' said Mr Knox. He seemed chirpy and unworried, but I thought Mother was being rude.

It was five o'clock, closing time, but no one was bothering to lock the doors or swing the sign to 'Closed'. Mrs Knox had swivelled her chair to face the empty fireplace. Mother passed Mr Knox another drink. He came over to appraise my book selection.

'So,' said Mother. 'Another week goes by, chaps. Don't suppose you've seen my husband by any chance? Hasn't dropped in to check up on my movements?'

Mrs Knox wiped her mouth daintily with her index finger and took another sip. 'No, no sign of Jo. But Rosa came in, didn't she, Barrington? Came by with desserts, would you believe? Left over from lunchtime. She sat with us for quite a bit, didn't she, Barrington?'

Mr Knox nodded.

'Seems she's got herself a new friend. Very nice for Rosa! Nice to see her looking after herself a little.' Mrs Knox smiled and cocked her head and I could tell she was genuine in what she said. 'Her friend's an artist too.'

Mr Knox nodded. 'Very good artist.'

'Rosa's forthright in her praise, isn't she, Barrington? Barrington thinks she's *smitten* with this Florence Oakey!'

'Well, she was very energetically admiring of her, that's for sure. But Oakey has a pedigree of a sort, a history ...'

Edith leaned forward to Mother. 'Rosa's trying to get her friend an exhibit at Works on Paper.'

'Oh!' said Mother.

'Yes,' said Mrs Knox. 'It's all somewhat *political*.'

'A great big bust-up, I hope.' Mr Knox rubbed his hands and then looked at Mother apologetically. 'Not that I have any, you know, ill-will toward Jo.'

'Interesting,' said Mother, looking not in the slightest bit interested, which was her current fallback position. 'What does my husband think about Rosa's new friend?'

FLORENCE HOKEY

Papa was all for exhibiting the drawings of Florence Oakey in Works on Paper. Florence Oakey had *great line*, he said. Furthermore, she had exhibited in London: a painting of a girl playing a tambourine; another of a society matron with beaked nose and ostentatious rings. Her paintings had drawn attention. But her drawings, Papa thought, in his humble not-really-knowing way, were better than her paintings.

James Parish, however, saw no merit in the drawings of Florence Oakey. Her line was *sloppy*, *curvaceous*, too *organic*. 'She's decorative, ultimately. Everything has overtones of *flora*.

Everything looks like it could be a bloody plant in human form.'

Rosa reiterated this, bashing down pepper-grinders, one by one, on table after table, as if hoping the tables would register, in the form of dents and knocks, her displeasure. It was the first time I'd seen her cross with Mr Parish.

It was Sunday. Papa was cooking for the Salvos. There was no need for pepper-grinders on tables. They could all stay packed away on the counter, with the napkin rings and skinny little vases with fake flowers. But Rosa seemed to need to smack them down on the tables anyway.

'I understand,' Rosa said, 'that Parish needs to show work *that sells*. But every time he takes a chance on an artist, he *takes a chance*. Florence is proven talent. She shows overseas. But suddenly, poof! the chance is *too* big to take.'

Rosa crashed a clean ashtray onto the centre of a table. Her anger about her mural paled in comparison to her anger about Florence Oakey's drawings.

By chance, I was at the restaurant maybe two weeks later when Florence Oakey visited to see Rosa. She was a small, sweet-faced woman in her mid-fifties. She wore a neat camel-coloured skirt and jacket and had pale ginger hair. Her nose was upturned like Kitten's, but her skin was less fresh-looking. She kissed Rosa on the cheek, left her umbrella in the doorway (it was raining), and sat down at the table across from me.

'Rosa,' she called out, looking smilingly at me while she took off her gloves. 'Rosa, sweet, can you make me a lovely cup of coffee?' Her voice was crisp, but also melty like buttercups.

Rosa left to do her bidding and Florence watched me drawing a giraffe being gnawed to death by a dinosaur.

'That's lovely,' she said. 'What a lovely giraffe, such a nice long neck!' She gazed at it a moment longer, putting her head to one side. 'But perhaps you could make the dinosaur more *vicious* ...' and she took the pen and in one fluid move transformed my dinosaur from common garden-variety giraffe-eater to seriously terrifying predator. She gave a *swing* and *dash* to the devouring motion of the dinosaur that I could not account for. Suddenly, the giraffe looked very dead in its teeth. I stared at her in wonder.

'Florence is a good drawer, hey, Owen,' said Rosa, who came beside us with coffee for Florence and chocolate for me. 'Florence Oakey: "Best draughtswoman in Melbourne". That's what the *Age* said.'

'Oh shush, Rosa,' said Florence Oakey. 'Let me drink my coffee. Then we'll go to the pictures.'

Florence Oakey was a good drawer. I wondered why Mr Parish didn't want her drawings in Works on Paper. Then I remembered what he said about her line being *too sloppy, too curvaceous*. I talked briefly to Kitten about it. I didn't see much of Kitten these days, but every now and then she popped into the restaurant after the gallery closed. Sometimes she had a telephone message to relay to Papa, but most often she just wanted to have a glass of wine and be around people. The gallery, she said, was very quiet, very boring. I was always glad to see her. Sometimes she stayed and ate at La Coccinella – 'It's such a waste of time,' she said, 'cooking for one' – and sometimes she quizzed me:

'What sort of a house does Mr Parish have, Owen?'

'What does Mrs Parish make you to eat? Is she a good cook?'

'How *old* do you think I look, Owen? Say, if you saw me in the street, do I look ... *twenty-five* or *thirty*?'

I couldn't tell the difference between twenty-five and thirty. I knew Mother was *thirty-six*, but between Mother and Kitten there lay a chasm of time and circumstance. Kitten was a sparky little cat-thing with new clothes and dimpled cheeks. Mother hardly ever bothered to dress in nice clothes anymore, and she had bits of grey in the sides of her hair. You, Ornella, cared about practicality before you cared about aesthetics these days. And Rosa and Mrs Parish, my two other measures of womanhood, were so ancient they were beyond age entirely.

Kitten lowered her voice. 'Do you know why Mrs Parish *never had any babies*, Owen?'

I looked up from my drawing of a pyramid on fire and shook my head. Mrs Parish's lack of babies had never occurred to me. I couldn't imagine her with a baby.

Kitten wound spaghetti around her fork. When she slurped the forkful up, a speck of sauce remained in the corner of her mouth in what seemed to me a rude and un-grown-up-like manner. She swirled wine around in her glass.

'I suppose,' I said, considering, 'that Mrs Parish didn't want babies?'

Kitten leaned forward at me, shaking her head.

'Why then?' I said.

She scrunched up her mouth and nose. '*Couldn't*,' she whispered. '*Couldn't have them*.'

It was hard to talk to her now without noticing the speck of tomato sauce. It made her look like she was only pretending to be an adult. 'Oh,' I said dully. I did some cross-hatching – Rosa had taught me about cross-hatching – on the right side of my pyramid where the shadow would've been, according to *perspective*.

I suspected Kitten was talking to me 'inappropriately'. More and more I heard that now: 'That's not *appropriate* for Owen', 'Don't say that in front of Owen, it's not *appropriate*.' 'I'm sorry Owen, that television show is *inappropriate*.' And yet I craved the inappropriate. The inappropriate was key to everything. If I had no access to the inappropriate, I lived in a different world to the other people around me. If I was let in on the inappropriate a bit more often, I might understand what the bloody hell was going on with everyone. *What the bloody hell!* It felt good to say the word *bloody*.

'Why can't she have bloody babies?' I asked.

Kitten ignored my swear word. She put a crumpled napkin on top of her dinner plate and pushed it away. 'It's a difficult situation for *Mr Parish* too,' she said primly.

It was half an hour before service, just starting to get dark outside. Rosa hadn't turned the radio off yet in the kitchen and Tracy hadn't started on the butters (there was a pattern of triangles you could chop the block up into and I always made sure I watched her do it). There was no one but me and Kitten in the restaurant.

'It's hard for a man too, *not having children*!' said Kitten. 'Think of your dad, if he didn't have you!'

I tried to think of this, but it didn't seem at all real or worth thinking about. I imagined he would just go on doing what he normally did, but a little more sadly.

'Really, imagine it, Owen!' Kitten took another gulp of wine and wiped the tomato off the corner of her mouth. '*You* are the closest thing to a *son* that the Parishes have. They're going to leave you all their money, you know. Do you realise that?' She glared at me as though she wanted to bore a tunnel through my skull with her eyes. 'Don't you think it's strange?'

I didn't know what was strange and what was not, but I knew now for sure that Kitten was being inappropriate.

'Some people don't have children,' I said. 'Rosa doesn't have children.'

'Rosa!' said Kitten, and laughed.

'Are you going to have children?' I asked her.

Now Kitten looked peeved. 'Well, a girl has to get *married first* apparently, Owen.'

I decided, at this point, while her peevishness otherwise occupied her, to forge ahead with my own questions.

'Have you met Florence Hokey?' I said. 'Rosa's friend?'

'Oh yes,' said Kitten, as though she wasn't really paying attention. 'Rosa's friend.'

'Do you think she's a good drawer?' I persisted.

Kitten swirled her wine around for a bit and then looked up. 'Owen. I can't tell anything from anything,' she said finally. Her voice wasn't right. She sounded tired. She sounded like she was imitating herself. 'Do you understand that? I know nothing about art. I know nothing about anything. I am a *complete vacuum*.' She drank another mouthful and sighed. 'It turns out I am just a very good *salesgirl*. Very good at getting people to part with their money.' Then she changed again. 'One day, Owen, I'll get married and have a whole *flock* of children.

Oh, yes I will! I'll have them *coming out of my ears.'* She gestured with her hands at the sides of her head, as though babies were popping relentlessly from her brain.

She was drunk now. Not drunk. That other word that means nearly drunk. Tipsy. I waited to hear what she'd say next.

But she didn't say anything. She sighed and sipped the last dregs of her drink. She got her jacket unravelled from the back of the chair and unhooked her handbag. She put the former on and swung the latter over her shoulder.

'I don't know about Florence Oakey, but *Rosa* is a very good drawer,' she said.

'Painter,' I said. 'Rosa is a painter.'

'Painter,' agreed Kitten. 'Rosa is a *very good painter.'*

She kissed me on the forehead and left.

EPHEMERA

Painting, they say, is real estate. It is an investment, a piece of property. It makes people money. Poetry isn't about money. Poets are poor. I knew this. Mr Parish was an *exception to the rule*. Mother's book would be an *exception to the rule.* Poetry, Mr Parish said, was a 'commitment to living intensely in the world. I couldn't survive without my solicitor or my broker – but I wouldn't *be* a solicitor or a broker. Life's too short to be wasted. Poetry is a commitment of the soul.'

I believed him when he said this. It helped make sense of Mother even if *living intensely in the world* didn't seem to be a particularly happy or pleasant prospect. What about Papa though? What was a meal a commitment of? Once eaten, you can never eat a meal again. You can't save it. A meal is a memory that you keep chasing. That's why you return to the same restaurant over and over. That's why you keep ordering the same thing on the menu – to make a memory alive again. Papa was in the business of making memories.

And a drawing? People bought drawings and framed them and put them up on their walls. They didn't cost as much as paintings to buy, and they weren't as big, but they were still worth money. I knew this from the success of Papa's gallery. Charcoal drawings and ink drawings and drawings made with pencil. Mr Parish said drawing was the *rigour* behind art. Artists usually made drawings to test out what they were going to paint in their paintings, he explained. But he also said drawings were by nature 'ephemeral'.

Rosa liked the word *ephemera*. Was it Italian in origin? Latin? No, she said, its roots were Greek. '*Ephemera*.' Rosa said it dramatically. But the word itself was all vapour. It didn't really have any drama. It was like smoke after a magician's trick.

Hearts got broken. Meals got eaten. Paper burnt. I got angry with my drawings and ripped them up and threw them away. *Ephemera*.

In painting, said Rosa, if you didn't like what you painted, you could *repaint the whole thing white again and start from scratch*. But the mistake would still be there, I thought, under the white paint, like colours on the walls of a house if you start chipping away.

One day, Mrs Parish made me a rubber out of bread-dough. I had made a mistake in a picture I was drawing with grey-lead pencil. The drawing was too good to throw out, but I couldn't find a rubber. She was making Mr Parish's bread – a kind of bread that went hard over the course of a day but was soft and malleable at the beginning. 'Here Owen, try this,' she said. She gave me a ball of dough about the size of a mouse. She was right. It rubbed my bad lines out very well. Only the shadow of a shadow! I thought I would tell Papa this. I thought Papa would be interested that bread-dough could rub out pencil lines. But when I did tell him, he said, 'I don't make bread dough, Owen. I make pasta dough.'

In school they started us onto grey-lead pencil in Grade 5. That's because the teachers know you can make a mistake with grey-lead pencil and rub it out, when you're learning. Grey-lead pencil is like L-plates for writing because you can make a mistake and rub it out and fix it. That's why, more and more, I chose to make my drawings in pen or texta. Because I couldn't rub them out. I had to be certain about a line before I put it down, before I committed to it. Because this was more dangerous.

At school, when we were in the junior classes, we drew horizontal rainbows of colour with our crayons and went over the top with black, deep and thick, until our fingers were encrusted with soft black crayon muck. It was laborious. It made a mess. Then, with the pointy end of a paint-brush, we engraved coloured pictures through the black overlay. Magical coloured pictures, like slivers of heaven through a thundercloud.

I used the word 'rubber' at school and all the sixth-graders in my composite class (four, five and six) laughed and I didn't understand why.

Mr Parish only pretended to like things that were *ephemeral*. But he didn't like things that didn't last. Not really. They upset him. He got cross, watching Mrs Parish's ikebana dry and change, the stems turning brittle. 'It's time for the bin,' he would say to her. Or 'For god's sake, June, can't we have something fresh?'

But Mrs Parish had her own time schedule. Her flowers were left to dry out around the house according to their individual life cycles. Sometimes she even started with specimens that were already dead. She arranged these with the same care she applied to the living. She made careful, thoughtful cuts. She restricted herself with her materials, and she eyed each cut like a painter eyeing a brush stroke. 'In ikebana,' she said, 'there is a thing called *wabi sabi*, Owen. It means that it's not only the fresh things that have beauty. I can put potato vine with an old shoe, Owen. I can make something I like out of a warty old pumpkin. Or ivy. Or weeds.'

I found this a strange idea. Imagine if people arranged vases of weeds and old shoes and put them on their dinner tables. When I mentioned *wabi sabi* to Mr Parish, he laughed and said, 'Ahh, yes, my wife's self-justifying philosophy!'

Mrs Parish put her secateurs to a dead branch and made a decisive cut. There was no green inside the branch. There was none of what Dicken in *The Secret Garden* would have called 'wick'. The branch was a smoky residue of its live self: when she cut, a little puff of grey dust came out. But I somehow understood what she was doing. When she hung the branch with wild berries, still shiny red, it was like Snow White in the forest with the apple. I don't know why. It just was. I don't know how there can be a story in something without words or, really, pictures even. But there was. Mrs Parish attached a frond of green – slightly off-centre, like a woodland creature's antler.

15 JAN 1969

Dear Tilde,

Yes, please send Hannah. I'm so bloody lonely in this house by myself. I walk from room to room completely aimlessly. Yesterday, I went to the shops to buy milk and a mother from Owen's school stopped me and took my hand and said, I'm so sorry to hear you've been unwell. I don't even know what she was talking about! Do I have a sick look about me? Or has Owen been telling fibs about me to his friends?

Oh, do send Hannah. Send her with shoes and socks and toothbrush and magazines and thick waxy white pimple cream and wild hopes and hopeless dreams. Send the whole bundle! Send her now, registered post. We will shop for outrageous articles of clothing and long-playing records of popular music. We will eat ham sandwiches on the run and fry up leftovers for dinner. Owen will be beside himself with happiness and will make her sleep in his bed and play downball against the back fence.

And gosh, of course we have the money. That is <u>no problem at all</u>.

Send her send her send her.

Signing out now,

Your sister, Veda x

† † †

24 JAN 1969

Dear Tilde,

This morning the first thing I noticed upon waking was a very odd aroma of citrus fruit. It was all through the house, the smell of leaves from a lime plant, or a lemon-scented gum on Pound Road. The whole house.

I wondered where on earth it came from. It wasn't from outside. When I opened the window, there was no citrus scent. I began to think I dreamt it, though I don't believe I've ever had a dream with a smell so real before, or even a smell at all come to think of it.

For a moment, I felt taken right back to childhood. Amazing that a smell can do that. I felt young again and hopeful, like the whole world was opening out, that I had all the time I needed, that there were hundreds of long slow days before me. Do you know what I mean? Do you know that feeling? Lying on the grass with a book for hours like we used to, or swimming in the creek all day, or hauling a picnic basket to the paddock for long lunches and chapters read out loud from novels. And Jane in a little bumpy wobbly pram or clutching your back and complaining in the heat. It seems both like yesterday and like a million years ago. I remember reading to you from poems I was writing. And you were all the while spotting animals, and birds, and plants whose names you were learning from books.

Sometimes I feel like everything exists side by side, Tilde. I'm still the same girl, you know, I feel very close to her, ten-year-old me, with all her hopes and vain loves.

It's very quick, in the end: childhood. When you're in it, it goes on forever and ever. It's only when you are a mother that you realise how fleeting it is. And how quickly Life comes along, with its curbs on playfulness and lassitude – for you need lassitude to have playfulness, it cannot be otherwise. Life comes down upon us and turns us into a reflection of our choices.

Anyway, taking the scent of citrus as a message from an unknown source, I have taken stock of myself and washed my hair today after a long period of stubborn neglect. I have no patience for the other business of hair anymore, the rollers and styling etcetera, but the washing itself – I am not averse. My hair now smells better than the rest of me, is almost as soft as Owen's, which I describe as 'gossamer' to anyone who listens. Mine of course is turning grey, and with greyness comes a brittle quality – it kinks and won't obey me.

Owen's hair is the kind of hair a girl wants: fine like spun gold – if it gets a knot in it, I have to extract every thread most gently, like I am untangling a spider's web. Of course, he is disgusted if I use such words as 'gossamer' or 'spun gold' to describe him. Such beautiful buttery bodies they have, our children – that is, until they're not children anymore. Owen is moving into the 'not children' world.

How does one protect them? Sometimes I think I would throw in every hope of my own, every dream of literary prowess or success, to protect him, even for one second, from any hurt that might come to him.

But would I, Tilde. Would I?

If it came to it, I wonder how I should make such a choice. I should hope that if ever given that choice I would make the right one, but I know I would resent it for the rest of my life. I would never be happy. I would be a bloody, injured banshee who ruined everyone around her.

What sort of a mother chooses a book over a child?

Sometimes I am not sure what I am capable of at all.

All my love,

Veda

† † †

1 FEB 1969

Dear Tilde,

Owen has asked for more Hot Wheels for his birthday. I'm giving you lots of preparation time, and I hope Hot Wheels means something to you – you are probably out of touch with the interests of young boys – but ask in any toyshop and they will know. Jo and I are buying him a complete racing track so any vehicular additions would be most welcome. His various hopes and aspirations have all congealed around the one current burning aim: to be a racing-car driver (or, if such options are beyond his reach, to work in a factory that manufactures racing cars).

Do what you will though, of course. If said purchase proves laborious, he will be made to compose a charming thank-you letter whatever the gift.

My book is due for publication 'some time in the next year' or so I'm told. The delays and postponements are heartbreaking. I have a small blunt-instrument headache at the mere thought of it. But I try to put the difficulties behind me. Have had, in the meantime, two other things published: one in Crosscurrents, a little magazine quite well thought of, and another in something called City Voo-Doo (which I have a feeling will exist for about three editions and then go defunct).

The thing is (and I admit this cautiously and own it as a challenge): I am still finding it quite difficult to work without a drink. I find myself wanting to write that in invisible ink, lemon juice, or in such teeny-weeny writing you need to get a magnifying glass out to read it. But I tell you because I know you won't judge me, and admitting it enables me to look it in the face, so to speak. My working days were always all about alcoholic beverages. The beverages knitted together the whole painful stop-start line-for-line word-for-word process. What does one do in the gaps without it? – there is a process, a pause, between thought and creation and it requires a prop. A cigarette is no contender. And they say cigarettes will kill me too.

Meanwhile, to help me on my way, my husband has purchased me an electric typewriter. I've said to him: 'Jo, I'm not a secretary anymore, I don't need to put down 80 words a minute, you know!' but he seems to think an electric typewriter, rather than the more modest manual chug-along type, will help me break my habits of the past.

I don't write poetry on a typewriter in the first place, of course, and never have – though it's true that publishers don't like to spend their time deciphering spidery hands from the nineteenth century. My new typewriter is a Smith Corona

Portable and it fits rather nattily in its nice little case. I wasn't sure at first, I admit, but it does truly make me feel businesslike. Should John Honey at Vellum muck me about any further, he may not get any more good poetry out of me, but he will get a ferocious business letter from me and my Smith Corona.

I am trying to spend more time with Owen, but he likes it so much at Ornella's little house, and the country air is so good for him at the Parishes, that I feel selfish if I object to the current arrangement. Hannah's presence here might tempt him home.

Have you heard anything more about her intentions? I had hoped she would write. But nothing yet. I guess she's still waiting to hear about university.

With all my love,

Veda xxx

27 MARCH 1969

Dear Tilde,

I realised yesterday that, reduced to an acronym, Works On Paper becomes WOP. I told this to my husband who became furious with me. I don't know why. I was quite calm and composed when I pointed it out. I would've thought he would've wanted to know?

I hardly go to the restaurant these days. And, being the bad wife that I am, I barely take an interest in my husband's charity work either. Jo is getting quite a name for himself on that front. There was even an article about him in the paper, with a photo of him, looking as though he'd got an unexpected fright. It seems to me, Tilde, that he gets younger and more energetic every day, while I get older and more enervated. I have a terrible furrow in my brow, deep and riven. And really, I can't be bothered with hair, nails, etcetera. Or not on a daily basis. Look at me: I can barely be bothered with complete sentences. That is what happens with poets eventually: they become so minimalist that they don't need words at all. Just a sound: a scream perhaps, like that picture by that German Munch (was he German? Or Austrian? Norwegian perhaps).

Might go and put my head in a bucket of sand or something. There's not much better to do.

Send reason for living,

VEDA xxx

† † †

2 MAY 1969

Dear Tilde,

Guess whom I spied with my little eye, after a hiatus of – perhaps a year or more – our friend Susan, aka Mrs G Bridie. And where did I see her? Rifling through her handbag, looking for her cheque-book – in the process of purchasing two 'lovely' drawings by Florence Oakey.

Florence is the first woman artist WOP has shown and this has caused plenty of friction. Especially because the red dots kept coming and coming. (They indicate a sale, you see.) Gosh, didn't I just nurse my wine glass (full of soda water) and cackle.

Jo's thoughts on Florence Oakey were all positive in the extreme, and he was sure Parish would feel the same once the monies had been counted. But Parish was in a funk – at being proven wrong is my guess – he was not a fan of the artist in question. Gallery assistant had to work extremely hard to jolly him back into sorts.

An all-round cracker of a night.

Susan has invited me to attend a group she has formed, lady patrons of the arts, something like that, but I'm not going to. I would only make some terrible class boo-boo and be sent home with my tail between my legs. Or find myself wearing the wrong dress or coat. You wouldn't feel equal to it either, I'm sure, though I imagine you think me silly for turning Susan down. I haven't much else to do, I know. I have a sort of mental paralysis, though, just thinking about such things: spending an afternoon talking, eating, talking, eating with a group of women I don't even really know ... I no longer feel capable of such feats. Yes, it would seem like a feat.

And I have neither the money nor the inclination for philanthropy.

Jo sends love. Owen sends thanks for Hot Wheels, belatedly I'm afraid. His note is within.

And no, I'm not thinking about having another baby. Are you joking? What sort of a mother have I been so far?

And no, no response from Hannah.

Love always,

Veda xxx

17 JUNE 1969

Dearest Tilde,

You won't believe the latest development: Owen has become a vegetarian!

I'm not joking, Tilde. He has sworn off meat in any form.

Jo is rabid with anger. He considers it a personal insult. I'm afraid I provide very little support. When Jo asked me to help him convince Owen to change his mind, I said: 'Let him eat beans!' at which my husband fumed.

What made O-yo come to such a decision, you ask? Well, to be honest, I think it was all due to my serving a particularly fatty old steak. (I don't often cook steak anymore, and so perhaps I was not paying enough attention and served it a bit underdone.) We were just sitting there, at the table, he and I, and Owen was prodding away at his steak, pressing the fork against it to see the blood squeeze out, and he said to me: 'Mother, is this from a cow?'

'Yes,' I said. 'Yes, darling. Steak comes from cows. As does beef. And milk. And leather.' (I was quite reasonable!)

'So ...' he said. 'Would this be a baby cow or a grown-up?'

I had forgotten, you see, that he has a little pet cow at the Parishes'. A little runty thing that has grown quite big now and has free run of the place.

'Oh, O-yo,' I said. 'An infant cow. But not a baby. Say, a year and a half old?'

'Paddy Cow is five,' he said.

'Well, isn't she lucky to get so old!' I said. 'Isn't she lucky: she's not ever going to end up on someone's plate.'

Owen considered that for a bit, and then pushed his plate away. 'This could be her brother,' he said.

'Or sister,' I said.

What else could I say?

'Yes, it could be Paddy Cow's brother or sister,' I said. 'And every chicken also has a brother or sister, as does every sheep, and every fish, and every pig.'

'I won't eat it anymore,' he said. 'I won't eat any animals. I want to care for animals, not eat them.' And so he didn't. I gave the steak to the dog next door, and heated Owen up a can of baked beans. Later, he stuck his head in the door to check whether there was 'animal' in salami (an Italian sausage), and though a little crestfallen by my affirmative response, he nodded valiantly and went back to his bedroom.

Italian cuisine, I have reminded Jo, is a cuisine dominated by vegetables. But Jo is disgusted. And I know he holds me responsible. He feels I have somehow feminised Owen. I did not know that the eating of meat was somehow masculine and the eating of vegetables, feminine. But it has put another rift between us. Yes, Owen's vegetarianism is another thing that makes Jo angry with me. But as Jo will not sit down long enough to discuss it, what am I to do? If I ask him to put aside a little time to talk about anything I am severely reprimanded for my selfishness: because don't I know he is feeding the poor and the homeless? Well, sometimes I want to shout all the poor and homeless fish and chips just so's I get a day occasionally with my husband.

Perhaps there's no point anyway: Jo and I, should we get stuck together for a whole uninterrupted two hours, might have nothing to say to each other. I feel like rapping with my knuckles on his head, 'Jo, Jo, Hello, are you in there?'

So there you have it.

And re your last query: No. I'm crestfallen – but not surprised. Of course I will go and visit Hannah. I will take her a cake and a stack of magazines. I understand her desire to be a young thing, free in the world, without a silly old aunt getting in her way.

Send recipes for hearty vegetable stews and soups with beans in them.

Love Veda xxx

† † †

28 JUNE 1969

Dear Tilde,

I have started something new. It crept up on me, a brooding idea at first, but getting clearer in the light of day.

Presumptuous of me before my first book even comes out … but I'm feeling a certain concreteness about my powers. Ambitious, even. Of course, I'm completely aware that ambition is a perilous path. Ambition is my downfall. Jo always says: 'Don't aim so high and then you wouldn't fall so low. You either think you're a genius or a complete failure. Think yourself into the middle of the road.'

Well, bugger the bloody middle of the road: that's where the animals get hit, is it not?

I was looking at my most recent poems and found I could see a certain narrative crystallising within them. Well, a theme perhaps, linking them, an elementary organising pattern. 'Youth' 'Middle Age', 'Death'. (The elementary organising pattern!)

For a moment it felt big and important, as though in one woman's life, I might bring to light many more. I began scratching down ideas, seeing how poems I am working on might fit, embryonic poems that have only just announced themselves but seem, almost miraculously, to fit this new scheme. I'm excited and hopeful, but am trying to be measured because I know how ideas work: they appear easy and exciting at first, but turn out to be complex and difficult in the execution.

It is good to have some thoughts on a follow-up to The Poems of Veda Gray, though. Yes, that is what the publishers are calling it – excruciating title, but they decide these things, not me. I wanted to call it Elephant in the Room but they objected on the grounds that it sounds like a children's book. Meanwhile, the cover: all of Vellum's poetry is published in the most dismal brown and cream cover art. Reminds me of the shorthand books I used to study at Goodwin's. My publisher says it is for the purposes of 'easy identification' – all readers will know a Vellum poetry publication by its puce and tan colour scheme. (All readers will be dissuaded from purchasing a Vellum poetry publication by its puce and tan colour scheme.) Anyway, I've given way on this like everything else.

My new work will be absolutely as I want it. That's the pay-off I foresee. Once The Poems of Veda Gray is out, I will have a little more freedom, a little more say, a little more leverage. I will write the book I want to write, and not feel corralled by the wishes of nervous editors and edgy booksellers and fickle book-buyers.

But I must go. Have dog (new). Needs walk. It's a fat little brick of a thing: a Boston terrier. Inherited it from my neighbour who can't walk it (or abide it) anymore. It 'gets me out of the house', as they say. The schoolchildren stop and pat it, and ladies in shops are clucky when they see me with him. Little did I know what an introduction to the community a dog might be. Name: Griffin.

Lots of love,

Veda x

† † †

3 SEPTEMBER 1969

Dear Tilde,

I'm sitting here alone in the living room feeling completely out of sorts. I am sure I am being punished for the sin of pride. I jinx myself by imagining I have something to offer the world. You should take my last letter and just put it in the woodstove.

I heard (on the grapevine, through the Knoxes) that Vellum Publishing is being bought out by a bigger publishing company. I don't know the details – but I'm just crossing my fingers that, whatever's happening, John Honey's staying on as editor-in-chief, all projects will proceed as per schedule, and this is just some money-salvaging operation that won't make any difference to my book. I've tried to call, but John's not answering the phone and I daren't send him a telegram in case he thinks me neurotic and unbalanced. Waiting to hear more. Will finish this letter in a bit. X

UPDATE

Talked to John. He says all is expected to run smoothly, just needed extra money on board. All systems go, as they say.

Had a lovely letter in the mail today from a woman in Newcastle who read my poem 'Brilliant-ine' in Crossroads. First bit of fan mail. (It went straight to my head.)

Write me soon,

X VEDA

† † †

12 OCTOBER 1969

Dear Tilde,

The new publishers are a 'consortium'. I'm not sure exactly what that means – I thought it a legal term denoting a husband's right of access to his wife – but I think it means they're not interested in books per se, only in the money that might be made from books. Perhaps all publishers are like that and I'm naïve to have thought them any different to purveyors of automobiles or insurance plans. Would Frank or our father be interested in sheep if they couldn't make money from them? Of course not. I'm entirely too naïve for this world, clearly.

Today, they have written me a letter seeking a further postponement of my book. Yes. I write this with my teeth gritted and my heart murderous. John Honey has phoned me and apologised and said we must do what we can do, keep it on track, go gently-gently, allow them time, et cetera, et cetera. Says they need to be 'brought around to poetry', be convinced of its commercial value.

I have bitten my nails down to the quick enough times over this that a little more can hardly hurt. Except it does. And blood is inevitably drawn.

The new bosses say they need to 'reconsider the content' and 'reassess the sequencing' of my book. They would like to remove 'Distraction in E' and 'Mild Summer Kill'. They would like to remove 'Coat and Coat-hanger' and 'Kindness When You Drove Me'. They think a different opening poem is required (perhaps a sonnet? they suggest, because *didn't Shakespeare write lots of those*?)

They would like an alluring picture of me for the back cover.

Alluring picture? Shall I drag something out from ten years ago? I'm about as alluring as a dead cat these days.

Why don't they just fling me into their incinerator of dead poets and stop wasting my time?

I feel like putting a needle through my eye.

V x

4 JANUARY 1970

Darling Tilde,

I'm really quite low and beyond anything.

I lay here all this morning doing absolutely nothing. The dog lay with me – he's a sweeter, stupider version of me. I didn't have the energy to make myself lunch. I couldn't be bothered taking the dog for a walk. I've retreated into a permanent Sunday. Could've stared at the wall all morning, listening to the wind and the screeching of the washing line.

The house feels vaguely dead these days, as when no one goes into a room for months: you can smell the neglect and abandonment. Outside there is unmown grass, soggy egg-cartons and cardboard boxes. Inside: filthy ashtrays, a leaking fridge. A piano to be dusted. Plants I have abandoned.

There is a terrible dog urine smell too, which has me down on my hands and knees sniffing the floor like a mad woman. If that creates a comic picture for you, I don't mean it to, I'm not trying to be funny or amuse you: it is actually me, going slightly mad all by myself here.

A rose-thorn has got into my knuckle and it is all swollen.

I'm depressed, fed up, exhausted. All I want to do is just sleep and have someone take care of me.

I know, I know, I mustn't slip into this mood, as it will just take me down down down and then leave me with all the horrible work of coming back up again.

I will pick myself up and dust myself off.

Are you getting my mail, Tilde?

Love Veda

† † †

20 FEBRUARY 1970

Dear Tilde,

Last night I dreamt I walked past a man buried up to his neck in concrete. He turned his head back and forth as I walked past and whistled at me, like we were in cahoots, like it was just a matter of time.

I have a headache. (Perhaps that is the first of the concrete being laid?) The headache causes me to furrow my brow so now I am acquiring an even deeper crevice in my forehead. I look at smooth-browed women, on the street, in shops. I'd like to stop and talk to them and ask them how they do it. 'What cream do you use? What exercises do you do before the mirror?' But it seems that in order to have such a brow, I would need to stop thinking all together. Is 'not thinking' really the remedy? Our mother's brow was prematurely wrinkled by the sun and the weather. She never worried about such things as smooth foreheads or greying hair or thwarted ambitions. And that is why she has lived a large, wholesome, satisfying life with only one of her children causing her pain.

There are people like our mother, and possibly you – indeed, I think definitely you – who are naturals at life. They understand and are at ease with the way things work. I don't understand the mechanism, Tilde. I am not properly in tune with the requirements. I don't have a natural affinity for anything. Not motherhood, not wifehood, not poetry. I probably would have been better off living in a century where women did not even learn to read. Perhaps I could have been happy brewing beer and fermenting goat's milk, had I not known differently.

Again and again, I see the same pattern emerge in myself: grand ideas, furious bouts of creativity, and then, a slow painful realisation. I look at the products of my efforts and see they are too small, too fragile to survive in the world. I see that the world will not want them. There is nothing grand or exciting about them at all: they are simply not interesting to anyone but me.

This realisation makes it very hard to work. It makes it very hard to believe in what I produce or see any merit in working to improve or perfect or refine. I cannot make head nor tail of The Poems of Veda Gray anymore. Working on it is fresh agony every day. All the solutions I come up with in the morning have created new problems by afternoon. I can't see clearly. I keep putting in words and taking them out again, and before I know it, a whole day is gone.

If only there was someone here to talk to. I thrash around by myself, getting nowhere.

The quality I really lack, Tilde, is humility. I had all sorts of opportunity to learn it throughout my girlhood – from our mother, from you, from women about us in church and at school, from other girls and teachers. It was one thing to be accomplished, but another entirely to make a song and dance out of it, as I did. Accomplishments are not things to greedily hold onto and turn into ambitions. That is where I went wrong.

Now I understand why girls are taught humility, modesty. It's not just to make us the quiet helpmates of others, it's to prepare us for our expectations of the world. It's to make us accept our fates.

No one liked Emma Bovary. Did you?

The dreams of girls are enormous air balloons, ripe for the pricking. We get to know early on that our balloons will not be lifted up, will not sail, will not land elsewhere in the world. It is apparent for us at a young age, just when boys are watching their own air balloons set sail. I sat with the boys, on the edge of the very same hill, and set my balloon sailing alongside theirs. I was as smart as them, I was as energetic and passionate and hardworking. I did not see the limitations of my equipment nor the many small darts aimed at my colours as I hoisted them aloft.

But now I am stretching my metaphor, just as I have stretched the patience and forbearance and better judgement of all around me.

I keep these thoughts to myself these days, though. I don't tell Jo anything, I don't worry Jo with things I want to say. I don't think of things to tell him, I don't remember things to tell him. I let him subside from my difficult annoying thoughts and feelings.

I tell them to the pot plants while I watch them die, and the leaking tap with the tea-towel round its throat. Drip drip drip.

Sometimes I just want to slice a big hole in my guts and let the whole lot fall out onto the floor. Relief!

PART 4

MONASTERY MAIDEN

1986

Mother's book made money for Bacchae Publishing. When it came out, in 1986, it was reviewed in national and international journals and newspapers. It was eventually included on a university curriculum. It went into a third reprint. It was translated into Spanish and French and German. Because the poems were accessible, people bought *The Poems of Veda Gray* who would not otherwise have picked up a collection of poems. Later on, there was a 'What happened to Veda Gray?' story in the *Age*, in which I was interviewed. Mother was, briefly, very pleasantly, Julia's cash cow.

Yet it wasn't only about money. Julia really felt something about Mother's poetry. She went back to the poems again and again. She still does. Her personal copy is dog-eared, bristling with bookmarks (cigarette papers in those days before sticky notes). I have often thought that choosing me was, in fact, a means for Julia to get close to Mother. But we have been together so long now, questions like that no longer apply. We are old battleaxes. We have no reason to stay together except for liking each other: we aren't married, we have no children. Julia is smart and kind, sweet and tough: a modern-day hard-working hedonist. When she turned sixty, she spent two thousand dollars on dinner and wine for her ten best friends. She loves food. She loves poetry. Perhaps I, in fact, chose *her* to get closer to Mother.

Still, she is not quite forgiving of Mother, not quite. Veda is a different story, but Mother and Veda remain separate in her mind. She cannot congeal the two women into one.

STEEL CHERRY-PITTER

'You're going to be a rich boy one day,' said Papa. I was sitting on the fence at Hawthorn and he was doing up my shoelaces. I guess it made him feel like I was a lord and he was my servant, the way he had to kneel down and bend his head, while my foot stuck up to regally accept his services. 'You're going to be Richie Rich, poor little rich kid. Got that, O-yo?'

I screwed up my nose. Was he crazy? I didn't want to be Richie Rich. I didn't want a stupid bow-tie and a dog with dollar-signs on its coat. He swung me down from the fence and I immediately trod my laces loose again.

Mr Parish wanted me to go to private school. I was already rehearsing to say no. I was going to work in a *racing car factory*: what did I need private school for? I was going to have a wife and some kids and I was going to work in the factory and race cars on the weekend. And when my racing career got going, well, then I'd leave the factory and be in the Grand Prix and when I won they'd shake champagne all over my head. I had a wife already picked out, well two actually: Monica Lloyd who read Trixie Belden books and was good at high jump or Vasoula Costopoulos who had big dimples and curly brown hair and the neatest handwriting in class. That was the future. If I was going to be rich, it would be from winning at the Grand Prix.

'Yeah, yeah,' you said, Ornella, but you got some fabric with racing cars on it and made 'drapes' for my bedroom – for some reason you wouldn't let me call them 'curtains'.

I've still got those drapes in a box somewhere. I remember all the early mornings, waking up and watching the racing cars as the sun rose: there were three cars racing across that calico vista – a blue, a yellow, and a red one. One had a snub nose like the Genesis, and the other two were sharp and speedy, like a Sharknose Ferrari. The man driving all of them was the same man with the same black hair. He looked French in a stripy red and white top and black moustache. Sometimes he looked like Papa. Sometimes, depending on the light, the cars looked, not like cars, but like strange coloured fish. Or, if I changed the angle of my vision, they looked like three different clown faces, all mean, all with frightening noses and mean eyes. I could stare at them for ages, shifting my vision, making them other things. Sometimes, if I started really hard for long enough, I could make them jump out into 3D.

Why did you throw out everything when you sold the house in Coburg, Ornella? Was it because you knew all those things didn't matter in the end, that without memories attached they were just junk shop rubbish? You put Nonna's things out on the grass for the neighbours to pick through. You didn't even keep a teapot, or a pair of earrings. You filled your new place with glossy new things with no memories attached. You thought Carlito was sentimental, the way he hung on to his christening bracelet. You rolled your eyes. But what are you now, without all those things? The other ladies here, they have display cases full of shells and trinkets and pictures of younger versions of themselves. Walking past, you can see their lives – not in summary, but at least in bits, in the things behind the glass. What could I put on your shelf? Your electric toothbrush? Your steel cherry-pitter? The nit-comb you dragged through my hair once a week, cursing other children's parents?

Julia says it really doesn't matter in the scheme of things. And she's right. Those things behind glass: they're not for the residents, anyway. They're for the visitors.

But when someone packs up after me, there'll be a truckload of stuff to go through. It's all in two locked rooms in Park Orchards. The tenants don't mind. Mr and Mrs Parish always had more rooms than they needed. Than the tenants need, too.

All those extra bricks Mr Parish laid for bedrooms for children who didn't eventuate.

FEAR OF FLYING

Mr Parish had a new collection out that the reviewers said 'eclipsed all his previous work'. One reviewer said it put him in place 'as Australia's preeminent poet'. The poems were in very small print on yellowish paper and they contained phrases like 'this morganatic marriage' and 'in the pocked shade'. It seemed like gobbledegook to me and I didn't know how he got away with it. There was not a single line that made sense. There were hardly even any rhymes. But grown men in suits came to discuss it with him at lunchtime so it had to be important. I heard them, trying to get to the bottom of 'morganatic marriage', and Mr Parish genially laughing in his accommodating laughing voice that meant he didn't want to answer. Mrs Parish said her favourite poem in the collection was 'The Cumquat Rose', which was not a real rose but she wished it was because she could imagine it, right down to its smell and its colour.

But as far as I was concerned, Mrs Parish was doing something much more exciting than Mr Parish's poetry collection, even if he did get his picture in the paper. Mrs Parish was planning a trip to Japan. She had booked an aeroplane flight to Tokyo. The only problem was Mrs Parish was terrified of flying. She could barely bring the subject up. 'Oh Owen,' she said, 'That enormous plane, and all of us passengers in it, I just can't see how the *physics* works!' Every time she talked about the plane, she put her hand on her chest and went a little white. I offered to go with her – I was desperate to go on a real live plane and I could hold her hand if it got bumpy – and she said, 'Oh Owen! I would love to take you with me' and squeezed my shoulder and shook her head. Then she tried to hold my hand, but I felt funny about it. So I took mine away and then felt even more funny.

So, while Mr Parish was having afternoon meetings with editors and men from universities in his turps-smelling study, Mrs Parish was wearing lipstick and going into the city to visit the travel agent. Once she even took the train to Sydney as part of her overseas preparations. She went on a sleeper and she said the bunk was so skinny and close to the ceiling she had to fold herself into it like a dollar note in a wallet. She had travelled to Sydney to meet with Norman Sparnon. He was her hero: she had all his books. He had first noticed her work at the Georges exhibition and it was he who had organised for her to attend masterclasses in Kyoto with Teshigahara

Kasumi. Norman Sparnon was impressed by 'the invisibility of technique' in her work. I remember these words, because Mrs Parish told them to me over and over again. Sometimes, when she leaned in to an arrangement with her big cutting-scissors, I could imagine her saying 'invisibility of technique' as she made snips and extracted superfluous foliage.

'But I am only an apprentice, Owen,' she said, 'and I must be taught by a master. You need other people to help you really *achieve* anything in this world. To teach you, Owen. To help you. You can't do it on your own.'

She tried to teach me.

'The samurai,' she told me, 'practised Ikebana for relaxation after battles.'

I liked this idea. I imagined the samurais going swish, swish with their swords and creating a perfect piece of *ikenobo* while blood dried on their cheekbones. But I wasn't good at Ikebana. When I put flowers together, they immediately fell apart again. Mrs Parish gave me 'props' to use, even though this was against the ikebana law: twine, foam, putty. But I never got the hang of it. I tried a flat dish, I tried a tall vase. My arrangements drooped. I guess I was not *Zen* enough. Zen meant leaving the past behind you. Mrs Parish explained this to me. 'It's more like simply forgetting to remember,' she said. 'Or just putting the past and the future aside for a bit. Quite hard to do.' Snip. Tilting her head to the side. Snip. 'In the end,' she said, 'ikebana is not about flowers, and not about nature, Owen, it's about you.'

I didn't really understand that, and yet I did. I was ten. I was still making drawings, but not so much. I had given up writing poems because they hurt my head. I had become a vegetarian.

Papa did not like my vegetarianism. But I couldn't eat meat anymore. I just couldn't. I could not put my teeth in a piece of animal flesh. The thought, the texture, the knowledge of where it came from. The mooning eyes of Paddy Cow when she came up to the window in the morning; the dumb glassy eyes of the chooks; the sightless orbs of a myxo rabbit, dead on the side of the road. *If it's got eyes, I'm not gonna eat it,* I told Papa. I didn't do it to spite him. But it made him furious. 'Potatoes have eyes!' he yelled. But I shook my head. He wagged his finger at me and said that the poor people of this world didn't have the luxury of not eating meat. He said I was a privileged little *shit*. He whacked the top of my head with his hand. And then he changed his mind and grabbed my head against his chest and hugged me and said, Sorry, Sorry, Sorry. And then slapped me again because he was still angry.

I was confused. But I was a vegetarian. It annoyed the men around me. It was the first beginnings of a separate me.

Only the women supported my new vegetarian self: Mother, Mrs Parish, and you, Ornella. Carlito ate a steak in front of me with relish, oohing and aahing over every forkful and smacking his lips. You just shrugged your shoulders and fried me up an eggplant. If you got it fried well enough, an eggplant oozed just as much as a piece of meat. You could mix up rice and nuts and crushed tomatoes and wrap it in vine-leaves like the Greeks did. Or stuff it in zucchini. You could even fry the flowers of a zucchini. If Papa had consulted me, he could've put vegetarian on the menu way before it was fashionable. He could've been ahead of the pack.

Mother used it as an excuse to have eggs and baked beans on toast for dinner. She said it would be like camping. We ate on a picnic blanket on the floor in front of the telly but she rarely finished her dinner, just mopped it round and round with toast and then butted her cigarette out in it. I liked the cans of tomato spaghetti best. I would even eat them cold, I didn't care. They were squishy in a way that was not like meat, but somehow satisfied me the same way.

Mother was in a bad phase. She called it a 'sprawl'. It was a big indulgent sprawl – she was taking up too much room with it and everyone but me was just letting her slob about and feel sorry for herself. I caught her looking in the mirror, grimacing at herself, investigating her teeth and the pores on the sides of her nose. She had a little scab in the corner of her mouth that she kept picking.

'Bloody stop it!' I wanted to say to her. In films, men slapped women around the chops to get them to come to when they were hysterical or comatose. That's what I felt like I needed to do to Mother, just give her a *bloody slap*. Just *snap her out of it* with a manly *slap* across the face. But I didn't have the guts. Who knew what she would do? She might hit me back or even punch me. Or she might cry. God help me, she might *bloody cry*.

'What's wrong with Mother?' I asked Papa, two weeks into her sprawl. I tried to sound like I didn't care.

'She's worried about her book. She's worried what people might think of it.'

But Mother didn't care what people thought. I knew that as a fact. An *actual fact*.

'She's really *letting herself go*,' I said.

Papa looked at me strangely. 'I'm not sure you should be staying with her at the moment,' he said. 'What do you want to do? Do you want to go to Ornella's? You can ride your bike there if you like.'

I had a new bike. A red Malvern Star Papa had bought me. I could ride to school in less than ten minutes, and to Ornella's in fifteen. And that's exactly what I wanted to do – ride my bike to Ornella's – but I didn't say that because I thought Mother might cry if I went. Or try to cry, or pretend to cry, all of which were awful possibilities. She had become horrible in her grey-blue dressing gown, which used to be soft and smell good, but now had the quality of a decaying bathmat.

'It's not very fun,' I said, 'when she's like this.'

'Hmmm,' said Papa. 'She probably needs a bit of company right now though.'

'Well, *you* stay home with her then!' I said. 'It's not *fun* for *me*!'

And then I felt sorry for Mother again and went and shook the picnic blanket out in the back garden while Papa put his socks on for work. He didn't know about her 'lolly-water', which was the colour of water, alright, but had no smell whatsoever and which she kept under the couch.

RED MALVERN STAR

I was broadening my social circle. I had a red Malvern Star and I could get to wherever I wanted on it. I rode along the river and met kids under the Richmond bridge to walk the undercarriage: the struts were big and geometrical; it was easy, it wasn't dangerous at all. It only looked dangerous from the ground. And if you fell, you'd just go into all that brown river water full of carp. The pink chemicals they pumped out from factories along the banks would probably hurt you more than the fall. We went in drains too, skinny ones where you had to crawl and big ones where you could put your hands out and only just touch both sides. Boys collected in these places, practising to be tough; names were not even important. Their younger sisters yelled at them to come down or come home. Some of the boys smoked cigarettes and occasionally someone brought alcohol which we snuck around among us, a capful at a time – it was horrible, but not as bad as the cigarettes, which made me feel like my guts would fall out. There were homeless men down there too sometimes: you'd come around a corner on the river path and find one up on the bank asleep or drinking from a paper bag and yelling crazy things. They were scary and sad and you stayed away from them, even though, by now, Mrs Parish had read *Great Expectations* to me and I knew a tramp could leave you a big fat inheritance if you played your cards right.

Ornella smelled the smoke on me, and smacked me, and then sighed ruefully when Carlito lit up a Camel and offered me the pack.

But there was civilisation too, in the broadened circle my bike-riding allowed. There were normal families. I went to Callum's for tea one day. He shared a room with his older brother. He went to bed at half-past eight. He had to eat green and orange vegetables every day and do chores in the morning before breakfast. At dinnertime, his whole family sat at the table to eat, like they were at a restaurant. There were rules for sitting at the table too. They were different to a restaurant, or different to Papa's restaurant anyway. We had to speak in quiet voices and no one clinked their knives on their plates. Salt and pepper were asked for and received politely. Mr Webster, Callum's father, sat at the head of the table and wore a shirt and tie and carved the roast with a big, white-handled knife that had got so thin in the middle it looked like it might break. I focussed on the knife handle so I wouldn't have to see all the pink juice coming out of the lamb. Once we were eating, everyone talked in turn about their day. Mrs Webster had been to the library and got a new lot of books for the kids (*The Cay* and *Charlotte Sometimes* for the girls, and, for the big brother, a science-fiction novel called *Do Androids Dream of Electric Sheep?*). Callum's sisters had had home economics class and learned to make shepherd's pie. Callum's brother had operated his first bunsen burner and asbestos mat. The grandmother's hydrangeas had got burnt and she wished she had planted them in a pot so she could bring them inside on hot days. Callum had been chalk monitor for the second day running.

And then they asked me.

No one had asked me about my day before. I had no idea what to say. Already I had shocked Callum's family by refusing roast lamb.

'I—' I said. I looked at my hands on my knife and fork and saw a speck of grit on the potato.

'Go on,' said Callum's mother gently.

But in that moment I couldn't think of a thing to say. Not a single thing. The day stretched out behind me like grey fog. Had I even gone to school?

Callum rescued me. 'He said the times table. The sevens. All the way through. Without a mistake.'

The family murmured approvingly, and I nodded, and eating – thankfully – resumed. The sevens were a hard times table.

Ornella collected me after dinner.

'Oh yes,' she said, when Mrs Webster told her I had not eaten very much. 'He's used to restaurant food.'

I didn't know why this was rude, but it was.

More and more, I was seeing mothers who were different to mine. I hadn't noticed it before, but it was becoming too obvious to ignore. Some mothers came and talked to the teachers and brought them gifts of flowers cut from their gardens or lemons from their lemon trees. Some came and helped on the school excursions. Others brought their kids Four and Twenty Pies and Wagon Wheels from the local milk bar. Mother did none of these things, though she had the time to do them. She could've come on our trips to the park or when we went to the Melbourne Zoo. I punched the pillow, or the couch, or my own arm, thinking about it.

In reality, however, I didn't really want Mother to come to school. She would either swan around or slouch, talk too much or too little, be over-nice or outright rude. She would be thinking about herself and not about me. That was her problem.

Even when she thought she was thinking about me, she was really thinking about herself. She thought she was the Queen.

When it came to the crunch, it was you, Ornella, who came to school and met my teacher, in your nurse's uniform. You yanked my arm hard crossing the road. And when you stepped out onto Church Street, you stepped out too quickly and a car blared its horn at you.

Miss Vella cocked her head and considered me, sitting silently beside you. I was less blonde by this time, my eyebrows were darkening.

'I've had Owen in my class two years in a row now, and I'm asking myself one question: Where's all that drawing he used to do?' said Miss Vella. 'And his poems?'

Ornella took a breath and went to say something and then didn't.

Miss Vella looked at me with sad hopeful love in her eyes. 'I hope you will continue to be creative, Owen,' she said. She said it like it was her dying wish. Then she looked brightly at Ornella again. 'But you'll be pleased to know he's doing very well in maths!' and swept before us a ream of roneo-ed maths worksheets smelling faintly of alcohol, with big red ticks all over them.

At the end of the interview, Ornella's sharp eyes caught Miss Vella's protruding stomach. I hadn't noticed it myself, but I did now – how could I not have seen it?

'You expecting?' she said.

'Yes,' said Miss Vella. She blushed. (I guess she was a Mrs not a Miss all along.)

'Gonna give up your teaching then?' said Ornella, pulling on her cardigan.

'Naturally,' said Miss Vella, 'though I'll miss it, of course.'

Miss Vella had big black hair sprayed into a fairyfloss shape. She came from Malta. She wore a beautiful soft white cardigan in winter that was knitted, she said, by her Maltese grandmother. She was young and pretty and everyone loved her. Even when she tossed her head, which she did now, her hair didn't move.

'I think that having a family,' she said, 'is the most important thing a woman can do, don't you?'

I don't think she realised Ornella was not my mother.

'For sure,' said Ornella. Her eyes were narrow. 'We'd all do anything for our families.'

Miss Vella smiled back and the two of you shook hands.

On the way home, I said: 'Would you really do *anything for your family*, Ornella?'

I must've used a mocking tone, for you stopped and turned to look at me fiercely.

'Of course!' you said. And when I kept looking unsure, '*Of course!*' as though you might still smack me.

We kept walking.

'So who *is* your family?' I asked. 'Your mum's dead, your dad's dead … There's only Carlito. And Papa, who's not your family *in actual fact* …'

You stopped again and I thought you were going to grab my shirt collars and throw me up against the wall.

'*You* are,' you said. 'Who else, do you think? Don't I come and pick you up, on time, *every time*? Don't I make sure *everything's* done for you?'

It was true. You made sure I had clean socks and polished shoes and buttons sewn on and hair nit-free and combed. You paid for school excursions and filled out forms and checked that I ate the fruit you put in my lunchbox. And yet …

But you're mean to me! I wanted to say.

Practical, reliable, and *mean*. Impatient. Short-tempered. You always talked with crossness in your voice. I had to be in bed at a 'reasonable time'. You wouldn't let me have a day off school even if I had a sore throat. Did I have homework I needed to do? You *didn't have a creative bone in your body*. That's because your bones were all made out of concrete. Carlito felt the same as me: he slammed his beer glass down on the table to let you know it.

For once, for a change, your voice went soft and patient. 'I'm not a smart person like your mother, O-yo,' you said to me. 'I'm maybe even a little dumb. So what? You don't have to be smart to have kids.'

What were you talking about, Ornella? You confused me. I was not your kid.

MIDAS

Papa was still unhappy about his success. The restaurant was making money, the gallery was making money. Everything Papa touched *turned to gold*. But he was like sad old King Midas in my Dr Seuss Beginner Book from Grade Prep. He sat glumly in La Coccinella and surveyed Rosa's mural. The colours were fading, but it remained a drawcard for the restaurant. 'A tourist attraction,' scoffed Rosa. 'A gimmick. A place that doesn't really exist anyway.' I didn't know why she didn't like it anymore. I didn't know why she said it didn't exist. Papa looked at it glumly now and smoked a cigarette. He had made me a plate of ratatouille. It tasted like it could have hidden meat in it. Rat-meat. Rat-tails. I picked it apart with my fork.

Then Papa said, 'Maybe I'll just whitewash the wall, huh? Start fresh.'

'No!' I said.

He was silent again, for some minutes. In the past, I would've absorbed this silence without difficulty, working away in my drawing-book, attaching spikes to the backs of dinosaurs and hubcaps to the wheels of Maseratis. Now, without such diversions, these silences of Papa's had become actual shapes I had to get past. I felt responsible for them, as though his happiness relied on something I could do or say.

'Maybe I should chuck in this restaurant business. Getting tired of it now. It's making me a sad old rich man. I'll get a face like I deserve soon.' He pulled an ugly face like a donkey's.

'But if you didn't do a restaurant, what would you do?' I was worried. I had an image of him and Mother living in the same house, sleepwalking past each other, passing the salt and pepper on auto-cue.

He gestured at Rosa's mural. 'Take up painting maybe,' he said, and then I knew he was joking. Papa could hardly draw a stick-man.

'Papa,' I said, 'Rosa is talented. You are not. You are talented at food, Papa. And that is all.'

He laughed and ashed his cigarette without looking. It went on the tablecloth.

'Still,' he said,' gesturing at the mural. 'Looks a bit *dull* these days ... Bit *hokey*.'

Fear came up in me in a surge, a panic. 'If you paint over Rosa's mural, I will—'

But I didn't know what I would do. I got up and left Papa looking sad, looking down at the tablecloth. I was sick of all of them. Grown-ups, it seemed to me, were children. They said things that were big as though they were small. They made me responsible for their feelings. I went to the kitchen where I knew there were several leftover cannoli. I ate three in quick succession, and then threw up in the rubbish bin outside the back door.

IN THEATRE

Rosa was having her first proper solo exhibition. She had continued painting all this time, exhibiting her works in group shows alongside her friends, at small rooms in town halls, and sometimes in her painting workshop itself, with glasses of cheap wine and plates with biscuits and cheese. A painting of hers was used on the cover of a local community magazine – but poorly reproduced, cheaply printed: 'All the colours,' she said, 'gone right out from it.' She kept going though, cooking, painting, living. She pretended she didn't care that no one had ever bought one of her paintings. 'Don't need the money,' she said. But now she had her own show and 'It's gonna be a ripper,' she said, which was not a word she usually used. It sounded strange coming out of her mouth.

Florence Oakey gripped my arm in hers and winked at me and nodded like she knew something I didn't. Then she pinched Rosa and Rosa cracked up laughing and slapped her hand. They were a funny pair, not at all in competition even though they were both artists. Sometimes they didn't even seem like women at all, but like little girls dressed up as women – neither of them were more than five feet in height: dressed up for going out, they were like a couple of ageing twins. They could be very serious and boring when they talked about art – such things as Dame Elisabeth Murdoch's trusteeship of the National Gallery of Victoria; the impact of sculpture on the status of painting; Burn, Cutforth and Ramsden's show at Pinecotheca. But when they weren't talking about art, they had more fun than most adults. They shrieked a lot, and laughed, and slapped and pummelled each other. They took me to Luna Park and Florence bought waffles and Rosa bought fairy floss and they clinked their snacks together as though they were champagne glasses. Later they almost cried with laughter on the Scenic Railway. Everything was an opportunity to laugh or shriek.

People were very glad Rosa was finally having her own show. But she was not having it at Works on Paper. She had found another gallery and she wouldn't tell anybody except Mr Parish what it was called. 'Rosa's gallery shows daring art,' said Florence Oakey. 'They take risks,' said Rosa. 'They're a lot of rot,' said Mr Parish. But he said it in Rosa's hearing so he must not've meant it.

It occurred to me that nearly all the women had reasons to be excited that year. Mother's book was finally going to get published. Mrs Parish was about to get on the plane to Japan. Rosa was preparing to have her first solo show ...

Those who had categorically declared themselves *un*creative (you, Ornella) were not, however, having so good a time. You spent your waking hours banging against objects that gave no reprieve although they sustained you with their utility: bedpans, ECTs, catheters, cannulas.

It was 1970. I told Mother I wanted a little sister and she laughed and pretended to shoot me with a make-believe gun.

There may not have been any creative ambition being realised in your life, Ornella, but you had a new job working 'in theatre'. This gave you a lot of authority. I imagined 'theatre' as an intensely serious, curtain-draped place, with a raised viewing area and classical music playing. 'Nurse, pass me the *endothoracic scissors*,' the surgeon would say from behind his gauze mouthguard. And you would display said item before him on a little stainless-steel tray, and a well-mannered audience would clap quietly in their elbow-length gloves. It would be a little like an exhibition opening at Works on Paper: someone like Kitten (but not Kitten herself) would serve refreshments, and at the end, cheques might be written out and coats collected from the cloak-room.

'The hospital,' you said, 'is a world *unto itself*. I was sure you hadn't originated this phrase, and had learned it from some doctor or surgeon on his rounds, but it helped me imagine the hospital as a kind of ant-colony, a sprawling community of worker-creatures all buzzing around busily, saving lives. You always loomed large over the other worker ants in my imagination: a Mother Superior figure with a clipboard and upside-down watch-pin.

You never took me to the hospital with you, but I wanted to go. Sometimes, when you weren't cross, you acted out fragments of your working day for my illumination. You showed me the sanitary procedure for hand-washing (far too thorough for me to bother with); the right way to tie a sling on a dislocated arm; the nurse's time-honoured method for making a bed so tight it could strangle its occupant.

But sometimes you came home sad. Carlito would be either asleep and snoring, or watching TV. He'd tell you to be quiet if you talked through his shows. He was tired. He'd been lifting stuff all day. You'd shuffle in next to me on the boat-sized corduroy armchair, and, keeping your voice down so as not to annoy Carlito, tell me about the sad things that had happened on your shift.

'The old scientist,' you said, 'he lasted through the night, but when I came in this morning, they were zipping up the bag, O-yo. Such a horrible sound!'

'The woman who fell off the boat ... her children came in today. She's not waking up, O-yo. So sad watching them kiss her goodbye.'

'They have to amputate in the end. That man Jack I was telling you about? Both legs gotta come off above the knee. Haven't seen a man cry like that before, O-yo.'

These stories were grave and real. Horrifying and banal. They were your everyday stories. Drip-buckets and lesions. Weeping sores and brain-death. I wondered about poetry and paintings when I heard these stories. Poetry and paintings didn't help a man who had his legs cut off or was dying of lung disease. Did they?

Mr Parish said they did. Mr Parish said art helped with all the big questions. It didn't give answers, but it made sense of questions that couldn't otherwise be made sense of. Like dying. And pain.

'And happiness?' I asked.

'And happiness. But less frequently,' he said. 'When you're happy, you don't need art quite so much, I don't think. And I'm not sure you make it as well.'

'Mother must make very good poetry, then,' I said. 'Because she's unhappy all the time.'

Mr Parish considered me for some time. 'It's because she has talent,' he said. 'Otherwise she wouldn't suffer. It's not fun suffering. See if you can remember that.'

'Do you suffer?' I said.

He stopped and thought and fed a log further into the fire. 'Probably not enough,' he said finally. 'Probably I've made others suffer more than I should.' He turned and looked at me. 'You'll have to ask *Mrs* Parish about that.'

I didn't ask Mrs Parish. I already knew the answer. Mrs Parish *had* suffered, but she didn't anymore. *That* was how art helped, I realised.

And art had taken Mrs Parish away. We'd seen her off at the airport, where she cried expressively, partly on account of leaving Mr Parish and me, but also because she was so scared of flying. She gave us brusque kisses, and squeezed her bag to her chest. In that bag, I knew, she had a pill she could take when she got on the plane that would send her off to sleep until she landed. She called it her Magic Aeroplane Pill. But until she had popped it in her mouth and swallowed it down with water, she would remain terrified. I gave her arm a squeeze and nodded to remind her about the pill – I couldn't say it out loud because Mr Parish didn't know. And then she was gone, beyond the big doors only the impending airborne could pass through. Mr Parish and I got the car from the carpark and drove a very sombre, manly drive home, with the radio on and no conversation.

I thought Mr Parish would be glad that Mrs Parish had gone away. He never seemed to like her being around; she always annoyed him or made him cross. But once she was away he became mopey, like a child. He was scared to be alone: I knew that. He'd argued fiercely with you, Ornella, to have me there, in Mrs Parish's absence. 'It'll be good for him,' he said. 'He can help me outside. We'll get along famously.' But he didn't know what to do most of the time: he'd put his head into my room to check whether it was tea-time or not, and what time did I reckon the fire should be lit, and was it cold enough yet anyway? These were not questions I had ever heard him ask before. Meanwhile, he failed spectacularly at such things as bedtime and teeth-brushing, and would happily have let me wear the same clothes all week – except for my shoes, which he complained about constantly and made a big fuss of putting out the back door sprinkled with Mrs Parish's talcum powder.

Actually, he was a different man.

Kitten drove up one Friday night in her green Morris Minor. She brought a casserole and a salad and said she was only able to come because I was there and I was her 'safety-net'. 'Otherwise, what would the neighbours think!' she said with a tinkly laugh, and I told her our nearest neighbours were at least half a mile away and they would not know if we had visitors or not. We ate the casserole in silence – I just had potatoes and gravy – and then Kitten became out of breath and uncomfortable and left. Mr Parish drove her car back out to the main road for her, because the driveway was so steep. When he came back he was grim and tired and asked me where Mrs Parish kept the headache powders. I hadn't ever known him to have a headache before. There was a lot of casserole left but he scraped it in the bin. 'Mrs Parish,' he explained, 'understands my digestion. Kitten does not.'

'I wonder what Mrs Parish is eating in Japan right now,' I piped up, thinking of her at a restaurant wearing a kimono, with chopsticks in her hair, and another pair between her fingers, poised over a bowl of white noodles.

'I don't know,' said Mr Parish. 'What do they eat in Japan? Fish? Seaweed?' He pressed his hand down on the table and looked at it. His gold wedding ring made the skin on his fourth finger bunch and wrinkle. It looked like the kind of ring you'd have to get off with soap or with pliers or possibly via amputation. 'She'll be missing her toast and jam in the mornings,' he said. 'And her milky tea. She's a country girl in the end, Owen. Mrs Parish likes the plain things.' He nodded conclusively and brought his hands together in a dull clap.

But I didn't know if he was right. I thought Mrs Parish liked plain things, but she also liked uncommon things, and things that other people thought were ugly. I didn't think she'd be missing her jam toast one bit.

HIJACK NO. 1

When Japanese Airlines Flight 351 was hijacked by men with samurai swords and pipe-bombs, and over one hundred hostages were taken, Mr Parish went to his study and drank from his whisky bottle. Then he walked up and down the house, bumping into things and straightening them, and talking to himself. 'Bloody Japs!' I heard him say. In the end, because he had not sent me to bed and it was nearly midnight, I took myself there.

I didn't mind him being drunk. I didn't feel not-looked-after. It wasn't like with Mother. I didn't expect a man to look after me. To be manly, a boy had to look after himself. That's what Mr Parish had said to you, Ornella. Carlito had agreed. And that's what they did at boarding school, too, in the olden days – a boy would be left on his own as soon as he was dropped at the front gates and that's how he toughened up. I was reading *Tom Brown's Schooldays*. It scared the life out of me. Tom Brown was from the olden days, but I knew the same lessons were still true for boys and men. They had to learn to fend for themselves. Carlito knew the truth in this. 'Owen needs to toughen up!' Carlito said. 'I'll take him down the wharves with me. That'll do it.' You looked at him, Ornella, as though he were an idiot – and gave me my beans and egg. Food went down Carlito's throat like he didn't taste it – I watched him with amazement sometimes. He could drink like this too. You said he had an 'open gullet'; he didn't need to swallow, he could just pour liquid down his throat as though it were an open-ended tube. It was manly to drink fast and eat a lot, I knew this. It was not funny for a woman to burp or fart – it was embarrassing and a disgrace. Sometimes you did a little burp in your throat, Ornella, I saw it: you had to press your chin down to squash it before it came up. But Carlito 'let it rip', as you said. You would make a big fuss if he farted, and make him go out of the house, even if it was late at night. The more you said '*Che schifo*!' the more he laughed and enjoyed himself. I could burp and I could fart – in fact, I trained myself to be adept at both. But my vegetarianism was a failure of manliness, utterly and completely, and Carlito had only contempt for it. 'What's that in your veins?' he said, flicking at my forearm, 'Celery juice?' If he didn't call me Onion these days, he called me Vegetable – and I *knew* what a Vegetable was. He called Ornella 'Ornary', which meant Ordinary, which she knew she was anyway. He thought it was hilarious to call us these things, but Ornella just rolled her eyes and went on cutting or washing or wiping.

At the Parishes' they called farting 'fluffing' and only Paddy Cow was guilty of it. At the Parishes', in the absence of Mrs Parish, I brushed my teeth and got into my pyjamas and pulled back my bedclothes; I was a completely autonomous nearly-eleven-year-old person who had no need for grown-ups. Paddy Cow was on the verandah and I opened the window and pushed out the broken corner of the flywire so she could nuzzle my hand. Sometimes I thought I would sneak her into the bedroom, but I never did. Carlito would think it was funny if I brought the cow inside; maybe I'd do it one day just to show him I was not a Vegetable and make him laugh and slap me and give me the thumbs up.

I was glad Mrs Parish was not on the plane that got hijacked, and I hoped she didn't hear about it because if she did, she would *never* have the courage to get on a plane and come back.

I had a TAA badge and a sample of 4711 perfume from a plane trip Mr Parish had taken to Sydney. He went to Sydney to discuss his work on a radio station and 'give readings', which I imagined as him sitting on the edge of grown-ups' beds orating poetry from his boring old book while they fell asleep. He also brought back from the plane two sweet biscuits wrapped in crinkly cellophane, an apricot jam sachet, and a sachet of Vegemite. I put them into the wooden box next to my bed where I kept loose coins, interesting bits of stone and stray meccano pieces. The box said: 'EXPLOSIVE Safety Cartridges Class VI Ammunition Division. Not liable to explode in bulk IMPERIAL CHEMICAL INDUSTRIES AUSTRALIA AND NEW ZEALAND.' The words had been stamped in red once but now they were pink. I imagined explosives would start out red and become pink too, if they got old and dusty. Sometimes I dabbed 4711 on my wrists before going to the dinner table to make the house feel cosier, as though a woman was in it. I wondered what Mrs Parish was going to bring back for me. I hoped it would be something from the aeroplane and not something cultured and Japanesey, like an origami kit.

'Dear Owen,' wrote Mrs Parish in an Aerogram addressed especially to me. 'I really feel at home here. In Osaka the cherry blossoms are out, and it is the prettiest sight you can imagine! We are not so far from Australia, but still, in Japan, it is Spring while there you are, in Autumn. Isn't it strange? I am working very hard and yet feel quite relaxed and happy. Mr Tatsuo has suggested I extend my stay another two months, and I think I will say yes. There is so much to learn! My billeted family are very kind, but I think I will take a little place by myself. Of course, I miss you very much, Owen! You would have lots of fun here. I wish you could have come with me! What would that have been like?! Going to a Japanese School! (I'm not sure you would like it – their schools are very strict.)'

HOUSE OF MERIVALE

Letters had become little stabbing missiles. I didn't like Mrs Parish's letter because it sounded to me like she was having too much fun on her own. It made me cross. It made me stuck at Park Orchards with Mr Parish, who was kinder than usual, but left the toilet smelling bad and didn't put butter on my toast. But when I wrote Mrs Parish back, I assured her Mr Parish and I had *everything under control.* This denial of my real feelings gave me a lot of confidence. I felt solitary and strong. Even Papa commented on the change in me. He knocked me with the back of his knuckles as though I were a shell he was testing to see if it was empty and said: 'You're not a baby anymore, O-yo! So grown up. Soon you'll be asking girls out.' Then he did a brief mooching action with the tea-towel, as though the tea-towel was a girl and he was me, and I was stunned into silent embarrassment.

But the most stabbing letters, the most missile-like, were the ones that came for Mother. Every time Mother got a letter in the mail I sucked in my breath and closed my eyes, hoping it was just a bill. A bill would go on the hall table under an old lead weight that said 8 oz, and Papa would sort it so that Mother never had to think about it again. But a letter, a letter with the logo of Vellum Press and revisions tucked inside, always spelled bad news. I wished the post never came on a Thursday, when I was there, but it always did, and it always seemed to be the day when the bad letters came. Mother would slam things around, and I would have to tiptoe about the house until she calmed down. 'Bastards!' she'd say. She'd have a drink from her white or yellow bottle, and then another. Sometimes she'd take herself to her writing desk and write manically for twenty minutes – usually a letter of outrage that she wouldn't send. Sometimes she'd read it out to me: 'Dear Mr Editor Bastard, No, I don't think removing the line *Bastards are everywhere* in any way improves this poem …' And sometimes she'd just wear herself out and fall asleep on the couch.

Once, when I got home from school, I found her asleep on the couch with her dressing gown undone and her underwear showing. What if I'd brought a friend home with me? The record was even bumping on the player. How could someone sleep through a record bumping? I crept into the living room, and threw a blanket over her. I moved the stylus off the record in the way she'd shown me, and then I felt like I was going to be sick, so I went outside and peeled some bark off the paperbark tree and listened to cars go up and down the street. *I hate you I hate you I hate you*, I said into the tree trunk, but I may as well have said, *I love you I love you I love you*. It would've been just the same, and just as awful.

She didn't make dinner that night but I knew how to work the can-opener and could easily heat up spaghetti from a can.

I gave her some on her own plate when she woke up and we watched TV together.

What did Mother do on the other days? I had no idea, but I imagined her sitting around in her dressing gown waiting for the mail to give her grief.

Mother was dragging herself into action. She had decided to go shopping for a dress for her book launch. 'C'mon O-yo,' she said. 'You're going to help me. What colour do you think suits me? Blue?'

She made me stay in her room with her while she got dressed to go shopping. I sat on the bed looking at the floor while she put on perfume. '*What* shall I wear?' she said, flashing item after item at me from her wardrobe. All of her clothes looked grey in the light of her bedroom. 'Can't I just wait til you're ready?' I said. And then she looked at me, hurt, and said: 'Yes, yes, O-yo. Stupid me. Go outside. Stupid old Mother, treating you like a girl.'

I got out of the room quick-smart and went and bounced a ball in the driveway where the bricks were wonky. I scowled and tried out some swear words. I tore a big chunk of bark off the paperbark tree and carved my initials in the soft, fleshy surface underneath. I checked the letter-box which contained a letter for Mrs J. Ferrugia, which I thought was funny because they had mistaken my father for a woman. But still she didn't come.

'Mother!!' I yelled through the open front door.

Maybe she was taking her time putting *eyeshadow* on. I didn't connect her, not really, with the girls in sixth grade at my school, but that's what they were all interested in, the girls at school – eyeshadow and lipstick and pretty hair. That's what it came down to. I was learning to be contemptuous of them, and their stupid interest in soft things like powder and eyeshadow and how their hair looked. When I mentioned this to Carlito, he lifted his can of beer in salute. 'Get used to it!' he said. But I didn't really understand, because you weren't like that, Ornella. Carlito *wanted* you to dress up. 'Make yourself look pretty, willya?' he said, when you pinned your hair back tight with a straight part down the middle. 'You look like a widow,' he complained, 'and not the good type.' You glared at him and applied a deathly smudge of black eyeliner. 'Shut up,' you warned him, 'Or I *will* be a widow.'

In the dress shops, Mother was embarrassing. A year earlier, I might've thought her amusing – flirting with the shop assistants, trying things on and admiring herself in the mirror – a year ago I had wanted her to admire herself in the mirror. I had wanted her to be happy and look nice in new clothes so other people thought *Owen's mother is nice, isn't she? Isn't she pretty?* Now it was too late. Now I hated it. I stood in the corner of House of Merivale and fumed. I was not a girl. I should not have been made to go into clothes shops, and wait in change rooms, and give her advice about embarrassing things. I could see other people feeling sorry for me. If a boy saw me in here, a boy from school or a boy from the park, I would never live it down. A lump came in my chest and then rose in my throat and, finally, settled in my cheekbones. It felt like when you eat bread too fast, only the bread was stuffed with razorblades.

When she'd decided, finally, on what she wanted – something stupid and blue with frills on the bottom – she got the shop assistants to box it up and announced we were going to the Knoxes for a visit.

NIGHTINGALE

I hadn't seen the Knoxes for months. Mr Knox had lost weight and, also, it seemed, energy. He was a sadder version of himself. His face hung differently. 'You'll have to excuse me, Veda,' he said, 'I'm off my game,' and ran his hand through his hair.

'It's been exhausting,' said Mrs Knox, getting out the sherry. 'Everyone's felt it. Barrington's been sick as a dog. We thought it was pneumonia!'

'But it was only bronchitis,' said Mr Knox. He smiled wanly. 'Bloody lungs.'

Mother tut-tutted. Mrs Knox got her an ashtray.

'Look at what I've bought,' said Mother. She pulled the dress-box out of its bag, fumbled through the tissue-paper, held up the glossy blue garment. 'Merivale.'

'Oh goodness,' said Mrs Knox, putting her head to one side.

'Brilliant!' said Mr Knox.

'Goodness!' said Mrs Knox again.

Mother's face fell. 'Is it not serious enough?'

'It's beautiful!' said Mrs Knox, putting out a hand to touch it.

'Oh!' said Mother, crestfallen. 'I've made a mistake, haven't I?'

'Not in the slightest,' said Mr Knox. 'You will look like a songbird in that, Veda. A beautiful nightingale.'

'Nightingales are brown,' said Mother. 'Oh I've made a mistake. I should've gone for something more serious.'

'Oh no no *no*!' said Mrs Knox. Mother had gone to bundle the blue thing up, but Mrs Knox took it and smoothed it and cajoled it back into its box like something precious and dear to her. 'It's perfect,' she said.

Mother sighed and picked up her cigarettes. 'Oh well ...' she said. There was silence for some time while she processed her mistake.

Everyone, not knowing what to do, turned to me.

'What?' I said.

'You're so tall!' said Mrs Knox, wonderingly.

'And handsome!' said Mr Knox. He looked at me with narrowed eyes.

'Beautiful, isn't he?' said Mother. She regarded me suspiciously for a few moments as though my 'beauty' were in some way related to her buying the wrong dress. I scowled. My eyebrows were darkening and I could feel my eyes sink beneath them.

'Rosa should paint him!' said Mr Knox, coughing and lighting a cigarette. 'Before the moment passes. Whilst he's in the *throes of his beauty*.'

'Yes, it's a metamorphic beauty, isn't it,' said Mother. She cocked her head again. I didn't like the look in her eyes. She was summing me up. 'It'll be gone in a year or so.' She took a sip of sherry. 'And then he'll be lantern-jawed and all knees.'

What was she talking about? *Lantern-jawed*?

Mrs Knox smiled at me. 'You are quite the young man, Owen,' she said. 'Don't listen to our foolishness.'

Mother nudged the dress-box out of the way with her bottom, holding her drink aloft so it didn't spill. I felt guilty now, ashamed. If she'd had a proper advisor in the dress-shop with her, she wouldn't have made a mistake.

Mr Knox took pity on me. He could see I was out of sorts. 'Have a sherry, Owen,' he said, and poured me one.

But I didn't want sherry. I wanted suddenly to be as far away from the three of them as possible. I didn't fit into their cosy little threesome anymore. I had become too big. Too lantern-jawed. You couldn't just give me a box of pencils. I had finished with dinosaur drawings. I got up and started looking at a shelf of books on China.

'What's the news then?' I heard Mother ask.

Mrs Knox considered. 'Well ...' she said. 'We've seen a lot of Rosa. She's come in a lot, hasn't she, Barry? She's been quite the regular.'

'Doesn't buy much, doesn't buy *anything*, but then we don't stock a lot of art-books ...'

Mrs Knox continued. 'It's been lovely, having her around. She's so friendly. We really like her. We've had a couple of *really* pleasant afternoons with her and her friend.'

'Florence,' said Mother in a voice that sounded almost cross. But then she said it again, more nicely. 'Florence Oakey.'

'Yes, lovely Florence Oakey.'

Mrs Knox, it seemed, had made friends with Rosa and Florence. I hoped this wouldn't aggravate Mother. But Mother seemed perfectly comfortable with the development.

'Yes,' Mother said. 'Cheers to Florence Oakey.'

'Oh yes,' said Mrs Knox. 'Wasn't her show wonderful! I won't forget that in a long time.'

'Wonderful bit of brinkmanship.' Mr Knox beamed and

looked, for a moment, more like his normal self. 'Has the drawbridge come down, then?'

'I think,' said Mother, 'the drawbridge stays up well and truly. Or, at least, comes down only under very special circumstances.'

What drawbridge were they talking about? I pulled out a book on the Great Wall of China. There were no pictures, just some diagrams and cross-sections.

'Well, it's a precedent,' said Mr Knox. 'A beginning. Not that that means much.'

'Oh I think it means a lot!' said Mrs Knox. 'You watch out, Barry. You just watch out. We can't wait for Rosa's show, Veda.'

Mr Knox rolled his eyes at Mother in a way that was amused but not mean. 'Rosa's concept is about as avant-garde as I've heard. Be interesting to see how it goes down.'

Mrs Knox leaned closer to Mother. 'She tried a good half a dozen galleries, didn't she, Barrington? And it was all, No, no, no, no, no. *No one* was interested. You've got to admire her persistence.'

'Yes,' said Mother. 'She's sturdy. Like a tank.'

'But this gallery – Katie Bitto, who runs it, a young woman, says she's *only going to exhibit women artists*! Can you imagine? No men at all! The newspapers are saying it's "galling female chauvinism"!'

'Brilliant stunt, I think!' said Mr Knox. 'I can just see them, bristling all over.'

Mother was getting tetchy and excited at the same time, I could feel it. 'You'd better tell me about this show of Rosa's,' she said. 'I don't know anything about it. I thought I was going to see Northern Italian landscapes. En masse. And I might start getting cross if you don't put me in the picture. With the concept, at least.'

'I never understand what *concept* means,' I said loudly. I flicked to an illustration of an elaborate pagoda. 'As a word. Is it the same as *idea*?' It sounded Chinese, I thought, if you said it quickly.

But nobody answered me.

'Come on. What is it Rosa's doing exactly?' said Mother. 'Tell me! Rosa would, you know, if she were here herself.'

'You're right,' said Mrs Knox. 'You're right, Rosa would. Well ... it's almost like a joke as much as anything really, isn't it, Barry?'

'Sort of.' Mr Knox was enjoying keeping Mother in the dark. 'No one's ever said an artist can't have a sense of humour.'

'Has Rosa got a sense of humour?'

'Oh yes,' said Mrs Knox. 'A very well-developed one.'

'Is *concept* the same as *idea*?' I asked again, more loudly now. I knew the word *avant-garde*. Kitten was always flinging *avant-garde* into her conversation. She'd say just about anything was *avant-garde*: a scarf, a way of arranging food on a plate. But *concept* felt important somehow. It felt bigger than its two syllables: it felt like a dangerous missile I had to understand to deactivate. I saw how it made Mother's eyes light up. I stamped my foot. '*Is* concept *Chinese for* idea?'

Mr Knox gave me his attention, suddenly and completely. '*Concept*, Owen,' he said, 'is the *intellectual thought that precedes the execution of an artwork*.'

'Oh God help him,' said Mother and laughed.

Mrs Knox considered me very seriously. 'Take no notice of Barrington.' She looked me straight in the eye. 'Yes Owen,' she said. 'You're exactly right: *concept* is Chinese for *idea*.'

Mother and Mr Knox burst into laughter. Mrs Knox didn't.

I relaxed. I trusted Mrs Knox. I didn't even care that I'd been the butt of a joke somehow. I went and looked at the Chinese bookshelf again. I found a book on the sayings of Confucius. Confucius says: 'You are what you think.' Confucius says: 'Choose a job you love and you will never have to work a day in your life.' Confucius says: 'He who knows all the answers has not been asked all the questions.' I put Confucius under my arm and wondered if Chinese and Japanese were pretty much the same thing. Mrs Parish was coming home and I thought I would ask her if they had Confucius in Japan. He seemed to think about things in the same way Mrs Parish thought about flower arrangements: slowly and with very few words.

And then I heard laughter break out and saw Mother, in the corner of my eye, half falling off her chair. 'Oh god,' she was saying and waving her cigarette around. 'What a bloody good serve! Here's to Rosa for being braver than the rest of us.'

Mrs Knox clapped her hands, and even Mr Knox laughed at Mother's hilarity.

I had chosen three books: one on calligraphy, one on Confucius, and one, from a neighbouring shelf, on the Trojan Horse. Mother said I was mixing my influences and she wouldn't pay for all three. But Mrs Knox put them in a paper-bag anyway, and Mother didn't notice and Mrs Knox didn't charge her.

HIJACK NO. 2

In fact, Rosa's exhibition was not Chinese for idea at all, not to my thinking, anyway. But it was definitely a *Trojan Horse.* She had got something *into the inside* that was not supposed to be there. She had performed an *artistic subterfuge.*

I went to the opening at Gallery K with Mother and Papa and Mr Parish and Kitten. We met first at La Coccinella for a drink. Mrs Parish was supposed to be there – we were supposed to have welcomed her back from Japan the night before – but she hadn't come home, yet again.

There had been a telegram, followed by an aerogram, followed by a four-page letter that Mr Parish took off to his study with his bottle of whisky. In the morning, the bottle was nearly empty, and he was asleep and there were strings of spittle vibrating in his mouth when he breathed. Luckily it was a Saturday and I didn't have to go to school. I had to make my own breakfast, but I had been capable for some time now of lighting the griller. I didn't know how to work the coffee percolator, which required the fitting together of complex metal pieces, but I understood about tea, about one spoon each and one for the pot, so I made a pot for Mr Parish and took it to him and he looked like I was rescuing him from drowning in a flooded creek.

It was very odd being in a bachelor house with Mr Parish. That was what he called it: our *bachelor house*, but he said it like a bachelor who doesn't want to be one. I was cross with Mrs Parish for changing her departure date, but at the same time the crossness was softening and I began to imagine her never coming back. I understood, strangely and completely, that I would be alright if she never came back. She was my companion, my respectful grown-up companion, and I wanted her to do all the things in life she wanted to do, because she did them without fuss and without anger. Unlike Mother, art made Mrs Parish calm and strong. It made her stronger and taller than it made anyone I knew. Art made Mother sad, Mr Parish silly, and Rosa overexcited.

At the restaurant, on the night of Rosa's opening, Mr Parish drank a lot of alcohol again – he drank so much that, when it was time to depart for the gallery, he couldn't get his arms in his coat properly and Kitten had to help him. Mother parsimoniously finished her single glass of white wine and placed her empty glass on the table. Only I knew it wasn't her only glass of wine for the day.

Outside, Papa hailed two taxis, one for us, and one for Kitten and Mr Parish, and we got to the gallery seconds before Rosa's patience ran out.

'Hello, my friends!' she said, relieved when we arrived. She stood just inside the gallery door, in a red suit and black shoes and her hair dyed so dark black it was almost purple. She had makeup on too: red lipstick and blue eyeshadow. Makeup did not suit her; she looked like a puppet version of herself. Florence Oakey swept up to us and kissed us coolly on both cheeks. Papa presented Rosa with a bunch of wilting flowers that had spent all day in a bucket in the restaurant kitchen. I took a photocopied catalogue from a lady wearing large black-rimmed glasses like Nana Mouskouri and went inside to look at the paintings.

I told you afterwards, didn't I, Ornella, about the paintings? I can't remember what you said: 'Stupid, *stupid*'. Or 'Smart, *smart*'. Depended how much money Rosa would ultimately make from it: your main point of reference for aesthetic value. 'I don't get it,' you said once to me, 'What makes one picture worth millions and another picture worth nothing? Who gets to choose?' In 1974, when the National Gallery of Victoria bought Jackson Pollock's *Blue Poles* painting for four million dollars, you screwed up the newspaper in disgust.

Rosa's catalogue had the big black word 'ERASURE' on the front, and then (in brackets) 'CANCELLAZIONE' which I knew how to say because I could read and pronounce Italian words even though I rarely understood what they meant. It was funny how the same words had different feelings in different languages. 'Erasure' sounded heavy and final; 'Cancellazione' sounded like a dance. I would ask you about this, I thought, folding the catalogue into my back pocket, but I never did. You would probably think it was silly: that a word could be like a dance. Mother would understand it though. *Why didn't I ask Mother about it?*

This is how I remember Rosa's exhibition:

Twenty-six paintings, all of which were white. Twenty-six white paintings on white walls with white lights shining upon them. Some people laughed nervously; others proceeded around the gallery a little hushed, as though all that white had *erased* their ability to think, or at least to put their thoughts in smart words the way people usually did at an exhibition. I'd been to enough openings at Works on Paper, I knew how it went: people stood around and said things that sounded smart, and then wandered off to get drunk. They didn't really care, but it made the artist feel good, to have all those people there, looking smart, saying smart things.

Rosa's paintings defied comment. They were like *ikebana*. What do you say about ikebana: 'It's very still. Very pretty. *Thank you.*' I wished Mrs Parish were here. She would understand Rosa's paintings. Because even though it seemed silly, like a joke – all 26 paintings being white, every single one of them – the effect of all that white wasn't silly at all. In total, all collected together like that, they had a kind of power. And when you went up close, you realised there was another trick: *they weren't just white at all.* You had to peer really hard through the white surface, but underneath it there were other pictures. Phantom pictures of towns and houses and people, skies and gardens and walls, mountains. All painted over in white. Shimmering shapes that didn't really exist, like mirages. They were like Pompeii looked, after the volcano came: dead but alive at the same time. Petrified.

Kitten elbowed me in the ribs and passed me a glass of soda water. Her hair was coming out of her combs, and her mascara had run. But she still looked beautiful: half movie star, half pet. 'Is this art?' she whispered. 'Is it, Owen?' She didn't wait for my reply, but linked arms with me and we went around together. '*I* think it is,' she said, slopping some red wine on my shoes in her enthusiasm.

I thought it was too. I was fully decided. I would tell Rosa when I saw her and it would make her really happy.

'You know what I'm going to do?' said Kitten. She let go of my arm and turned to face me. 'I'm going to buy one!' She looked around the gallery. 'Which one, O-yo? Which is your favourite?'

And then it was really funny, because we went round and round the gallery deciding which painting Kitten should buy.

'This one?' 'No, this one!' 'Hmmm,' said Kitten, pointing, 'that one's too white!' and we burst into laughter.

'What are you up to?' said Mr Parish, sidling up to us. 'What are you two concocting?' He was still drunk and I could tell he wanted to put his arm around Kitten.

But Kitten nudged me and put her finger to her lips, and we burst out laughing again, and the joke was on Mr Parish. It seemed so hysterically funny, all of a sudden, that the joke could be on Mr Parish. Kitten pinched me and we ran away.

I was glad to be with Kitten. Kitten was the perfect person that evening to be with. She had no artistic pretending to do: she was not on duty. She had no responsibility to me beyond making me laugh. She bought a white painting with the very faint outline of a garden behind it. Hers was the first red sticker. But others followed. And Rosa's joke was not a joke at all. Not a trick. Not a joke. Not even a concept. It was a Trojan horse.

Kitten and I laughed and laughed and when she smoked, she laughed so much it came out of her nostrils like a dragon.

AFTERMATH

The morning after the exhibition, Papa took me to your house, Ornella. He was dishevelled and hungover. I'd told him I could ride my bike but he dragged himself up and started the car still wearing his dressing gown. You already had your grocery bag in the fold of your arm and your purse in your hand, waiting. Carlito was snoring, and you closed the bedroom door so we didn't have to hear him. 'I will buy you one cinnamon doughnut,' you said to me. 'Two, if you're very good. What is *wrong* with your hair?' You scrabbled at it with your free hand and glared at Papa, who retreated to the car and reversed without caution from his parking spot. 'That man!' you said. 'He's a disgrace.'

The Richmond market was full of people. There was squashed fruit on the bitumen and a smell of dirt and bracchia. I saw an old woman put her hand in between other people's hands and steal three tomatoes from a stall. She had a string bag with single items in it: an orange, an apple, an onion. She put her three tomatoes in the top. Her hair had bits of bracken or tobacco stuck in it and her clothes looked like they had come out of a bin. I elbowed you. 'That old lady just stole tomatoes,' I said.

I expected you to be outraged. I expected you to run after her and say, 'Excuse me, *madam*!' Instead, you glanced up and then returned your gaze to me coldly. 'Just be quiet, Owen,' you said. 'Just be quiet, will you. So rude of you. Just be quiet.'

I dug my hands into my pockets crossly.

Everything was topsy-turvy and stupid. Nothing made sense. An old lady took things from a stall without paying for them and *I* got into trouble.

At the doughnut van, you gave me my measly paper bag with its one measly doughnut and it went down in two stupid bites, like nothing. What was the good in a doughnut when it went down in two bites? Nothing was satisfying. Nothing lasted. 'I'm still hungry,' I said. 'So rude,' you said. 'I shouldn't've got you even one doughnut, rude boy.'

All the good feeling from the night before, the fun with Kitten, the buying of the painting, evaporated. I was beginning to understand that that was the way things worked. Everything that made a person feel good ran out. That was it. That was how it was.

'Cruel to be kind, O-yo,' you said later, as we walked back up Bridge Road and I still wasn't talking to you. You kept walking for a bit, then, 'You've got to learn compassion for people, Owen. Like your father has.'

What were you talking about? I thought you said Papa was a disgrace.

Nothing made sense. I was in Grade Six. Puberty was the explanation for my bafflement. That's what you told Carlito when we got home and I shut myself in my room. Carlito thought the idea of me having puberty was hilarious. But puberty was not hilarious. Puberty meant nothing was fun anymore, and none of the fun things lasted.

The reviews came out for Rosa's show. There were several. Two or three were cruel. One was humiliating. Two were positive. Merely getting that many write-ups was a *coup*. Rosa now had press-clippings. Mother cut them out of the paper with her nail-scissors. She pinned them, scallop-edged, to a corkboard above her writing desk. 'Rosa Rosa Rosa,' she said, swaying slightly.

In the same week, there was a feature in the local press about Papa. Not about La Coccinella – La Coccinella didn't need press because it had as many customers as it could take – but about Papa and the Salvation Army soup kitchen. 'Mr Ferrugia,' the article said, 'restaurateur and art collector, is tireless in his efforts for the underprivileged. "Everyone deserves good food," Mr Ferrugia says. "We are blessed in this lucky country and we should share what we have with those less fortunate. For me, I share my skills and my good fortune in having been successful in my business." The Salvation Army kitchen has become a reliable focal point for the unemployed and homeless of Melbourne.'

Mother did not cut out this article and put it on her cork-board. Nor did Papa. It embarrassed him. 'I look stupid in the picture,' he said. But I cut it out and kept it. Because even though photographs can lie – Papa *does* look stupid in the picture – words actually tell more than pictures, despite wisdom to the contrary. Those words, aligned with that picture, are a kind of documentary evidence that memory can't compete with. In fact, you need all three – words, pictures, *and* memory – to piece together the truth.

The good fortune of the homeless and unemployed of Melbourne was the bad fortune of Veda and Owen Ferrugia. That was the bit not told by the newspaper. Papa spent hardly any time at home because he was so busy with the restaurant and the soup kitchen. If we wanted Papa we had to go to him, and Mother wouldn't, and I had better things to do than watch him make small talk with diners and fuss over culinary details. I loved Papa, but love had become duty. And part of my duty was to show him I didn't care or need him. Fathers were supposed to be busy with other things. That's how *the bacon made it home*. That's how *the wolves were kept from the door*. Papa wrote out the cheques and Mother put the stamps on the envelopes and took them down to the letterbox with her fat little dog trotting by her side. 'My husband's mistress,' she told Mrs Mathers next door, 'is his work.' 'Oh yes,' said Mrs Mathers. 'Yes, that's how it is, dear.'

PLOTTING

Mother was plotting. She had spent a horrible amount of time sleeping, and lazing around, and being generally an embarrassment to me. I was glad she had got her energy back, but it was a feverish, unpredictable energy. She wasn't a writer anymore, she said; she was an inventor of plots to foil publishers. 'I'm going to write a sonnet,' she said. 'They want a sonnet? I'm going to give them a *beautiful* sonnet. A sonnet they'll never forget!' She was almost rubbing her hands in glee.

I was reading *Asterix*, with a plate of lamingtons balancing on the chair-arm next to me. 'What's a sonnet?' I said idly, not really caring.

'A sonnet, O-yo,' she said, 'A sonnet, my *dear dear O*-yo, is a fourteen-line poem, usually in iambic pentameter, and ending in a rhyming couplet.'

I nodded and she drew her breath sharply inward and retreated to her writing desk. I did not see her again that evening.

When I got hungry, I whipped an egg with milk and grated cheese and scrambled it in the crepe-pan. There was no bread, so I buttered two Weetbix and added Vegemite. Sometimes I mixed the Vegemite and the butter so it was an indistinguishable paste: pale brown. Papa had beer in the fridge, and Carlito had already begun teaching me how to drink beer, so I had a glass of beer. No one minded me falling asleep on the couch anymore. So I fell asleep on the couch. It was as good as my bed, which was never made, and had a strange sour smell where I'd spilt a milkshake.

It was only at your house these days, Ornella, that I was actually 'put to bed' in the old-fashioned sense of being regulated and bossed around. No one else bothered with 'lights out, school tomorrow'. In this sense, you had become the bane of my life. 'A child your age needs eleven hours sleep a night. Do you hear me? Eleven hours!' And then, in the morning, over breakfast, you punished me by making me recite the times tables. Then there was teeth-brushing. Shoe-polishing. Hair-combing. Where was my library book? Why hadn't I eaten yesterday's banana? What would you do with a kid who didn't eat his bloody banana?

At Mother's house, I sailed to school in the same clothes as yesterday, with money for the milk bar I'd got out of her milk-and-bread-jar. I could get a pie. I could get a piece of battered flake. I could get Redskins or Milkbottles or even Fags. I was scared, sometimes, by all the choice.

'You've started to drink again, Veda,' said Papa. 'You need to get a grip on yourself. You don't want to fall back into it. You've been doing so well.'

We were home, in the house in Hawthorn, all of us together for a change. Papa had unbuttoned his vest. He ran his hand through his hair and looked tired. 'I'll cook a *banquet* for your book launch, okay? You can invite whoever. I'll do whatever you like: lamb, veal. We'll have a big celebration. Then, after that, you've got to stop drinking. Once and for all. For good.'

Mother's eyes looked brightly unseeing at Papa. 'Yes,' she said. 'That sounds fair, Jo.'

I thought she was mocking him, but Papa seemed satisfied with her answer. I knew Mother hated Papa these days. She had an iron glint in her eyes when she looked at him.

'Good,' he said. 'Well. I'm going to bed. You'll take Owen to school in the morning?'

'Oh yes, Jo,' said Mother.

What was Papa even talking about? Didn't he know I rode to school by myself?

'Alright, well, I'll see you in the morning.' He went to go to the bedroom and then turned back. 'I'm serious – you've got to do something about it after the launch, Veda. Okay?'

'Okay Jo,' said Mother.

Papa eyed her strangely. He hesitated again and then came over to her and put his hands on her shoulders. But it wasn't a patient loving-hands-on-shoulders; it was a listen-to-me-and-do-what-I-say hands-on-shoulders.

Mother was an alien to those hands. She looked at Papa, clean in the eyes, and smiled the strangest smile. I felt panicky. The house smelt bad. Some of the washing had fallen into the flowerbeds and every time I looked through the windows and saw it I felt strange.

Mother angled out from under Papa's hands. 'Just give me a second, Jo,' she said and went into the bathroom.

They had forgotten I was there, both of them. Maybe they thought I was in bed. Or maybe I was supposed to be in bed, and was hiding behind the yellow velvet curtains, watching? How else did I see these things, Ornella? It doesn't make sense.

I heard the toilet flush and Mother came back into the room, swaying a little and waving her hairbrush. It was a large old-fashioned hairbrush: yellow, made of some kind of bone perhaps, heavy. I knew it could be lethal. She wove it around in front of Papa's face while she talked very low and very determinedly at him. I couldn't hear what she was saying. Papa put his hand up at the hairbrush, and pushed it away as though it annoyed him.

'Yes, *push* it away,' Mother said. '*Push* it away, Jo.'

Because she couldn't wave it in front of him anymore, because he'd put his hand up, Mother turned as if she had had enough. But then she turned back suddenly, lifted her arm and brought the hairbrush down on the side of his face. It thwacked hard on Papa's cheekbone.

'Jesus!' Papa said. He caught hold of Mother's wrist. He tried to pry the hairbrush out of her hand but couldn't. 'You're a lunatic! Stop this!'

Mother broke free, still holding the hairbrush.

'You've hurt me!' Papa said. He put his hand to his cheekbone.

At this, Mother started laughing a horrible laugh.

'*Jesus*!' said Papa. 'You're a madwoman!'

Mother laughed and laughed and laughed and I wanted to run over and push her, right in the middle of her stomach, so she went crashing up against the wall and had the laughter flung out of her. I wanted to push her and ram a cushion over her whole laughing stupid face. *Why couldn't she say Yes Jo and mean it? Why did she have to ruin things when he was just trying to be a good husband?*

Papa lunged for the hairbrush and Mother shrieked, jumped back, threw it on the floor at his feet. Only it bounced, and when it bounced its trajectory was clear and inevitable: it went straight through the back window, the glass coming down in little shaky diamonds around it. Papa yelled again,

'You're a fucking madwoman!' and came toward her as though he wanted to kill her, but Mother leapt away and locked herself in the bathroom.

She spent the whole night in the bathroom. It was cold there, I thought: those tiles, they were so cold. And dirty. In between them, where the grout was, was all black and mouldy. They really needed scrubbing with a toothbrush or a nailbrush, they needed a damn good scrub, and they were cold and hard.

My bedroom was on the other side of the wall. 'Owen!' Mother said to me through the wall. '*Owen*. Owen! O-yo. *Please, O-yo*. Bring me some blankets, will you, and a pillow, *O-yo!*'

But I wouldn't come. Why would I come in the bathroom with her? Why would I go and look after her? She didn't look after me. Not properly. Not like a real mother. *Why would I?*

There were towels in there, weren't there? She could make a bed with them in the bath.

2016 DOLL THERAPY

Last week, I tell Julia, they did doll therapy with some of the dementia patients at the care unit where Ornella lives. Mainly the women, but some of the men too. All sorts of dolls were brought in: rag dolls, hard plastic dolls, even china dolls. One resident took to her doll with particular passion. She nursed her doll all day. She brought her doll to meals and we had to set up a makeshift highchair for it. She tended to her doll, brushing its hair, tying on its bib. And then yesterday, we noticed that the doll had gone. There was Rose-Marie, at the breakfast table, eating her Weeties as usual, but the doll was nowhere to be seen. When we asked Rose-Marie where Baby was, she just smiled a strange sated smile.

At the end of my visit, one of the carers found the doll under Rose-Marie's bed. It had been cut down the middle with something – a knife? scissors? They don't even allow residents to have such things in their rooms – and all her stuffing had been pulled out. The head and feet and hands were still connected by threads of fabric, but the doll was otherwise dismembered, disembowelled. There was something gluey in her hair and in her eyes that we couldn't work out unless Rose-Marie had broken into the craft storeroom and stolen a bottle of PVA.

I tell this to Julia, who is correcting university papers and perhaps only partially paying attention. 'I don't understand,' I say. 'She was getting such joy from the doll.'

Julia, ever able to multi-task, does not look up from her papers. 'Maybe she felt the baby was threatened,' she says. 'That happens, you know. When a mother animal feels her baby is threatened, she eats it sometimes. To protect it.' She makes a mark with her red pen. 'Cats,' she says. 'Mother cats will sometimes do it. Particularly if they're inbred. Siamese cats, for instance.'

THE POEMS OF VEDA GRAY

One morning, not long before Mother's book was due to be published, John Honey turned up on our doorstep. He looked exactly like his name: yellow hair, tanned face, brown corduroy jacket. 'Veda,' he said in a waxy voice. He had flowers and a gift-wrapped copy of her proofs.

Mother had let me stay home from school that day because I had hurt my leg in a crash on my bike. The front wheel of my bike was mangled beyond recovery; my ankle was twisted. It was all because of a dog running in front of me. I didn't like dogs. I didn't like Mother's dog, Griffin, who salivated when you patted him and left everything he touched feeling damp. I was on the couch with my leg propped up on cushions, reading an abridged version of *Moby Dick*. I was struggling to understand how it was that Herman Melville could write so lovingly about whales, and yet so matter-of-factly about killing them. When they stripped the whale blubber off the dead whale, it went round and round like orange skin being peeled from an orange, and I wanted to be sick. It made me think of Paddy Cow. The whale babies were even called calves. Whale mothers had two teats in case they had twins, just like human women.

Mother made John Honey real coffee that filled the kitchen with a good rich smell. I could tell she was embarrassed, him arriving unawares like that, and her without any makeup on. Nobody visited her just on the off-chance.

Her conversation with John Honey, as she made the coffee, was stilted and boring. John Honey praised Mother, and Mother thanked John Honey. John Honey loosened his pale yellow tie and took off his brown cord jacket. Mother apologised about the state of the house. John complimented the coffee. Mother said she'd need something stronger than coffee pretty soon to get her through 'this publishing malarkey.' And they'd both laughed.

I kept reading. Mr Parish said *Moby Dick* was a classic, and all boys should read it if they wanted to understand what being a man was all about. I thought Ishmael was a nice man, and Herman Melville too. That's why I couldn't understand about killing the whales. I would rather have candlelight forever than kill whales to get oil for lamps. I would never eat a whale steak, not even if I were starving on a desert island.

It wasn't till Mother reached over to open the parcel John Honey'd brought that I wrested my attention from Queequeg and Stubb to watch.

Mother opened the parcel very carefully so as not to rip the paper. She looked up at John Honey and laughed and then parted the paper and there they were: her creamy new page proofs. A cover in brown and tan with her name on it. 'Gosh!' she said, 'Somehow it hadn't occurred to me that my name would be there, like that, so big!'

She turned the pages over. They looked quite beautiful, I had to admit, peering over the top of my book. All that space around the lines, and a very nicely chosen font. *The Poems of Veda Gray*. 214 pages of them. Measured out, on cream, in black, with serifs.

'Gosh!' said Mother. 'Oh John!'

'Congratulations,' said John.

'I feel like an imposter!'

'Oh, that's normal.'

Mother turned over the pages, a few at a time, and then referred back to the Contents, with her finger marking where she was up to. 'So, what do I do now? Do I read over them?'

'Well, that's the point, I guess,' said John. 'Check them. Make sure there are no typos, errors.'

Mother kept going through the pages, not quite rifling, but with a certain subtle agitation. She spent quite a bit of time looking through them, and then referring back to the Contents page, and I could tell John Honey was getting nervous.

'John,' she said at last, not looking at him. 'I think one's missing.'

John Honey grimaced and swallowed his coffee. He reminded me of Papa when he was guilty of letting Mother down. Or Jimmy Panageorgiou when he got in trouble in class and blamed me or George or Callum. 'I know, Veda,' he said and put his coffee cup down. 'I've got to say the coward in me hoped you wouldn't notice.'

Mother's mouth hung just a little more open than normal but otherwise she checked her dismay admirably. 'They've cut "Monastery Maiden". Why?'

'It was McMannish who decided, in the end.'

'But why?' said Mother.

John Honey's honey colour had deserted him; he had gone red in the face. 'McMannish thought it was a little,' he grimaced again, '*lewd* for, you know, a book of poetry by a woman.'

Now Mother's mouth fully dropped open.

'Lewd!' she said. 'But – but it's all so heavily veiled. That's the whole point of it.'

'There's the line,' John continued, 'about the mortar and the pestle, the grinding, etcetera, of the grain. I know it's a, well, sort of a *joke*, on your part, but he thought it was coming on a bit heavy.'

I was listening now. Even Queequeg couldn't distract me and he was, currently, my hero.

Mother burst out laughing. 'But that's all deliberate!' she said. 'The whole poem is about the ludicrousness of those images, those symbols, and how people are too coy to just call a *spade a spade*.'

'Yes, but you see, Veda, for McMannish, it goes too far. *You* go too far. In amassing those images, veiled or not, one after the other – even if you are sending them up, you make the whole thing weighted with, well, *sex*. He feels the poem stops being *veiled* and starts being *lewd*. He doesn't like it. They don't like it.'

Mother put her head in her hands, still laughing. 'Oh *god*,' she said.

'I do agree with you,' said John Honey. 'It's ridiculous.'

'Bloody hell,' said Mother. She got her cigarettes out and lit one and I even thought for a moment she was going to throw her lit match down on the page proofs and watch them catch fire. But she didn't. She kept looking through them, one-handed, as though seeking another insult. 'I feel like I need to re-read the whole thing now,' she said. 'In case they've changed words, or whole lines, without telling me.'

'Well, do read the whole thing! Of course you must. Read it through. Check it over. But I can assure you, they've touched nothing else.'

Mother folded the brown wrapping paper back over the stack of proofs and sat up straight, with her arms crossed and her hand smoking. 'So, I'm just looking for typos then?'

John Honey blinked. 'Mainly. But it's your last chance to change anything. It'll go to print and that will be it. You won't have another chance.'

Mother nodded sagely.

'Keep the changes down, though, Veda. We don't want to

give the buggers another reason to postpone.' He smiled weakly. 'Or complain.'

Mother ashed her cigarette with supreme contempt.

'Hard not to want to tinker, I know,' said John.

'Well, I won't. I'll be disciplined, I promise. Might briefly revisit the sonnet, that's all. Looking at it now, it's a little under-baked.'

There was silence. Mother stubbed her cigarette out and took the coffee cups away without asking John Honey if he wanted more.

I went back to *Moby Dick*. Stubb secured his flat spade to its long handle and bunged it straight down into the head of a shark so blood spurted into the water.

'How are you going there, son?' said John Honey. He seemed to have forgotten I'd been there for the whole conversation. I wondered if he knew he'd said the word *sex* in front of me.

'It's a challenge, reading *Moby Dick*,' said John. 'You a prodigy like your mother, Owen?'

'It's abridged,' I said. 'Which means, the writers have made it easier.'

'Ah,' said John.

'Oh, he is a prodigy,' said Mother. 'He's going to grow up to be very rich and famous.'

John Honey raised his eyebrows and laughed a laugh that was waxy like honeycomb but not the slightest bit sweet.

Mother ran water into the coffee cups and then dumped them on the drainer. 'Oh bugger it,' she said. 'Let's go out for champagne, John. Shall we? It'll only take me a minute to get ready. We can go into the city. Owen'll stay here, he'll be fine. Won't you, Owen?'

John Honey seemed relieved at this idea. I was relieved at this idea. Mother hadn't gone out anywhere for ages. I nodded my assent and let Mother pretend to fuss about the state of my twisted ankle so it looked like she was a good mother who cared.

And they left. The house was much easier to be in when I was on my own these days. Still, as they went laughing out the front door, something nagged at me: *Was it alright for a woman to go and drink champagne at lunchtime with a man who wasn't her husband?* I didn't know. I suspected Carlito would get angry if you did it, Ornella. But you weren't publishing your first collection of poetry. That made everything different.

GREEN FOAM

Coming off the plane, Mrs Parish looked longer and thinner. She wore a red skirt and carried a flat leather case under her arm. This was her folio, she said, full of photographs of the work she'd made in Japan. She presented her cheek for Mr Parish to kiss and put her arms around me – just for a second or so, but filling me with assurance that she was definitely back and would definitely have some kind of present for me in her suitcase. She smelt of something odd that wasn't perfume. Tea or soap or face-powder. We picked her luggage up off the luggage belt – it was the first to come out, and there was only half as much of it as she had left with, in new red leather that matched her red skirt – and Mr Parish wouldn't let her take anything, except for the flat leather case, which she kept tucked under her arm as though it were entirely natural for a woman to walk around with a folio under her arm. At another time, Mr Parish might've ribbed her – he might've said, 'Oh, that's a new pose, dear!' or 'Going out to teach the world a lesson, are we?' – but tonight he was fussing around her and seemed to want to make everything pleasant for her. I wondered if she was as surprised as me about this, but she remained composed, and not in the least surprised, not even when he opened the car door for her and pulled out the seatbelt end from where it habitually got stuck between the upholstery and the metal.

'It's good to have you back, June,' he said, and she nodded and felt in the back for my hand to squeeze.

The morning after Mrs Parish came back I woke up early. The sun was just starting to rise and there was Paddy Cow at my window. I was feeling happy and relaxed, glad that Mrs Parish had returned, glad Mother's book was being published, glad of everything. Paddy Cow was snuffling and her nose was banging against the glass. My eyes closed again and I let the bangs lull me. Bang – snuffle – bang bang – snuffle. It sounded like a boat bumping softly against a pier, as if the wood were padded and old, or coated in rubber bitumen, or wrapped in sheets of whale blubber. I tried to go back to sleep only then the bangs got stronger in intensity, and Paddy Cow made a strange, high-pitched sound that was not normal. I opened my eyes and sat up. There was froth coming out of Paddy Cow's mouth: green froth like a lime spider.

I got out of bed and ran onto the verandah.

Paddy Cow was a proper cow now: a small one, a runtish cow, but as fully grown as he was going to get. She'd moved away from the window and was coming towards me on the verandah, very big, with green foam spewing from her mouth.

'Mr Parish!' I yelled.

Paddy Cow's body was shivering, and her eyes were rolling like *Where the Wild Things Are*. Her hooves skidded on the verandah tiles and she fell and, upon hitting the ground, started bucking, just bucking like she couldn't stop, rolling in the green foam that came out of her mouth. I screamed.

And then Mr Parish was there, in his pyjamas. 'Jesus,' he said. 'Jesus Christ! It's that fucking brown snake. I saw it yesterday.'

And then he was gone again.

I couldn't get close to Paddy Cow because, even though she was on the ground, her legs were still kicking and foam was going everywhere. Part of me was scared that the foam was poisonous – like I might start going crazy if I touched it, like rabies – but finally I got near enough to reach out and put my hand on her back. I rubbed my hand back and forth. Her hide was wet and cold. I knelt down. 'Paddy Cow, it's that *fucking brown snake*!' I said. 'Come on, Paddy Cow! It's just that *fucking brown snake*!' Paddy Cow made a gasping mooing sound, and then another one, and then she vomited blood and grass and yellow stuff like jelly.

I heard Mr Parish come back. I saw his bare feet in the corner of my eyes, his toes all squashed to the side.

'Owen,' he said. 'Owen, you need to get out of the way.'

Paddy Cow was less trembly now and I could feel her heart

going bang-bang-bang. 'She's alright now!' I said. 'Good girl, Paddy Cow. Good girl!'

But then a terrible, terrible sound came out of her. A sound like a whole lot of different animals in pain all at once, and she rose up suddenly. Her leg came out and got me in the forehead.

'Owen,' said Mr Parish. 'You need to move away, now.'

I knew what the black stick was, pointing down next to Mr Parish's bare feet.

'Owen, I want you to come up. Just stand up and move over to the windows. Paddy Cow's in pain, Owen.'

I was sobbing, but I got up, and moved over to the windows and leaned against them. My face throbbed where Paddy Cow had kicked it but I watched as Mr Parish lifted the gun and put his finger on the trigger. I felt the BOOM! in my body. It was one straight hit and it dropped Paddy Cow into silence. She was immediately still. A big red blood patch started up above her eyes.

Mr Parish slumped against the wall and rubbed his head. 'I'm so sorry, Owen,' he said.

I stayed quiet for some time, looking at Paddy Cow with her eyes open and the blood from the bullet leaking into them. Her head lay at a strange angle to the rest of her body. And then finally I went over to her. I rubbed my hand on her dead wet body. My knees were covered in green froth and my face was covered in blood. I don't know if it was blood from my forehead or from Paddy Cow's bullet-wound.

'I'm so, so sorry, Owen,' said Mr Parish.

But I understood. I didn't blame him. 'It's alright,' I said.

We didn't wake Mrs Parish. Mr Parish went down to his

studio where he had a piece of old carpet he didn't use. He brought the carpet up the hill on his back while I sat with Paddy Cow. Then he unrolled it on the verandah, and we turned Paddy Cow onto it and wound her up. It was very difficult. Paddy Cow was very heavy. But it was a nice carpet. It had faded oriental patterns on it. It was a nice thing to put her in.

'It's her funeral shroud,' said Mr Parish. 'Now, let's clean up this verandah before Mrs Parish gets up.'

And so we did.

MOBY DICK

In days to come, I told Papa about Paddy Cow. But mostly I talked to him about *Moby Dick*.

I took the tram to the restaurant with my schoolbag and my cricket bat. Papa wanted to consult me, man-to-man, about the banquet he was preparing for Mother's book launch. I had been thinking about it too. I knew what I was going to say.

'Have you read *Moby Dick*, Papa?' I asked him, as we sat down and he put a bitter Italian soft drink in front of me.

'No, but I know what it's about,' he said.

'It's about whaling, Papa,' I said.

Papa nodded his head. 'Yep.'

'You know my cow got bit by a snake,' I said.

Papa nodded. 'Yep,' he said.

'Mr Parish had to shoot her with his gun.'

'Yep, I know. That's called a mercy killing.'

I considered for a moment. Mr Parish had used the term *euthanasia*.

'Herman Melville says whales are like elephants, but bigger.

He says elephants are like dogs when you compare them with whales. In size. Like if a whale was an elephant, an elephant would be a dog.'

'Sounds about right,' said Papa. He kept looking towards the kitchen as if he had a pot on the stove.

'Mr Parish shot the gun straight through Paddy Cow's head,' I said.

'I know,' said Papa. 'He told me. He said you were very brave about the whole thing.'

'I wasn't,' I said. 'I just didn't show him, that's all.'

'Well, that's brave. That's courage, not to show it.'

'We buried her in the garden. We had a sort of funeral. Mrs Parish was there, she's come home.'

'I know. Mr Parish said.'

'But she's going again …'

'Is she?' Papa's eyes flitted back to me.

'Didn't Mr Parish tell you?'

'No, O-yo. He didn't mention that. That's very hard on Mr Parish. Are you sure?'

I nodded. 'She's just come to sort her things out.'

Papa nodded. 'Well, that's sad for Mr Parish, Owen. But that's what happens sometimes with married people. They stop getting along well together.' He looked at me properly for the first time in the conversation. 'Does it make you sad?'

I picked at the bally fabric of the tablecloth. It'd been washed too many times. Papa needed new ones. 'Nup,' I said. 'She said I could come with her to Japan if I wanted.'

'She did not!'

'She did! She said I could go to Japanese school and live

with her in an apartment where you can see a snow-covered mountain right outside the window.'

'But you know you can't go, don't you, Owen?'

'Why can't I?' I didn't want to go, not really – but I wanted him to suspect I might, that it wouldn't really matter to me, going away from him and Mother, that I wouldn't really care.

'O-yo ...' he said.

'The Japanese,' I continued with great restraint as I made my way towards my point, 'are commercial whalers, Papa. They use harpoons just like in *Moby Dick*. They do so much whale-hunting that whales could become extinct.' I squinted my eyes at him, checking if I still had his full attention. 'Japanese people eat whale because it is in their tradition. They eat it in their soups. In *Moby Dick*, Stubb – he's the first mate – he eats whale steak under the light of the ship lamps. Just cuts them off the side of the whale. The ship lamps are lit with whale oil, Papa. The oil comes from its head. If you shot a sperm-whale in its head, Papa, it wouldn't spurt blood like Paddy Cow's did, it would spurt oil.'

'Like a geyser,' said Papa.

'Yep,' I said, though I didn't know what a geyser was.

'We hunt whale in Australia too,' said Papa. 'But I don't cook it in my restaurant.'

'The Aborigines never hunted whales,' I said. 'It was not part of their diet.'

'It's not in the Aborigines' tradition, or not that I know,' said Papa. 'Though I bet they would've made good harpooners.'

'Why is it in our tradition to eat pigs and sheep and cows, Papa?'

'I guess it's just because we're used to it. I've eaten other animals than those, though.' He was distracted by the kitchen again: an imaginary pot boiling on the stove. He barked something at the kitchenhand.

'Well,' I said. I felt suddenly bigger and more knowledgeable than Papa, with his apron round his waist and his stupid soft drinks that no kid would ever like. 'Well,' I said. 'It's not *ethical* to eat cows and sheep. Or chickens and pigs. It's sort of like eating whales in the light of their own oil from their own heads, Papa.'

Papa looked mystified.

'The animals we eat only eat grass and hay. And vegetables.'

'Not pigs,' said Papa. 'Pigs'll eat whatever you throw them. Pigs'll eat a dead man, Owen, if you chuck one in their feeding trough.'

'Pigs eat acorns, Papa.' I was stubborn. 'Does it seem fair, Papa, to eat animals that are vegetarians? I am a vegetarian. Would you eat me?'

My thinking was not yet refined but righteousness was on fire within me.

Papa looked tired. 'Don't be ridiculous, Owen,' he said.

'And you know something else, Papa?'

Papa shook his head wearily.

'Cows are smart, Papa. And pigs are like dogs, in their intelligence. And lambs are so cute. How could you want to eat one?'

He threw his hands up in the air.

'So,' I said. I felt a strange rush at what I was about to say. 'So, Papa. For Mother's launch, we should have a vegetarian banquet. In honour of Paddy Cow and Moby Dick.'

Papa didn't even bother to look at me. 'Oh, Jesus, Owen, don't be stupid,' he said. 'I'm not doing vegetarian food for Mother's launch.' He stood up and wiped his hands on his tea-towel even though there was nothing on them.

I felt tears come behind my eyes. They made my jaw ache. 'I just got my cow shot, Papa. I just got my *cow shot*!'

The tears were right there, right in the sockets of my eyes, and the more I tried to stop them, the more they grew.

'You're being stupid, Owen,' Papa said. 'Grow up. I'm really sorry about your cow. I won't cook beef, alright? But just grow up. Imagine how it is for kids living on a farm. When I was your age, I could skin a rabbit without even thinking about it. I wasn't so bloody soft. Jesus!' He threw the tea-towel onto a table on the other side of the restaurant and made for the kitchen. 'Your mother likes *pork*, Owen. So *that's* what I'm going to cook. *Jesus*!'

The tears were not going to get me. I felt for my cricket bat under the table. I found its peeling rubber handle, and I brought it up to elbow height, vertically, like a sword, just above the table. Then I brought it back so I could get a good swing, and I belted my Chinotto bottle across the restaurant so it shattered against the wall. It shattered all down Rosa's mural – a brown stain like creek water.

Then I bolted. I ran so fast, with my bag banging on my back, and my tears going backwards into my eyes where no one would ever see them. I bolted out the door and onto Collins Street where the commuters were lining the streets, waiting for their trams. I held my cricket bat aloft as I ran and everyone coming toward me, *everyone*, knew that I meant business.

3 JULY 1970

Dear Tilde

Did you get my last letter? I've been running to the letterbox for your response. Every day, such a disappointment! Now, I know you're a busy woman, but spare me a line or two. I don't care how short. All right? I don't care how short. As short as this will do!

Xxx Veda

† † †

11 JULY 1970

Tilde, you've got me worried!

Have I said, done, intimated something that has made you cross? Do you not approve of my latest gallivants?

Have pity for me, won't you. Let me know that, whatever I have done that has offended, it is ultimately forgivable. Go on. You've a lifetime of that behind you.

X Veda

18 JULY 1970

All right then, Tilde.

I apologise over and over and over. I simply do not believe

you're too busy to write to me. Please, Tilde, darling, write me a letter and let me know all is well.

I know it's not Mother or you would have telegraphed.

Veda x

† † †

25 JULY 1970

I think I have to write to you differently now, Tilde.

Because I don't get a response from you anymore.

And as no one cares cares cares I will speak of my despairs.

Oh, I'm sick of poetry. So fussy. Always asking to be cleaned up.

And prose: prose is full of nicety. Nice things are the only things that ought to be said in a letter, our mother advised.

Ask after the weather. Describe the view from your window.

That was the very essay topic prescribed at school all those years ago: Describe the view from your window.

Hundreds of years of women staring out of windows, describing views, imagining things on the horizon.

What did I spy with my little eye: peonies, hollyhocks; in the distance, gums. Ghost gums shimmering in the summer heat.

I must've dealt out poetry of some kind to impress the examination markers. Cleversticks old me.

Visited the Egyptian museum, went up and down a promenade in a big city.

Teeny weeny me on the head of a pin!

Oh the things they did and didn't teach.

No, prose and poetry are done and dusted.

So I will write to you in a spool
Neither script
nor screed,
a spool I imagine as
long
and ongoing
and unbroken.
More like a cotton reel than a scroll.
An endless unwinding of something
very
very
easy to break
I can unravel in a spool, the process is endless.
(So much thread in one standard reel!)
I will unspool my self, it feels a very
cathartic process.
I will hang my anger out to dry,
another white among the whites
(or grey among the greys
as the case may be).
The house is quiet, Tilde.
Tick-ticking. Plock-plocking of a tap somewhere.
A smell comes over, goes, returns,
something cooked and forgotten.
Soiled washing.
A child will bang a door soon,
A husband will tiptoe through the flotsam jetsam.
I am at sea on a large
beached

lounge suite
in the centre of nothing

31 JULY 1970

Tilde

I have been feeling mildly fascist all day.
I wanted to kill the postman.
I wanted to eliminate the unignitable gas jets in the kitchen,
the slippery green shoes that don't properly connect with the floor,
the hot and cold heater that doesn't obey.

There are wheels of dust in the house.
Actual tumbleweeds. Matted loops of dust and dog hair.
You just leave a house to stew and it creates hours of labour.
Years.
Sleep on a bed and the sheets go grey.
Cease movement and *voila*! A carapace of dust.
Everything makes me want to scream.

Had a dream in which Owen is making soup. I pour in the boiling water only to discover it is coffee. I find Owen has put tea leaves in it too. We try and salvage several floating olives.
So hard
To pin down
With a fork.

† † †

II AUGUST 1970

Tilde

Sat in the living room and looked at the light fixture until Owen came and asked me for calamine lotion.

I pasted it on chalkily where the itches itched.

Oh a mother doesn't have to do much.

Just open a jar, and dip in a finger.

I imagine there must be things that bite that have not yet bitten me.

Should I feel his bites as my own?

The dog makes a weeping sound when I leave the room.

I shall sit here in the corner with my wooden crate of booze.

I shall drink a glass or two or three then have a little snooze.

I'd write for the Tivoli you know, a sketch show: modern woman goes up

in flames!

Forgive me Tilde: because you don't answer, I just write whatever comes into my head.

30 AUGUST 1970

To get inside my house you must open a big dead door on a silly little hinge,

progress through a garden with shadows and dead things underfoot,
a fence keeps out the curious,
a letterbox lets bits of the world get in,
sometimes there's a sickly smell of daphne,
the footstep of a husband and the key in the door.
(Oh, the key in the door!)
When I cough, what a tremendous chorus of smokers!
A dead house has such wonderful echoes.
Have you ever known a fridge to hum the tune of an advertising jingle?
The hum of our fridge is the blood of the house.
It is one enormous placenta.
(Is that a word one might use safely?)

I am not sure of words anymore.
They have not got me anywhere.
They don't love you, for instance, and they can't look after you.
Quite possibly they can kill you.

The leaves are very still outside and the trees don't move.
There is a noise of gravel in my ears.
I'm a little scared, Tilde. I'm not sure what I've done.

PART 5

SABOTAGE

1989

Julia says my childhood was all about the adults in it. She chops carrots and shakes her head. 'All those selfish adults,' she says. She bangs the knife down and takes a mouthful of wine and a long puff on her cigarette. It is 1989. She is thirty-four and I am twenty-nine. She loves Mother's poetry, but she is not sure Mother was really cut out to be a mother. She is not sure if Julia is cut out to be a mother either. We have been together for four years. I help her in the business, and I run an imprint of my own: ArtBook. It's just started up. I'm not sure where it's going. Do either of us have the requisite business sense for success? Julia looks at me, her eyes narrow. 'Let's not have children, Owen.' I nod, gratified by her decisiveness. 'Let's not have children. Because God knows what we would do to them, not even meaning to, just by being selfish.'

But by that logic, should anyone have children?

CINDERELLA

'I'll be leaving after the launch,' Mrs Parish told me quietly.

We were in the kitchen at Park Orchards. She was making a batch of bread for Mr Parish. She had been making loaves of bread every day since she'd got back. They were going in the freezer. 'I don't want to leave him wanting,' she said. 'His digestion.'

'You could teach him,' I said. 'You could give him the bread recipe.'

'Oh, he couldn't *bake bread*,' she said.

'But why not? Papa can cook. He makes all his money out of cooking. If Mr Parish wasn't sure about how to cook it, Papa could show him.'

She looked at me dubiously.

'Or *Kitten* could show him,' I said.

Mrs Parish kneaded the bread dough and put it near the window with a damp tea-towel on the top. 'Oh Owen,' she said.

She stood next to me and I could tell she wanted to stroke my hair or something, but it was too late for that.

'You can come and visit me in Japan,' she said.

'I know,' I said.

'I hope you don't feel like I have ... abandoned you, or something?'

'No,' I said. I was pretty clear on this. 'You have to go and learn ikebana and become a master.' I thought about this for a second: could she be a master or would she only be a mistress? 'It would be very sad if you couldn't. It would be a waste of talent.'

Then Mrs Parish did hug me, but I didn't mind: she was so spare with such things.

'All right then,' she said. 'You've given me permission, Owen.' She washed her hands under the hot tap and wiped them on the tea-towel. 'Thank you.' It was her last batch of bread. 'Go and get your good clothes on, Owen. I'll meet you at the car in half an hour. Wear something your mother will like.'

What would Mother like me to wear? What would Mother like me to wear? *What would Mother like me to wear?* I stood at the wardrobe and could not answer this question. Coats hung on good quality wooden hangers. Shirts were pressed. There was even a jerkin, and – on a thin arm of plastic-coated metal inside the wardrobe door – two ties.

I knew Mother would plan to wear her blue frilly expensive dress, but would change her mind at the last minute, possibly ripping it slightly when she tore it off. She'd leave it inside-out on her bed like children do. She'd put on a secretary skirt instead and a brown twin-set and a pair of shoes that were too high and too tight. Then she'd look at herself in the mirror and see that she was plain and ugly and frumpish, and she'd pull off the twin-set and wriggle out of the skirt and look for something else, something elusive, something her wardrobe didn't contain. She'd pull out piece after piece, and as she tried things on, she'd get rougher and rougher with them, and more and more exasperated, with her wardrobe, and herself, till the clothes would layer the bed and the armchair and the floor, and she'd sit among them and weep for a bit, and wish she had someone who could advise her. Then eventually she'd stalk out and put the record player on and pour a drink, and go through the whole thing again, slowly this time, and as the first drink went down and she poured a second, gradually those discarded, inappropriate clothes would acquire a new life and she would begin to feel different. She would begin to feel special. She would begin to feel like a movie star going to the premiere of her new film. She would dress herself again and this time she would keep her wardrobe door open where the full-length mirror was and she would admire every bit of her form, the way the clothes fit so well, the way the buttons did up so neatly, the way her throat rose so elegantly from the collar. Because *the fact was* she was still beautiful and her hair was still golden, and, you know, you *could* mistake her for a movie star. And she *was beautiful* in the light of that room, and the aura of that drink, and the sadness of that music. Her ensemble, finally devised, would thrill her – only her, only then, in that moment. And then she'd leave the house and it would be too late, it'd all change back again. The outfit would be the wrong thing after all: the bad thing, the ugly thing. And she would not be able to be happy.

That was the story of Cinderella. I didn't need to have read it. All the girls knew it by heart.

I put on a cream shirt, a blue jacket and a green tie. I went and waited for Mrs Parish at the car.

Mr Knox had put up signs in the front window and Vellum Press had taken out adverts in literary journals and writers' society newsletters, so there was quite a crowd in the bookshop when Mrs Parish and I arrived. There were people I didn't know, lots of them. Mother was talking to three or four of them at once and had two glasses of champagne in her hands. Her eyes slid across the room and registered me.

The room was warm. Mrs Parish took a fan out of her handbag and flapped it discreetly. Mrs Knox had a tray of drinks and was hopping around the room with it like a bird. Mr Knox was putting his hands through his hair and laughing. Mr Parish was talking to people I didn't know and writing something in the notebook he kept in his suit-pocket. John Honey was looking at his watch. The man from the newspaper had a flashbulb that went off every now and then and added to the hilarity, the warmth, the drunkenness. Papa was nowhere to be seen.

A table was stacked high with Mother's books, brown and tan, over and over, her name going on and on and on unbearably: *Veda Gray Veda Gray Veda Gray.* Someone I didn't know who reminded me of Kitten was sitting behind the table with a cashbox and a docket-book.

Papa arrived. John Honey tapped his watch. Mother stood up. A sea of people parted and pushed backwards and I felt myself become suddenly compressed in the crowd. My ears were hot and burning at the tops and I had to try and cool them with spit on my fingertips. A wave of sickness came into my chest and my legs went quivery. 'Owen?' someone said in front of me, and then I was going backwards, into the crowd, and a honeycomb of yellow fogged my eyes and I fell.

'Owen?' you said again. 'Owen!'

Outside on Collins Street the air was cool and crisp and grey and it was raining softly.

A pigeon with touches of green in its feathers pecked at a crumb next to a cigarette butt. A broken umbrella stuck out of a rubbish bin.

'You alright, O-yo?' you said. You put your face in my face and your breath smelt like Juicy Fruit. I was sitting on the ground, propped against the window of the bookshop. You didn't have water so you fanned my face with your copy of *Veda Gray*. 'Cool down,' you said. 'Don't worry about your mother. She's fine.'

Inside, the voices were rising and falling, and there was clapping that started, and built, and fell off again. And then a different voice started speaking.

'How about we just go around the corner to the restaurant, huh?'

I nodded. 'Did I faint, Ornella?'

'Think so,' said Ornella, helping me up to stand.

'Don't tell Carlito,' I said. Ornella pressed my hand and then tucked it inside her elbow, and we strode through the cool air and the grey people, with their hats and their bags and their raincoats. On the corner of your street in Richmond, a plum tree had started sprouting pink blossoms that week; I could see green buds on the trees in Collins Street. What sort of trees were those?

'They are elms,' you said to me. (That was when I realised you could read my mind.)

We missed the launch, in the end, you and I, Ornella. It didn't matter. It wasn't the end, after all, was it? We'd thought it would be the end – Papa and I thought it would be, anyway. 'After Mother's launch ...' had become a catchphrase, a marker of future order and harmony. Everything would become normal after Mother's launch; years would fold backwards on each other as if they'd never been, and there'd only be 'Veda Gray, the respected poet, with a sunlit desk and a stack of publications'. Papa would come home and kiss her head and hassle me to do my homework. Mother would be sure and mild, with a long elegant neck and a cashmere twin set like Mrs Parish.

Back at La Coccinella, you and I helped the waitstaff by folding napkins into shapes like birds and placing them on side plates. Yours looked like dying ducks collapsing in a pond, but mine were lithe and young and sat up on the plates like little lapping tongues saying 'hello' and inviting the diner to sit down and open them out. The restaurant was filled with the smell of meat. It made me feel sick again.

By dinnertime, though, I'd fully recovered. The heat of the restaurant had acclimatised me to the heat of people, so when they all came through the doors, holding Mother aloft on their praise – I imagined her on a kind of bier, strewing petals, like Cleopatra – I was able to laugh and let myself get pummelled by the men who knew me and kissed by the women. Mother made me sit by her and then changed her mind and went and sat somewhere else. Mrs Knox gave little nervous sighs and picked at the bird I had so cleverly composed for her side plate. Papa went straight to the kitchen, not even stopping to check on me first, like the food in the oven was more important than his son who had *fainted* in the bookshop. *Fainting is for girls, Owen.* He would only blame it on vegetarianism.

There was a seating plan. It went like this, clockwise: Kitten, with her hair in a long braid over one shoulder like a schoolgirl. Then Mr and Mrs Parish. Then you and Carlito. Susan and Gordon Bridie. John Honey and the curious blonde woman who had been at the cashbox. Rosa and Florence Oakey. Me. Mr and Mrs Knox. Mother. Finally, a newspaperman who kept trying to get his arm around Kitten, which she resisted, valiantly and cheerfully. A hundred cigarettes burned in a hundred ashtrays. *The Poems of Veda Gray* was everywhere. It was, in duplication, a strangely unsettling mirror, a reflection of something that didn't exist: Mother's mind, in book form.

There was nothing concrete in the conversations that night though; they were all featherweight. Or lighter, because feathers tend ultimately downwards, towards the ground, and these conversations just went up up up and dissolved into nothing. 'And I couldn't believe it when …' 'And she really thinks that he …' 'And it *is* a wonder, after all …' 'But you never *said* that, you only *insinuated* …' 'Oh *of course* it's too much money …' 'I don't go for it, I'm afraid, and I never will …'

In their wafting gaseous forms, the conversations that night were antithetical to memory, Ornella. They were a chain of present moments, popping like bubbles colliding with other bubbles.

But if the talk was elusive, forgotten in the next minute, the menu was pressed into archival service by ink. It is a fact separate to all others. I still have it in my Safety Cartridges Class IV ammunition box, where I keep the documentation of *Life Before*, should anyone ever need it.

On heavy cream paper, Papa offered his diners two choices for first course, but only one for second:

I primi

Pappa al pomodori
This was his accommodation of my vegetarianism. I consider it a significant compromise. A soup made of stale bread and

milled tomatoes, rich with sage and garlic. No one had ever contemplated vegetarianism on a menu before. He was the first. He said this to me over and over.

o

Risotto agli Scampi

Prawns and fish stock, stewed into arborio rice, that weird tough nutty rice. Papa had been at the South Melbourne market that morning. That's where you got the good prawns. The diners sucked the smell into their nostrils, but they did not call it a smell, they called it an *aroma.* I had long ago concluded that seafood was the worst of all meats. You could see their whole creature-hood. You could actually *identify* their spines, complete and intact. The speckled grey of fish skins. The bones. The feelers and crunchy transparent casing of a prawn. Black eyes. Heads and tails you could rip off with your teeth and spit onto the side of your plate …

I Secondi:

Papa's special dish to celebrate Mother and alienate me:

Maiolino da latte intero arrostito:

A suckling pig, six weeks old, roasted in its entirety, in an enormous pan, covered in salt and slices of lemon. 'The most delectable way to eat pork,' I heard Mother whisper to Mr Knox. Papa brought it out, with help from the kitchenhand, on a tray like a bed-base. It was orange-coloured, in places brown. An effigy. A small sleeping baby pig on a baking tray. The smell was intense. The pig's eyes were closed in two small crescents on either side of its face. Its snout curved upwards – Papa had propped something under its chin. Kitten's lips glistened as she watched. Hot roasted suckling pig. Mouths opened around me, and Papa got his knife ready. My soup came up into my mouth.

I didn't care about the dessert menu. Fruit. Cheese. Torte. I stood up. I pulled out the napkin I had tucked in my shirt collar. I knocked a *Poems of Veda Gray* onto the floor. *Cannibals*! I said to the whole lot of them. The baby pig on the table like a fruitbowl! It felt like some kind of ancient sacrifice. Like the Aztecs. Or the Mayans. Mrs Parish rubbed my arm absently. Rosa speared a piece of baby pig on her fork and opened her mouth wide. *Cannibals!* I roared. A pig was like a dog in its intelligence. I hated them.

The air outside in the courtyard was crisp, but the rain had stopped. A steady drip fell from the guttering. The seats and the table were wet. My old tricycle was still there, tangled in the ivy. I pulled it out. The ivy felt poisonous, like a snake.

I sat on the tricycle even though I was too big for it. I rolled slightly forwards and slightly backwards over the concrete. There was an outdoor light rigged up to the eaves on the back of the kitchen wall, and I rolled in and out of the yellow pool it made on the ground. Drip drip went the rainwater into a terracotta pot plant base filled with wet cigarette butts. I stayed there for a long time, it seemed, long enough for plates to get cleared, and mouths to stop chewing and throats to stop swallowing. I heard Mother's voice coming down the passageway.

'O-wen,' she called. 'Are you out there?'

Her shoes were drunk. They clittered and clattered like wobbly old goat hooves. When she got to the doorway, she stopped to steady herself in the doorframe before coming down the step.

She carried a bottle of wine by the neck and two glasses between thumb and forefinger.

'Oh bloody hell, it's saturated out here,' she said. She put the bottle and the glasses down, wiped the seat with the back of her hand, then sat and poured some wine and lit a cigarette. 'So *hot* in there,' she said. 'And all of that food! Poor O-yo. Suckling pig and the whole lot!'

I rolled back and forth on my tricycle.

She looked at me patiently for a few moments, breathing her smoke in and out, watching me push the concrete back and forth under my feet, as if noticing for the first time how much too big I was for a tricycle.

'I heard you had a bit of a *fit* back at the launch. Are you alright now?'

'Faint,' I said. 'Not fit.'

'Did I say fit? I meant faint. Sorry O-yo …' She waved her hand with its cigarette and poured more wine. 'It wasn't a really good time for you to have a fainting fit.'

'No,' I said. I thought hard about what a person who didn't care might say. 'Sorry about that.'

She looked at me curiously. Her hair was golden in the light, though streaked with grey, and her face was still pretty, with white teeth and smooth skin. I had always believed her eyes to be grey, a little sickly, not normal, but they were actually quite blue tonight, not grey at all. She sat there, silent, looking straight at me, as though she were sizing me up. I thought something important was only a fraction of a second away. She was going to say something I would remember – on purpose or accidentally, it didn't matter. She was going to say it. She took a puff of her cigarette and watched me. 'What do you make of all this, O-yo?' she said.

She was asking me a grown-up question. I was sitting on a little kids' tricycle.

'Come on, O-yo. What do you think about everything that goes on? Do you think all this is normal?'

I didn't know what she expected of me. Was 'all this' a big thing or a little thing? Was she asking me how I felt right this second or in the whole complete history of my life? Did she really care or was she just making conversation with me?

'I think ...' I said.

She looked at me intently. The blood rushed to my brain, trying to complete the sentence with a phrase of insight or wit – or honesty, even – but I couldn't think of a single thing to say, not a single word. 'I think ...' I said again.

And then a sudden chiming started up inside, like a hundred glasses being rapped by a hundred spoons. There were whooping voices. Mother sat instantly upright and put her hand on my arm. Her hand was little and cold. 'Come on, it's the speeches,' she said. 'Come on, O-yo. Papa's had his *pitcher* in the *paper*, now it's my turn!'

SABOTAGE

I can't go on much with my memories of that evening, Ornella. Because of course, Mother did get her picture in the papers.

The Age put Mother on page two. *The Australian*, somewhat further back, in a smaller column, using a smaller photograph.

Would Mother have got her picture in the papers if it hadn't been for Mr Parish? Would anyone have noticed her transgression? She might've become merely a respectable published poet. Maybe somewhere down the line, an enterprising postgraduate student would have figured it out and there'd be a relevant footnote in a thesis somewhere.

Did she really *want* to be a respectable published poet?

Do you remember anything of Mr Parish's speech, Ornella? Back there, deep inside that plaque-ridden brain of yours that never put any stock in memories in the first place?

Mr Parish was flushed. He had his shirt unbuttoned and a handkerchief knotted around his neck as though he were on a boat, and I watched him roll his sleeves up in preparation for getting down to business. But he was crimson in the face, and when he called everyone to attention to hear his speech, there was something frantic about his manner. I thought for a moment he might bang the table with his fist. He was more like a town crier than a poet laureate.

'Pay attention, cryptic crosswordeers,' he said, or something along those lines. He held up a drink in one hand and *The Poems of Veda Gray* in the other. 'Listen in, veterans of acrostic subterfuge. For Veda Gray has your measure!' And then, in his clever, well-practised way – searing each letter into the heart – he spelt it out so no one could miss it. Mother's sonnet.

Mrs Parish wouldn't look at Mr Parish while he read the sonnet. I do remember that. She spent the time pulling on a pair of very tight long black driving gloves, smoothing them over her wrists, tugging the fingertips and pulling back the cuffs.

Perhaps it was her lack of interest that made Mr Parish betray Mother. Maybe he was trying to get his wife's attention. Or maybe it wasn't even a betrayal, in the end. Just a moment of bad judgement. Even famous poets can have moments of bad judgement. Especially when they're drinking too much alcohol and feel themselves unloved. I have always given him the benefit of the doubt. Mrs Parish sitting there, ignoring him, putting on her gloves. It was her he wanted to hurt, not Mother.

Or womanhood in general. Perhaps. I don't know.

Mother's eyes flickered between people nervously, and she tried to laugh.

No one recognised the seriousness of the revelation for some days. To its credit, while the *Australian* merely alluded to it, the *Age* published the sonnet in full – in the same breath that they denounced it. Was this *hypocritical*? I had recently learnt the word *hypocritical*, and found it to be a highly valuable word, for all around me, everywhere, I saw it.

Then there was the Letters page: 'No decent woman uses *that word*. What sort of a model to her children?' 'An abomination: if this is modern literature, I'll have none of it,' and 'If this is modern *womanhood*, we're all in trouble!' There was an opinion piece that referenced, and opposed, the still-recent lifting of the *Lady Chatterley's Lover* ban. A counter-opinion, published the next day, quoted Harry Whitmore quoting Bertrand Russell. The book, the newspapers said, would surely not be stocked by decent bookshops.

INVITATION TO THE READER: A SONNET

F or all those readers contemplating here
U nrousing afternoons of quiet calm:
C oy men and women, fobbing off their fear,
K illed in their beds by every false alarm.
P repare yourselves for small incessant wounds
U nduly actioned on your hearth and homes
B urnished into bits of black and gold
L ike sequins from the very oldest bones
(I n patterns from the very oldest caves.)
S o sequins too! make dancers of dull feet
H arangue old bodies into quadrilles vain
E nriching life despite what life depletes
R *espondez s'il vous plait* to truths so bold,
S it by me, let our blood warm hands we hold

It's a curiously classical, even stilted, poem for Mother, who did not write in closed form very often (bar a couple of villanelles that Julia most particularly admires). But at the time, I merely spelt out the letters vertically, like everybody else did.

The consensus was clear, however: women who hoped to be respected for their literary pursuits could not possibly expect to *use language like that and get away with it.*

There was a lot of talk of this: of Mother *getting away with it.* But Mother didn't seem to be getting away with anything.

Mother couldn't move.

She was dumbstruck.

It was as though she had planned and executed her literary revenge without any understanding of what it was, exactly, she was doing. Papa questioned her, but she just sat there, on the couch in the living room, white-faced, clutching her dog, saying: 'I didn't think it would come to this!'

'I'm frightened,' she said, 'about the fate of my book.'

'Why didn't you just use the word "Damn"?' asked Papa. 'For god's sake, Veda. Are you a complete *idiot*? Why didn't you just use the word "Damn"?'

'Because,' said Mother, truculently, pressing her face into the dog's fur. 'That would've been a different poem entirely.'

'And why the first poem in the book? Couldn't you have buried it somewhere further in? James might not even have noticed if you hadn't drawn his eye to it like that, plastering it on the front page.'

'The sonnet was called "Invitation",' said Mother. 'It had to go at the beginning of the book.'

Papa looked at Mother with disgust. He looked at her as though she were an alien. Papa loved *My Favourite Martian*, but he didn't like his wife being a Martian. 'I can't trust you, Veda,' he said quietly. 'You're not a wife if you don't tell your husband you're going to do a thing like this.' He put clothes in a case he had open on the floor. He folded a shirt and then dropped it in so it landed unfolded, which was stupid, I thought.

And didn't he care that I was there: watching, hearing him? They didn't even pretend to spare me anymore.

'I've got to *defend* you to people,' Papa said. He put a rubber band around a stack of bills from under the 8 oz weight and dropped it on top of the shirt. 'I don't know if I can.'

Then he left Mother on the couch with her fat dog. His tie was sticking out of the case where the hinges closed. He didn't say a word to me, like I was invisible, like I was not even part of the story. He didn't ask me what I wanted to do. He didn't ask me if I wanted to go with him. Mother cried and banged her head against the back of the couch a few times and asked me if I would stay home from school to keep her company the next day.

'Of course,' I said, patting her on the shoulder, and looking at the floor, wanting to run as far away from her as I possibly could.

It was Thursday night. Mother and I slept with blankets on the couch with the telly on in the background. On the third of September, Hamish McMannish, her Scots editor, wrote a blistering repudiation of Mother that was published in the *Australian*. I was on newspaper duty. I got it first thing from the milk bar, but I kept it folded all the way home. I had hoped there would be nothing in the paper, I hoped that *Veda Gray* had been blown over by other, more important things. Couldn't there have been another aeroplane hijacking? But there it was, a headline that said: 'End of Line for Disgraced Lady Poet'.

Mother tried to call John Honey in Sydney, where he was 'advocating on her behalf'. Nowadays they would call it 'damage control.' But she couldn't get through and at 2 pm his telegram arrived: 'Book being pulped stop so sorry veda stop will telephone.'

I imagined all those *Veda Grays*, all those identical reflections of Mother's mind, going through an enormous industrial-scale shredder, coming out the other end like grated cheese or the stuffing from packing crates when they're filled with china. *Excelsior*, it's called. It's what burns up Leroy in *The Bad Seed*. Mother's books: turned into murderous old *excelsior*. Totally unreadable. Lines with all the tops cut off. Or like when you write appleappleapple over something you don't want anyone else ever to decipher.

Mother got the telegram, and her body went into complete abeyance. She stopped moving and even seemed to stop breathing. It was like she was a statue.

I sat by her with my hand on her shoulder, squeezing occasionally. I didn't know how to comfort someone who had turned suddenly to stone. Eventually I got her a tissue and pushed it into her hand.

'Get my hairbrush too, darling,' she said.

So I did. And she brushed her hair and blew her nose and put on her pale pink lipstick, which was a stupid colour for lipstick because it was the same colour as her lips. And then we took the tram into the city to the Knoxes.

'Barrington will know what to do,' she said. And she was quite calm and composed and smoked out the tram window with her back straight and her eyes on the trees.

IT NEVER RAINS BUT IT POURS

'It never rains but it pours.' This was one of your sayings, Ornella. On your windowsill you kept a strange plastic felt-covered creature that changed colour according to the weather. White when it was cold, blue when it was overcast, orange when it was warm. When it rained or poured, the creature showed no differentiation: dark dark grey like the dark dark sky. When Mother got betrayed, she got good and properly betrayed.

REAL CIGARETTES

Because it was September, the sun was warm but the shadows were freezing. The commuters were commuting. Women were wearing very short skirts. I hadn't noticed that before, but now I saw it, as Mother dragged me down Collins Street. Women's skirts hardly even covered their bottoms. Maybe it was because the sun was out. Maybe they needed to air their bottoms in the sun. All these thoughts going through my head, new thoughts I hadn't had before, as Mother dragged me towards Knox Books with her sun-glasses on and a cigarette in her hand and her handbag swinging from her elbow.

The sign wasn't out at Knox Books. Usually there was a sandwich board on which Mrs Knox wrote the bestsellers and new releases. The sign wasn't out and the door was closed.

'Well, this is funny,' said Mother. She dropped my hand and put her bag down.

It seemed that Mrs Knox had failed to turn the *Open* sign. The sign still said *Closed*, and it was four o'clock in the afternoon.

'Silly Edith!' I said to Mother.

Mother tried the door handle. Nothing. She put her sun-glasses up on her head and her hand like a visor to her forehead and peered through the window.

'Maybe they're sick?' I said.

Mother pushed at the door with her foot.

'They might be sick,' I said again.

She kicked the bottom of the door with her toe. I could see a spill of mail on the mat inside the door, maybe a few days' worth.

'They must be sick, they're not picking up their letters,' I said.

Mother had gone back to peer through the glass and I came up next to her and pressed my nose hard against the window to block out reflections from the street. All the books were in the shop like normal. All the books on all the shelves. But there was a trail of paper on the floor, and none of the wine glasses from Mother's launch had been picked up and put away. I could see them, some of them fallen over as if they hadn't been touched since that night. Copies of *The Poems of Veda Gray* were still in a motley pile.

Mother turned around and put her back to the door. 'Jesus,' she said. She was white.

'What?'

'They've gone under. *Jesus*!'

She slid down the door till she was squatting with her back against it.

'What?'

Her mouth opened as if she were going to yell something, and then closed again. She sat there, looking out at the street for some moments, and then she started banging her head. She banged it backwards against the glass door first, and then turned and banged it forwards on the sharp bit where the wall became a corner. Bang-bang-bang-bang-bang went her head against the sharp corner. A bad sound came out of her mouth and I saw blood on her forehead.

'Mother!' I said. 'You've got blood on your head!'

I got a hanky from her handbag and tried to wipe the blood off, but she pushed my arm away, and got up and took off her shoe. She stumbled and hopped and then, holding the soft toe-part of the shoe in her hand, she aimed the heel at the window.

'Mother!' I screamed. I grabbed her arm. 'Stop, Mother!! STOP IT!'

She pulled her arm back as if to get momentum, and then, abruptly she did stop. She looked at me and sort of slumped and dropped the shoe. 'Come on, Mother,' I said, pulling her arm. Already people were looking at us. Someone would call the police. They would put Mother in jail, and there, in jail, *there* would be a wall she could really bang her head against.

'Come on, Mother,' I said.

She leant her weight on me to put her shoe back on. I gave her the hanky. I spat on it first so she there was something wet she could use to get the blood off her forehead. We proceeded with dignity to the tram stop. I lit a cigarette for her with her Glomesh cigarette lighter. She puffed absently on the cigarette, and the blood, wetted by the spit, smoothed away until it was really just like she had a bit of a bump on her forehead. 'Good boy, O-yo,' she said to me. 'There's money for the tickets in my purse.'

Poor Mother, she was quiet as a lamb on the way home. I don't know where Papa was. I don't know where Mr Parish was. I don't know where you were, Ornella.

Where was everyone?

Mother looked out the window and she hardly even puffed on her cigarette now. It burnt down and down until I had to remove it so it didn't burn her fingers.

On Friday I went to school, even though she hadn't wanted me to. She got up and made me toast with honey and sandwiches with white bread (also with honey) for my lunch. I had already decided I would go to La Coccinella after school. I didn't think I could bear to see Mother anymore with her bunged-up head and dead eyes. I couldn't think about her book going through the shredder either. The story was in the newspaper again that day, I checked at the milk bar. It was on page seven: 'Author's book to be pulped'. 'Mr McMannish of Vellum Press has signalled the publisher's intention to withdraw *The Poems of Veda Gray* from sale on the grounds of indecent language.'

So that was it. I left the newspaper on its stack. I bought a packet of cigarettes. Real cigarettes. Not Fags, which were training cigarettes made of sugar. You could still get candy called Nigger Boy in those days. You could get Blackie Toothpaste. But you couldn't say *fuck* in a poem, not if you were a woman. Not if you were a respectable one.

I bought a real packet of cigarettes. I had pinched enough money from the jar in the kitchen. Cigarettes didn't cost much. No one cared if a kid bought cigarettes – how many times had I bought them for Mother? The shopkeeper didn't flinch. I bought a packet of Craven and I smoked them in the lane off Church Street. I smoked three of them in a row and then I threw up in the gutter.

By the time school had finished, the sickness from the cigarettes had receded, so I smoked another one. I loitered outside the school grounds and kicked the dust and didn't know where to go. *Which home should I go to?* I couldn't bear to see Mother.

I couldn't bear how the fight had gone out of her. I knew she needed sympathy, but I wanted to shake her. I wanted to shake her and then give her a slap *whack* across her cheekbones. *Toughen up, you stupid broad. Stop feeling sorry for yourself.* I didn't want to go to Papa either – La Coccinella was the scene of a crime, and now he'd gone off with his stuff in a suitcase, I was the man of the house. He'd stepped down. I was not going running back. And I wouldn't go to you Ornella because you'd purse your lips about Mother and shake your head, and I couldn't bear that either. And of course I would not go to Mr Parish. I wanted to kill him.

The cigarette made me sick but it also made me feel tough and self-possessed. Cigarettes made Mother feel elegant. Cigarettes made Mr Parish guilty, Kitten saucy, Rosa cough. Cigarettes ruined Papa's palate.

Cigarettes made me separate from all of them. I went and sat at the Yarra River, under the bridge where the graffiti and broken bottles were. No one was around. A dog came past. A factory belched something that bubbled into the brown water. The trams rattled overhead. *I could just climb up into the undercarriage of the bridge, I could just hold on for a bit, and look down at the water and let myself go …*

The light got lower. I was looking west. The sky was getting orange. The sky was getting darker and darker orange. No one knew where I was. I wasn't going to climb into the undercarriage of the bridge. But if I'd had a blanket, I could've just rolled up in my blanket and gone to sleep …

I didn't have a blanket. I shivered. I zipped up my jacket and put my satchel on my back, and I walked along the ragged river pathway to Pridmore Park, where the loneliest trees in the world lived. Once, the river flooded and all the trees in Pridmore Park were up to their middles in brown muddy water. The whole park became a dirty big lake. Right up to the fence-lines. Right up to where the concrete began. It was spooky.

I would go home to Mother and she would see what a good son I was.

It was a short walk home, up a not-very-steep hill. I went past the house with the manicured hedges, and the house that looked like a birthday cake. I went past the brown and white block of flats with arches over its parking bays, and past the falling-down house where the little old lady lived. I went past the red-brick units where you could cut through to Laws Street, and the black house with the evil dog. I went past the house with all the lavender out front, where a politician lived, and the house with two cars in the driveway up on blocks. You couldn't see through the garden to our house, it was so thick with plants. In summer, the temperature dropped two degrees when you opened the gate and walked into our garden. 'Gosh,' said Mrs Parish once, 'You could die in here and nobody would ever find you.'

Our soft brown gate made no clink when you opened and shut it so it was always a surprise when someone came home. A letter was poking out of the letterbox, so I pulled it out and took it with me. It had Aunt Tilde's writing on the front: Mother would be glad. I opened it and read it, though I knew I shouldn't:

Dearest Veda,

I'm so so sorry for my silence. I have been in hospital with pneumonia. I've been so sick, Veda, for weeks, and Frank didn't bring all my letters until I was recovered enough to read them. I'm so sorry. He should've written to you and told you. I don't know why he didn't think to do so.

I'm still weak but am penning this now so you know I am thinking about you and not for one second reserving judgement. You do what you have to do.

Write me soon.

Love always,

Tilde

On the wall near the front door Papa had hung a large white flower-shaped ornament, and that's where Mother kept the key. She kept it in the three o'clock petal, which I could only reach standing on my tiptoes. I fished out the key and opened the door. I hoped Mother had not seen the newspaper.

Mother must've been out. Or asleep. The house was dark. That sometimes happened when she was asleep: she would leave the lights off. Her dog was nowhere to be seen. I felt my way down the passage and into the bathroom, where the toilet was.

At first I didn't understand the warm slimy stuff under my feet; then I thought the pipes had burst, like they had once before. The bathroom light flickered and flickered again, two three four times, before erupting like a sky across the room. It lit up the floor, the tiles and cupboards. Had Mother left the bath on? The floor was flooded with water. The shower curtain was pulled around the bath, but bathwater was trickling over the top. Mother's hand poked out around the curtain. Had she fallen asleep in the bath? *Silly Mother. I'd tell Papa about this, this was dangerous, she could drown.* I wrenched back the shower curtain.

How do I ever unsee that scene, Ornella? How will I ever unsee Mother under the water in her bath? Her white face awkward on its neck and her grey eyes sunk beneath their lids. I can't unsee the bottle drunk down to the base with its cap off. I can't unsee all that water flooding over the sides of the bath and onto the floor.

I turned off the tap, but the water kept going. It just ran and ran and ran. It ran out from the bathroom to the hall and into my bedroom; it drenched, it stained the carpet and the walls; it ran down the laundry steps and into the garden. It pooled at the base of the washing line, and then it went on running, into the flowerbeds, down the gutters into the street, down onto the tramline, and on and on, all the way out to the river and into the city. It ran and ran and ran.

Lights were suddenly on that hadn't yet been on. People were running, gates were crashing. I was in the street. I don't know how I got there. I stood in the street and I could hear someone screaming and it was me. Voices rose in the air, there was yelling. Someone got me under my arms and lifted me high and away. Some man with a big white and red face was talking to me: quietly, urgently. There was water all over my shoes. I was looking downwards, folded like a hinge, while the man held me under the armpits. I could see the bitumen littered with shreds of paperbark, and my wet shoes, and for some reason, my hands. My hands and my arms, all wet, all wet with water. 'It's alright,' the man was saying, over and over. 'It's alright, son. It's alright, son.' But who was he? I wasn't his son. *Who was he?*

It took no time for the ambulance to arrive. The whole street came out to watch the lights and Mother's body on the stretcher. They'd covered her up, right to the top of her head, so everyone knew.

And they were all silent, and horrified, and all they could hear was me screaming in the arms of the man I didn't know who kept calling me son but wasn't my father.

Mr Parish finally collected me. I don't know why. Was Papa talking to the police? Was he putting his hand through his hair and feeling sick and talking to the police? And you? Were you at work that night, Ornella? Were you on the ward, changing someone's drip, wheeling a body to the morgue?

Mr Parish collected me. On and on and on went the road, the car moulding itself over the bumps and tick-tick-ticking at the intersections, and when it at last came to a halt, almost touching the mud-wall at the top of the driveway, the ignition turned off, and I was carried, like a sack, like an enormous dead human sack, to my bed where the sheets were cold but my body, clenched into a comma, managed still to warm me.

PART 6

THE POEMS OF VEDA GRAY

You could get a cheap place by yourself in the eighties in St Kilda, live alone and pay your bills, even if you were poor, which I wasn't. I didn't have to rent like other people my age. I could have bought whatever I wanted. But my requirements were modest. I bought a two-bedroom flat in St Kilda. It's now worth over a million.

What would Mother have thought of that?

When Mr Parish died, he left everything to me. Mrs Parish wanted nothing. I travelled to Osaka a few times and she put me up in her tiny apartment with its simple floors and walls and decorations. Her life was good, she was content.

Mr Parish's estate was significant. I don't imagine all his money came from poetry – maybe it came from various chairs he occupied, positions on boards, family inheritances he'd received, I don't know how that world works.

I could've rejected Mr Parish after what happened with Mother, but I didn't. He wasn't a bad man. After Mother died, I continued to stay with him on weekends, I helped him build fences and we sometimes put flowers on the grave of Paddy Cow, though a wild woolly grass had grown up there, and it wasn't necessary: she was wrapped well enough in her carpet.

Mr Parish died of a stroke when I was twenty. Mrs Parish wasn't with him, of course. Nor was Kitten, who had long gone, to a younger man and the prospect of children. He was on his own, in his study, with dried mud on his shoes and a pen in his hands. I like to think there was a half-written poem on the page before him ... No, you're right, Ornella: this is not true – I never liked his poetry. I would prefer to imagine him dying in the middle of building a wall or making a firebreak. He did these things with great energy and competence; they seem realer to me than his poetry. He didn't get a state funeral because poets don't get state funerals in Australia. But it was a big funeral and I was a pallbearer. There were obituaries in all the newspapers.

I was twenty years old. I suddenly had a lot of money. I didn't need to finish my university degree. I didn't need to do anything.

It wasn't much of a life though – the solitary life I lived, at my flat in St Kilda. I said the bare minimum to my neighbours. I had a balcony with a few plants on it. I had a view of the sea. I didn't really think it could get much better. Life didn't really get better for people, just more complicated. I'd learnt that. You can't rely on anyone. You need to be self-sufficient.

And then I met Julia.

'There's no question,' said Julia, 'that your mother loved you, Owen.'

We were well past business lunches by this point. We were toing and froing between houses, my flat and her flat, leaving bits of clothing behind.

'You think she abandoned you,' Julia said. 'Of course that's what you think. And she did, in a way. But ...' Julia considered me and I saw myself, for a moment, through her eyes: a grown man feeling sorry for myself.

'All those other people there for you,' Julia said. 'Your mother left you in good hands. It's not for us to say what another person can endure, Owen. And *how* they should endure it. *That* would be selfishness.' Julia swallows more wine. She drinks way too much, in this she is like Mother. 'Your mother wasn't cut out to be some firebrand heroine. She didn't have the temperament of a Joan of Arc. Why should she have? She's left work that other people can enjoy. That's enough. Why do we expect women to be armour-plated? And you were fine, Owen. How it all turned out. Maybe even better off.'

I must not have looked convinced.

'There are only so many bricks you can lay upon someone before they collapse,' Julia continued.

Or maybe the opposite was true: it was all the bricks taken away from Mother that killed her: there was nothing left to stand on.

Julia reached for my hand.

Julia keeps the books she has published over her career on particular shelves, chronologically ordered. Poetry begins in 1980, the year she started Bacchae Press, and ends in 2011, when she let it go. She was winding it up, actually, for most of its life, but it puttered along, borne up by small publishing grants and then courtesy of the Parish Estate. Her poets were a diverse bunch. Fragile men who looked exactly like poets. Defiantly robust men who didn't look like poets at all. Well-kept middle-aged women with frumpy dress sense and furious, pretension-puncturing wit. Long-haired, side-parted youthful beauties who mingled their souls and their sex lives with adroit intertextual references and crisp parsing. Apart from Mother, Julia has not made much money publishing poetry. Nor have her poets. I don't think anyone makes money out of poetry.

When Mother's book came out, its success emboldened Julia. She was thrilled by her own role as discoverer of posthumous genius – 'I feel like the publisher who found Emily Dickinson! Or John Kennedy O'Toole!' The story of tragedy implicit in posthumous publication appeals to the public's hunger for biography, for sensation. Dickinson, upstairs in her locked room, meting out her en-dashes. John Kennedy O'Toole and his rejection slips. It's only recently I've learned the history of *Moby Dick* – after its publication, Herman Melville returned to his job as shipping clerk, and if it hadn't been for the furious championing of early twentieth-century male writers, we might not know the novel today. Success is, not wholly perhaps but partially, a matter of luck and good timing. Tragedy is a fabulous marketing bonus.

'It's true that we don't read a book anymore,' Julia says, 'without wanting to know the story of its author.' She sighs. 'One can't sell a book anymore, without manufacturing such a story. The booksellers need these hooks to hang their books on.'

Poetry has not been a staunch investment prospect. The market for poetry has shrunk and shrunk.

Julia mourns this too. 'People don't understand it,' she says. 'I don't really understand why they *need* to *understand* it. A poem is not a code that needs to be deciphered.'

Once, Julia started writing a book of her own but found she had no talent for it. 'I am a rearranger and fixer,' she said.

'I can see the beautiful skeleton and I carve away the excess flesh. I have an eye that goes for the throat of a thing.'

On Tuesdays, at 1:30, Ornella, you play bocce with the residents and a group of respite patients. Erin, the carer, unrolls the green rubber field on the concrete, and we distribute balls of varying colours and weights to the players. Estelle always has yellow and Colin chooses light blue. Some of the men are incapable of heeding the word 'Gentle!' and they propel every bocce ball out of the field and onto the concrete. Maybe they think they are playing ten-pin bowling. Maybe they remember that they are men and rise to the challenge with too much enthusiasm. You don't care what colour balls you get, Ornella, you don't notice. Each time they are placed in your hands, you look at them freshly, oddly, and then look up to me for explanation. You worry about not knowing what you should do.

But the body remembers. It remembers things the brain no longer can. It remembers the sipping at cups, the cutting of food, the perambulation of hips required in order to walk. It remembers. It swallows and breathes and sleeps, it drinks and eats. These are the last things it forgets.

You took on the job of raising me after Mother died, Ornella. The majority of the job, anyway. When it came down to it, there was only you, who *didn't have a creative bone in your body*. I'd already learned to live with Carlito, who'd taught me the more cartoonish foils of manhood, before settling softly into middle age and letting himself go: teeth, hair, stomach. He worked on the docks til retirement, and then, like so many men of his era, when the work stopped and the pension started, he was dead of a heart attack in a matter of months.

Papa was good for nothing after Mother died. He was good for work – he didn't stop working – but he was no good at being a father. He had to stop that, he couldn't do that anymore. Meanwhile, you got up every morning, Ornella, and went to work; you came home and cooked and cleaned; you checked I had done my homework; you made plans for my birthdays and carried them out, read my reports and told me off if I was not up to scratch. Reliably present in your no-nonsense shoes. You were brisk, but your bedside manner was always good.

After Mother died, you made me a bed on the couch in front of the television where I could eat toast dipped in runny boiled egg and watch Skippy. I was way, way too old for Skippy but I stayed there a long time – days, it seems. And every time Skippy's big brown eyes came up in the close-up, I thought of Paddy Cow, and how, when eyes are dead, they stop being intelligent and feeling and go like marbles. It's such a little thing, such a little difference. The way seeing just stops.

You ran the bath, and you washed my hair. My hair had got so long that sometimes people thought I was a girl. You washed and washed my hair till the whole bath was full of soapy bubbles right up to my chest and then you let me soak, with my eyes closed, and my hands across my chest, and the deep burble of under-water in my ears. And when I got out, you warmed up the towel in the tumble-dryer. I stepped into the big warm towel and it came around me and dried me without me having to do anything.

In the reissue of *The Poems of Veda Gray* – the thirtieth anniversary of Bacchae Publishing's first edition back in 1986 – Julia has decided to include all the variations on FUCK that Mother came up with. There are over thirty of them. They comprise a sort of appendix at the back of the book.

FUCK FUCK FUCK FUCK FUCK

Julia asked if I wanted to include extracts from Mother's letters in this edition. This time I said yes. The selected correspondence are printed in a slim companion volume, and the two books are paired in a cardboard sleeve, with notes. It's a beautiful little publication, no expense has been spared.

I'm not going to get you out of care for the thirtieth anniversary, though, Ornella. It's not worth the discomfort and confusion it would cause you. They've just put a new bed in your room, and that's enough for you to get used to for now.

And I'm not sure I'll tell Papa. I'm not sure what the purpose would be. Papa has no interest in the past, even though the life he lives now is the sum total of it.

The old house in Hawthorn is too big for him but it's derelict enough to keep him busy patching, mending: he pulled up the carpet recently and there in the dust and damp were sheets from the *Age* newspaper, July 20 1969: 'Man Walks On Moon'. He pinned the sheets on the corkboard in his living room – which is not really a living room, but a bachelor's workshop: disordered papers, tools, half-eaten plates of food. The house smells of apples when he's been buying cheap bags of apples, and cinnamon at Easter time when he stocks up on discounted hot cross buns, but generally, it smells like bins that should have been emptied last week, and rooms that should have their windows opened. The hallway and living room are lined with crumbs he won't sweep up; the contents of his fridge are an exercise in self-denial.

For a man who loved cooking, I can't understand this refusal to indulge his own appetite. Maybe it was only ever something he did for others. 'Owen!' he says to me when I come to visit, 'Help me with this, will you?' and he shoves some large object at me that he wants me to hoist onto a high shelf, or attach to a wall, or break up with a tomahawk. He collects bits of furniture from everywhere, side of the road, deceased estates, and little by little it leaves his house and enters the lives of others: chairs that need re-upholstering, a lamp that needs its wiring mended, a kitchen table with missing stoppers. His house is a holding-station.

He sold the restaurant in 1997. He never remarried.

Rosa? Rosa will come to the launch. She might not stay long but she'll come. Rosa, who most recently fought a legal battle because she refused to allow the National Gallery to print her images onto tea-towels. She has enough money to live on and she doesn't need more. 'Who does, Owen?' she says. 'Why do you need more money than you need? They can shove their tea-towels. I am not a gift shop.' She is old and dried as a prune, but she is also a household name, and she loves it though she pretends not to.

Today, in Music Therapy, I got you to shake the maracas, Ornella. You haven't shown such interest in a long while. But you're not going to get better. Your words are going. Even a simple sentence is no longer intelligible. I have to read what you mean in your eyes and usually what I see is merely a plea for reassurance.

Some time soon, you will stop speaking altogether. You will stop speaking and you will stop eating. You will move your thumbs, back and forth, and that will be it. Memory will stop being an argument, even theoretically. I will be the sole repository of my own experiences.

They fixed your bed. You have a choice now: bed or chair, banana or apple, water or wine.

On the night of the thirtieth anniversary of *The Poems of Veda Gray*, Julia is dressed in green – deep jade green, a voluptuous dress for a voluptuous middle-aged woman. She wishes she could forgo her glasses, but she can't bear contacts, and she can't bear not being able to read. She is very pleased with the publishing deal she has brokered. There is not much money involved, really, but that's not the point: keeping Mother in print is the point.

'Veda is still so relevant,' she says. 'Because it's still hard to be angry, if you're a woman. It's still not allowed.'

Julia is a feminist but her feminism rarely turns on me. Generally speaking, I have gone through life outside of the circle of blame. Perhaps if we'd had children, it would be different. Children seem to polarise the sexes, or at least fix in stone roles that were previously less regimented. But in the absence of children, Julia and I have been free to make what we want of our relationship. We each have faults. We each have habits the other can't bear. I won't give up smoking. Julia will not give up meat. We have a balcony. We have many frying pans. Accommodation of each other is not difficult. Sometimes I am in need of support and sometimes Julia is. 'But times have changed,' Julia says. 'It was not always so. Forty years ago, we would have been considered a very specious, very dubious little unit, you and I!'

The years have rolled away in a gentle manner, very few ripples.

Do you need ripples to have a satisfying life?

Money insulates you; it smooths the sharp edges so you don't get caught on them.

I watch Julia talking to a group of interested young women, all clutching their *Veda Grays*.

'Veda was years before her time,' Julia is saying. She has been saying this for three decades. '*Years*.'

The young women are nodding. Veda Gray now has a dramatic biopic glamour. The photo on the flyleaf is one of Mother well before she even embarked on this book: she is flighty, blonde, winsome. She never finished her own university degree. I don't even know what she was studying. But the press that is putting out this thirtieth edition is a university press. There are academics here at the launch and many talented well-dressed female PhD candidates, writing on Luce Irigaray's philosophy of sexual difference and Maurice Blanchot's orphic philosophy of literature. Someone has already written a PhD on Mother: there will be more. The new edition is nicely packaged – not in brown and tan, but in sea-blue and green, rather in keeping with Julia's dress colour-wise – with quotes on the back from distinguished scholars. I can't help wondering whether Mother's precocious adoption of the word *FUCK* is finally paying dividends.

Julia drinks too much champagne so it is lucky she doesn't have to officiate. Local poet Lin Yiu, much lauded and this year's winner of the Gwen Harwood Prize, is making the speech and cutting the figurative ribbon.

Yiu's speech is full of high praise and elevated, if abstract, analysis. It's difficult to say things publicly about poetry, I've noticed, and remain comprehensible to a general audience. Sometimes, there's a retreat into further obscurity, because where else to go? Academia sometimes seems to require impenetrability. Mother would have made short shrift of that.

Outside, on the steps of the Wesley Anne pub, Julia falters. She is really quite drunk. Her heels are too high and she is probably due for a new glasses prescription. She needs my arm around her, I realise. So I put it there and steady her, and help her not just down the steps but up the skinny by-lane to the car park. 'Lovely man,' she says to me tenderly. *The Poems of Veda Gray* is falling from her hand. I retrieve it and try to stash it in her handbag amongst the lipsticks and biros and sunglasses with broken arms. She fobs me off. She's not worried about *Veda* right now. I put *Veda* in the back pocket of my trousers.

She strokes my face with the palm of her hand, her torso enfolded within mine as I guide her along the concrete and then out along the bluestone cobbles.

'Lovely, lovely man,' she says, 'You're my lovely lovely man, Owen.'

† † †

In 1961, Australian poet Gwen Harwood, tired of being rejected or paid less than male poets by literary editors, published a hoax poem in the *Bulletin*, which spelled out FUCK ALL EDITORS when read acrostically. The scandal made newspaper headlines. Harwood wrote that, in the aftermath, '[S]omeone I thought a friend said ... "I thought no woman would ever use that word," and made it clear I was cut off from decent motherhood ...' (Letter to Tony Riddell R 24.8.61).

Harwood went on to become one of Australia's most-feted poets.

† † †

Acknowledgements

There are some people I need to thank: firstly, my wonderful editor and publisher, Jo Case, whose belief and conviction in this book has been so important to me; my agent Jenny Darling who stuck with me through the thick and the very very thin; my readers – Deborah Crabtree, Gerard Elson, Jan Robinson, Lianne Broadbent, Angela Howard, Harry Howard, Johanna Preston and Liz Preston. Thanks to Lara Telford for the ikebana education and the loaned books. Thanks to Janine Burke and Christos Tsiolkas for reading this novel prior to publication and for their kind and generous words. And, for encouragement and enthusiasm: Peter Salmon and Robert Sessions. Finally, Greta and Sukey, for teaching me to be a mother and a woman and a writer all at the same time.

I also thank the Australia Council for the Arts for funding the writing of *Bad Art Mother* through a new work grant.

An early version of 'Milk' was published in the *Griffith Review* in 2010.

Sincerely, Ethel Malley

Stephen Orr

In the darkest days of World War II, Ethel Malley lives a quiet life on Dalmar Street, Croydon. One day she finds a collection of poems written by her late (and secretive) brother, Ern. She sends them to Max Harris, co-editor of modernist magazine Angry Penguins. He reads them and declares Ern an undiscovered genius. Determined to help publish the poems, Ethel moves in with Max and soon becomes a presence he can't understand, or control. He gets the feeling something's not quite right. About Ethel. About Ern. Then two poets come forward claiming they wrote Ern's poems.

Based on Australia's greatest literary hoax, *Sincerely, Ethel Malley* explores the nature of creativity, and human frailty. It drips with the anaemic blood of Australian literature, the gristle of a culture we've never really trusted.

'I bloody loved it, devoured it in a couple of short sittings. Funny in exactly the right way, unique and – perhaps most importantly – entirely plausible. Ethel Malley is easily one of the most vibrant and glorious literary creations I've encountered in a very long time.'

– Chris Womersely